# Cragside

## *A 1930s murder mystery*

## M J Porter

**M J Publishing**

Cover design by Flintlock Covers

ISBN 978-1-914332-84-5 (ebook)
ISBN 978-1-914332-83-8 (paperback)
ISBN 978-1-914332-82-1 (hardback)

# Contents

# Dedication

This book is dedicated to all the hard-working staff at Cragside, and most especially to Alan, who is always smiling, come rain, shine or blizzard, as he welcomes visitors to the estate. His enthusiasm is impossible to contain.

Thank you for all you do and all you have done to secure such a beautiful place for future generations to enjoy.

# Chapter 1

Rain thuds onto the black roof of the Rolls Royce Phantom, but that doesn't concern me. No, my eyes are drawn to the flurry of activity taking place around the main door of Cragside house, despite the sheeting rain that makes everything appear elongated and out of focus. I can see little despite my best efforts.

What's happened now? I want nothing more than to luxuriate in the Turkish bath complex with its beautiful blue tiles, soaking away the stink of the local police station at Rothbury, but that isn't about to happen. Not if the bustle I'm witnessing is anything to go by.

Eagerly, not waiting for my chauffeur, Williams, to open the door, I swing it outwards, noticing how my sleeve darkens beneath the deluge, able to hear the hub of conversation as I skip over the gravel driveway. My red driving shoes are drenched between one heartbeat and the next. I can already feel the leather chaffing my cold feet. I hadn't precisely been dressed for a cold and draughty police station when I was led away in handcuffs the night before.

Now I wear Williams' overcoat over my sensible travelling clothes of a green skirt and thick stockings. My favourite blue coat and hat are still on the coat and hat stand. I was given no chance to put them on before being made to leave the house.

I've been gone for much of the day—darkness shadows even the brightest of the light pouring through the open doorway.

"My Lady," a startled housemaid meets my gaze, bowing and

curtseying all at the same time as we almost collide. I don't get so much as the chance to ask what's happened. She runs past me, a dark coat flung over thin shoulders, covering the smart black dress and white pinafore she wears. Her frightened eyes, hollowed by her short-cropped hair and pale face, reinforce my belief something is badly amiss.

Hastily, I stride into the sheltered stone alcove, grateful to be clear from most of the rain. I wince as I step into a puddle that hadn't been there on my arrival the day before, cresting the flat and wide stone steps. Above my head, the weight of the house, cast almost into darkness, is telling. Chill water from the puddle slips over wet shoes and onto my cold skin. The rain is streaming at an angle, able to sneak into the stone alcove, whereas normally, it would do no such thing.

Bright lights welcome me into the house, for all the large double wooden doors hang entirely open, the trickle of flowing water attesting to the direction of the biting north wind even through my borrowed overcoat. I don't want to consider the state of my hair, and I'm not even a vain woman.

I can see into the far reaches of the well-appointed property from my location. And there, the activity comes to an abrupt stop. There's no one inside, not even the efficient butler, Mr Underhill. I can hear no noise from the kitchen. No noise from the dining room. Nothing at all. Can the upright Mr Underhill be out in the rain? I hardly dare think he'll risk getting his immaculately shined shoes muddied. And if he has, then it's indeed some new catastrophe that's befallen the inhabitants of Cragside.

So then, where are the remainder of the weekend guests? Where are those who'd been so keen to see me sent away, slim hands held cuffed before me as the police smirked at having caught the culprit so easily? I turn, the pull of the unknown too much to ignore. I wish there were a handy torch to light my path into the impenetrable dusk that beckons to me.

The rumble of another motorcar outside pulling onto the gravel-strewn drive with the distinctive crunch beneath the thin tyres is all I need to hear. I swivel. All thoughts about luxuriating in the Turkish bath complex are forgotten. I need to see. I have to know.

As I hope, the other motorcar has been brought alongside that of my Rolls Royce Phantom, Williams still inside and just about visible behind the rain-soaked windscreen. Now both vehicles' thin, yellow beams attempt to drive back the mizzle and the gloom. I've experienced rain like this before on very few occasions. Williams warned me when I mentioned our destination was the far North-East of England in November, but well, I didn't believe it could be so torrential.

I step outside once more, pulling the hood of Williams thick woollen coat over my head, wishing for an umbrella. I meet Williams' eyes through the fogged-up interior of the car. I incline my head questioningly, but he shakes his. I'm not the only one to be unaware of what's happening.

Carefully, wary of the deep ravine that lies below me if I take a wrong step, I make my way to where the beams of the two vehicles are being directed. There are yellowed glimmers from small torches, and an amber glow spills from the curtains of the study and the staircase. Still, it isn't enough to truly see the focus of everyone's attention. I consider the time. It can only be just after 4 pm. The blackness of the storm shocks me.

I crab closer over the grey stones. They're almost flat beneath my feet, but prior knowledge warns me that there are dips and hollows to trip me. No one here is my ally. Not one will mourn if I tumble to my death, down to where the river flows, crossed by the elaborate iron bridge on either side of the Debdon Valley. I'm not about to allow that to happen. It would make it all far too easy for the people who already hold me responsible for something I vehemently deny.

It's the splash of red fluid that catches my eye first in the pools of light. I sigh unhappily. I feel as though I'm becoming a magnet for such shocking events.

But, I have no idea who it is that lies on the hard stones of the most magnificent rockery I've ever witnessed. Not for this house, small and perfectly placed pieces of shimmering stones, all different colours, a promise of a rainbow in the basest of rocks. No, here, giant boulders from the quarry, the thing that has given Cragside its name, tumble in a graceful arch towards the seething river. Far below, the rush of the water assures me that it's been raining throughout my containment. Not that I can see any of that. Not through the blackness pressing in at the edges of the light, trying to blind me.

"Who is it?" I ask of the sobbing housemaid. She dashes past me and into the house through the main front door, her feet flying up high, no care for the threat of the fall just behind us. Of course, there's no response.

A throat clears. I follow shining black boots upwards until I meet the eyes of Underhill, the butler.

"You've returned, My Lady. Perhaps you should shelter in the house. Out of the rain." His voice wavers only slightly. He gives no sign if he's surprised to see me sent back to the property. It's more than I expect from the guests staying at Cragside for the long weekend.

"Here, take my torch." And so I take command of the long metal tube. He does not indicate what's happened in my absence. Perhaps, he suspects I know, or maybe he doesn't feel it's his place to inform of this fresh tragedy that's occurred at the majestic house. Maybe, it doesn't matter. Not to me. The blood speaks of more than I can ever say to clear my name of any involvement in a new crime.

As I pass Williams again, I open the door on the Phantom, peering inside, a cloud of warm air passing over my chilled face.

"Who is it?" I ask. I'm sure he must know.

"I've no idea, My Lady. They told me to get back in the car and shine the car lights where they pointed. I do hope that's acceptable?" The question speaks of servitude, but the tone doesn't. His voice is warm with a northern roll, although he tries to mask it behind a more bland accent. We've known each other for a long time. We've both endured and remained loyal to one another through some terrible events. Williams has never let me down.

"Carry on, but tell me if you hear any news." I hesitate. "I'll have them bring you tea and sandwiches. And make sure you don't use all the petrol. I don't wish to be stuck here a moment longer. And goodness knows where you can buy more of the stuff out here." I indicate the general area with my hand. We can't see, but we're sheltered on the side of a steeply sloping hill. Behind me, the sway of the trees and the drumming of rain on the leaves promises nothing but an expanse of countryside. While there's a road running close by in front of us, it leads only to the small settlement of Rothbury. The promise of civilisation lies more than thirty miles away in Newcastle.

Williams nods and then smiles, his white teeth stark in the darkness.

"Watch yourself," he warns me.

"I will." I close the door. I'm wrong. One person will care if something happens to me. And it isn't that he's my chauffeur and dependent on me for his livelihood. No, he's my friend as well. Such base matters as money and inheritance have been dealt with years before. Such as we've endured has made friends out of the strangest of allies.

Inside once more, a blast of warm air rises around my feet. My shoes are drenched. I kick them aside, swirling Williams' overcoat from my shoulders, feeling the weight lift from my arms. But there's no one to take either item from me. I pick up my sodden and dripping shoes, hang the overcoat over my arm and make my way, stockinged feet, along the inner hallway towards the source of the heat. Below my feet, wooden floorboards keep some of the cold from the stone edifice from chilling me further.

"Ah, Lady Merryweather." The voice of Detective Inspector Aldcroft is uncertain, far from the confident man I was forced to speak to yesterday. He's not at all the confident man who ordered my apprehension for a crime I hadn't committed.

"Detective Inspector," my words are like ice. I see him shiver at them as he comes to an abrupt stop in front of me, as I do the same. I raise my chin, refusing to be cowed by the state he finds me in, with my blond hair dishevelled by the rain and by not seeing a brush for over twenty-four hours. I've slept in my travel clothes. I know I smell of the damp police station, but my eyes are ice blue and clear. My fury ensures I'm thinking clearly.

The detective looks little better than I imagine I do. His overcoat is dark with rain, and beneath his feet, a trail of water pools that one of the housemaids will need to clear up before someone slips.

Silence falls between us, the sound of the kitchen drifting to us. Perhaps the sobbing housemaid has returned inside to make tea. Or maybe Mrs Underhill has taken refuge in what she knows best; providing for the household living at Cragside.

Evidently, Aldcroft has been outside. Aldcroft knows what's happened in the rain. He knows the identity of the victim who's been injured on the rockery.

"Well. Um. So I see you've been released." He licks his lips before he speaks. I try not to note how snake-like the action is.

"Of course I have. It seems that even the Northumberland County Constabulary actually require proof of a person's guilt before holding them indefinitely on suspicion of murder."

"Ah, yes, well, um, apologies, Lady Merryweather. My humble apologies."

Aldcroft runs his wide-brimmed hat through thin fingers, his eyes trying to look anywhere but at me. He's a man of moderate height, a few inches taller than me now that I've discarded my shoes. His lips are covered with a fine brown moustache, although no beard. His police-issue overcoat is black, his boots filthy, the hems of his trousers spotted with what I hope is mud. And I feel just a single moment of pity for him, quickly banished. This man doesn't deserve any kind thoughts.

"Good day," I turn to continue my path to the library, thoughts of hot tea and something to eat driving me onwards to hunt down one of the housemaids who aren't assisting the butler and whoever else is on the rockery. I know I'll pass the stairs to the Turkish bath on the way, but right now, I'm cold and hungry.

Bathing can wait.

Only Detective Inspector Aldcroft speaks. Somehow, I sensed he would. I consider whether he has, in fact, been seeking me out, having heard the growl of the motorcar engine pulling up on the gravel drive.

"Well, actually. If I could. If you wouldn't." And Aldcroft pauses again. "You're cold. Let's talk before the fire. There's tea and biscuits," and he indicates with his hand that I should lead into the library. I open my mouth to speak, to proclaim my innocence, but I bite down on those words. I won't beg. I never have before, even when facing the noose.

I wish I'd kept my shoes on then. My passage makes no sound on the wooden floor, robbing me of the chance to make my displeasure felt in such an obvious way. Instead, I have to rely on rigid shoulders and tight steps. It won't do. Not at all.

I bend and place my shoes before the vast fireplace in the library, noting as I do that there's a fine spread laid out on the dark wooden table but that none of the other houseguests is partaking of the delicate sandwiches or gently steaming teapot. The library, which only a day ago had housed twelve people, is now silent and empty, even if every single electric lamp is turned on, including the converted cloisonné vases. The glass pendant shade over the table adds a warm glow to the cold food.

The fire is well-stocked with burning coals and logs, no doubt from the many trees on the estate. The smell is fragrant with pine and the promise of the coming Christmas.

I pull out one of the wooden backed chairs surrounding the table and hang Williams sopping overcoat over its back, stifling a shiver. My eye catches the hem of my sopping skirt. Aldcroft hesitates in the doorway, his eyes peering back towards the open front door. I believe he might attempt to escape at any moment, although he's asked for this conference.

"Well, come in, or go out, but don't hover," my tone is reassuringly acerbic. I'm pleased to be feeling so much myself, despite the tribulations of the last twenty-four hours.

"Yes, well," and Aldcroft casts a fleeting look along the inner hallway one more time, as though the answer lies out there.

I begin to pour myself tea into the delicate china cups, thinking of Williams. I can't leave him without sustenance, but I need to see what the Detective Inspector wants first. Equally, I wish for a huge mug so that I can grip it between my two white-rimmed hands.

Carefully, I place two lumps of white sugar into the dark brown mass and then liberally apply the milk.

Only then do I remember my manners.

"Would you like one?" But Aldcroft shakes his head miserably, his lips fixed in something similar to a grimace.

I stand and take a sip, wincing at the tartness of the too-long brewed tea, but welcome the warmth and the sweetness. It soothes me like nothing else. At least it's better than the mixture they'd given me in the police station, which had not been worthy of the name tea. I don't even think it deserved the name mud. It had been something indescribable, but I'd needed the warmth.

"Lady Merryweather."

"Yes?" I meet his eyes keenly, noting the furrows in his forehead, the way he licks his lips with indecision once more. I have half an idea that he might be about to apologise to me using more effusive language than earlier.

"You might want to sit again," Aldcroft suggests. I decline to do so. I'll stand while he stands.

"Very well. While you've been," and once more, the detective inspector struggles for the right word to use.

"Detained?" I ask, eyebrows arched, frustrated by his desire not to insult when our earlier discourses have shown none of the same hesitations.

"Away," he interjects at the same time, jaw tight as he snaps out the word. "There have been some developments, other than those of which you're aware. They leave me in an awkward situation."

I'm sure they do, I think to myself, as I continue to sip my tea, wincing once more. I've forgotten the taste of it. Where's the housemaid? I should like fresh tea and food for Williams and a new pot for myself. I don't want to move and ring the bell on the wall, not until Aldcroft has finished spluttering his way through whatever it is he's trying to say.

"There has, as you must be aware, another murder in your absence. The nature of the .... death means that it's impossible, out of everyone else here, for it to be you who was the perpetrator." Despite my best efforts, I'm intrigued, even as a spark of delight splutters to life inside me. I pity the person who's been murdered, but the timing is quite opportune for me. Not them.

"And what was the nature of the death, and who is dead?" I speak too loudly, but Aldcroft doesn't notice, so consumed with his personal misery.

"I. Well. I'm afraid that Mr Harrington-Featherington has been murdered, in a most cruel way, his throat slit." I grimace as Aldcroft rushes to share this information with me so that it comes out as though a river in flood and without empathy. A good job I'm not Mr Harrington-Featherington's nearest and dearest.

Aldcroft slaps his hand over his mouth on realising what he's done. I nod, trying to maintain some equilibrium. A slit throat would easily account for the pool of blood I've witnessed beneath the glow from the car lights and pouring from the study and garden alcove.

I'm suddenly aware of a rush of footsteps from outside. Aldcroft again gazes at me as though trying to decide. His following words astound me.

"As someone with a great deal of experience in these matters, if admittedly for all the wrong reasons, I must seek out your assistance. If you'll give it to me."

"With what?" I can tell we're about to be disturbed, so I snap the words.

"With solving these crimes. First, Lady Beatrice Carver drowned in the basin tank, and now Mr Norman Harrington-Featherington, throat slit on the rockery. You know these people, and you can't be responsible, as it's been proved."

I want to argue with him; to demand an apology for my earlier detention at his hands, but this is better than an apology. Much, much better than that.

"But you must do it secretly," he quickly stipulates. I nod eagerly, unhappy with the caution and yet thrilled at the same time. I can't deny this is the perfect means for me to gain some vengeance against those who've spoken out against me not once but twice. Their accusations are without foundation, and yet I've been led away in handcuffs on two such occasions in less than twelve months.

"I'll do it. And thank you," I offer, head high, peering down at him over my nose and teacup.

"Don't thank me yet. There's a blood-thirsty double-murderer on the loose, and I've no idea if they plan to kill again."

"There, there, Detective Inspector," I caution. "We'll solve this, mark my words." I have even more desire to gain answers than he does. For him, it's about pride. For me, it's about refuting allegations that have seen me deprived of my liberty for nearly a year.

And then the inner hallway is filled with noise. I hear the unmistakable sound of a body being dropped on the wooden floor. I frown at the wet sound, eyes closing in sorrow. When I open them, Aldcroft is gone, his angry voice reaching me along the echo of the hallway.

"Be careful," he urges them. I dread to think with what.

I reach out, take a dainty cucumber sandwich from the tray and bite into it. The cucumber has lost its crunch, but I hardly care as I carefully chew.

There have been two murders in less than twenty-four hours of my arrival at Cragside. I'd been accused and arrested for the first until the police had been forced to release me. I smirk. The fact another murder had since occurred is perfect. My absence is my alibi. None of the other screeching women or supercilious men is above suspicion.

I'll have my revenge and avenge the two murder victims simultaneously.

I'm almost gratified for my arrest now, for all I've been raging about it since late last night. It is, I admit, a shame that my good driving shoes have been ruined as a result of it.

# Chapter 2

I missed breakfast and luncheon while away, and my stomach growls. Whatever was served to me in the police station wasn't a meal. I select another cucumber sandwich, noting that my fingers are so white as to be almost blue. Only then do I make my way to the library door to investigate what's happening.

Aldcroft is there, and so too are four of the male servants. Not all of them are footmen, although two of them wear the uniforms of the indoor staff, black and maroon. They look wretched as they drip water onto the hallway floor. Neither of them wears a coat. The two footmen are joined by one of the chauffeurs, and I also think Lord Bradbury's valet. He won't be pleased with being involved in this. He'll think it beneath him.

All four men are uncomfortable at Detective Inspector Aldcroft's cross words. But, half of Mr Harrington-Featherington's body lies on the wooden floor, his chest and head. Even though there's a white sheet over the poor, murdered man, it's come loose, caught in the hands of the footman who's dropped his part of the bargain. The gaping wound around Mr Harrington-Featherington's neck is easy to see; a violent slash that's almost severed his head, the jagged edges of the slice mismatched and greying in death.

I scowl, my stomach curdling. I think my sandwich might curl just from such a sight.

"Lady Merryweather, there's no need to see this." Aldcroft words are kindly meant.

Never one to admit another is correct, I merely nod and turn aside, the sandwich turning to paste in my mouth. I swallow quickly, making my way back to the table for my tea and then back to the warmth from the fire. It's impossible to feel concerned with the merry dancing of the leaping flames and the soft glow from the electric lights. I distract myself by examining the collection of vases on display on the mantlepiece. They're bright pieces, blue and white. Scrutinising their beauty, I labour to forget what's happening outside the comfort of the well-stocked library.

"My Lady." At last, a housemaid appears. She's busying herself picking up Williams' discarded overcoat and my shoes, her brightness a stark contrast to the darkness of this new crime. The words of an apology are on my lips, but then my persona reasserts itself.

"Leave those, please. But could you bring fresh tea and take the same to Williams, outside, in the Rolls Royce Phantom. He's assisting the Northumberland County Constabulary."

She bobs quickly, auburn curls running free from the confines of her hat, testifying to her youth. She barely stifles a sob. I think I might need to comfort her, only to watch her sweep from the room as though the lady, and not the servant, head held high, shoes tapping over the floor, reminding me that my feet are mute and shoeless.

I watch the housemaid go, feeling somewhat callous. But then, I have too much experience of events such as these. I've not grown used to them, far from it, but the shock will pass. For both of us. In good time.

I make a concerted effort not to listen to the whispered but heated argument taking place in the inner hallway, the unmistakable sound of lifeless limbs thudding to the wooden floor once more. The sound is altogether too final. I stand and choose another sandwich consisting of orange cheese and sweet pickle. Orange cheese, is such a northern delicacy. It brings a smile to my face.

There'll be nothing left to eat soon. I eye the half-consumed plate of white, delicate sandwiches. Well, it's the least they can offer me; I decide.

Eventually, the dragging sound disappears, one step at a time, and all is silent, other than the ticking of the grand old clock, counting down the seconds since the death, adding up the minutes and hours since I'd been led away in handcuffs. Where are they taking the body? I hope not to the Turkish bath. I still wish to bathe away the smell of the police station.

Why have I come here? I'd known, even as I accepted the weekend invitation, that it was no place for me. But then, I've also started to enjoy my minor celebrity, even if it's tempered with frustration. I'm not a murderer, and people need to realise that. I'm not some act to witness in the circuses and curiosity shops.

Yet, I'd come all the same, and now, in a departure from all other such weekend parties, someone has actually been murdered while I'm in residence. And not just one person.

Well, one of them was murdered while I was in the vicinity of the vast estate. Poor Mr Harrington-Featherington has met his end when I can't have had anything to do with it. I'm not foolish enough to think that there won't be some who might say I've ordered the killing. What matters is that my chauffeur, Williams, and I had both been travelling from the cold building where the police had kept me locked up in Rothbury itself. Neither of us can take the blame. I reconsider then. Has my release come because of the new body? It is possible.

I hear another's footsteps, the jangling of cutlery and plates, and I appreciate that the young housemaid is on her way outside. It's taken so long to organise; I half expect to hear Williams voice coming from the main door. But of course, he'll need to use the servants' entrance in and out of the house.

I muse on the significance of the similarity between this house party and the one that led to my first incarceration. I think of the remainder of the guests and my hosts, Lord and Lady Bradbury. Is it all quite by chance, as I'd thought, or has this been planned? I could perhaps ask the detective inspector about my suspicions.

And then I hear a flurry of conversation and steel myself.

The rest of the vultures are returning to the library. How surprised they'll be when I greet them, sandwich in one hand, cup of tea in the other.

They think me still locked up in the police station, hounded by ineffectual police sergeants and constables who believe that because such a tragedy has tainted me in the past, I'll merely crumble before them, admitting all. I have no intention of doing that at all. The solicitor I summoned to assist me had been both startled and devilishly effective. How often, I consider, does he receive such a phone call, and on a Friday evening, no less? In a sleepy place like north-Northumberland? I hardly needed him to assist me, but it's about how it looks, not what was truly happening. And my usual man is far away in London. I had to take what was offered.

In that regard, the local solicitor has served me well, although perhaps he would have done better to bring me a blanket and a thermos of decent tea rather than his briefcase and spectacles. My defence is even better now that this second murder has taken place.

Not that I can feel any sympathy for Mr Norman Harrington-Featherington, a wholly awful man. I doubt I'll be alone in not mourning him. I can mourn the nature of his death, if not the loss of the man himself.

They come pouring into the library. I eye them all. I can't say that any of them notice me favourably. Once, surely, we must have held one another in some regard, but not anymore. In all honesty, I'm not sure I can remember why I ever thought these people worthy of the title of friend.

My hosts, Lord and Lady Bradbury, are of a similar age to me. Lady Bradbury, Margot, to people who know her as a close friend, wears a jewelled circlet threaded through short grey hair. Margot's dressed for dinner, not that I believe we'll be retiring to the cosy dining room anytime soon. Her drop-waisted dress of shimmering yellow silk is out of fashion for London, but here, in the far reaches of Northumberland, it's probably regarded as the pinnacle of fashion. I can't deny and don't even do so begrudgingly that it suits Margot. Around her shoulders, she wears a turquoise shawl with a fringe of dark blue. It matches her eyes, or would if they were visible in the gloom, for she hardly stands before the warm lights. No, on seeing me, she comes to a sudden stop and eyes me uneasily. I watch her with contempt.

Lord Bradbury, Edmund, as he'd been to my husband, is a tall man with a fringe of jet-black hair, curling almost too long around his ears. He wears a dinner jacket and stands, left hand in one pocket, the other holding a pipe that he's clearly keen to puff on but won't do so because it will upset his wife. Margot will make a point of coughing, quite impolitely, if he succumbs to his desires.

At his feet, two hounds circle and then lie down, one over his foot, the other as close as it's possible to get. Both animals are the sleek auburn of autumn ferns, and they're more loyal to Edmund than his shrew of a wife.

Edmund Bradbury had been a life-long friend of my husband's. I know I'm here on Edmund's invitation. Margot wouldn't have stooped low enough to invite me. I'd have liked to be a fly on the wall when Edmund informed his wife of my imminent arrival. Even now, Margot's face elicits shock that I've been returned to the house. Not just shock, but a tendril of disgust as well, visible in the way her lips curl over her teeth, as though a dog about to growl because someone threatens its bone or ball.

I meet Margot's look with an arched eyebrow. If I could mock her, then I would. But beneath the gaze of everyone there, I attempt to behave myself. If I'm to assist the Detective Inspector, I must pretend these people mean something to me, even if they don't.

Lord and Lady Bradbury have no children, but the next guest that draws my attention is Hugh, the heir-apparent and Lord

Bradbury's nephew. He's perhaps twenty-five years old. I've lost track of his age. It seems to happen that children are children for many years, and then the next time I see them, they're adults with professions.

Not, it seems that Hugh Bradbury has a profession. He's toyed with the law, but it hadn't agreed with him, as his uncle has explained to me. Now he's merely waiting for his inheritance. Hugh will be waiting a long time and living on his uncle's charity until then. Of that, I'm sure. As much as I no longer count Margot as a friend, I wish Edmund a long and happy life.

Hugh is a similar build to Edmund. It's impossible to ignore the family likeness. Hugh even has his uncle's intelligent flashing eyes and jet-black hair.

Not that his blonde fiancé seems to have considered that Hugh might not inherit for decades to come. While Hugh dresses in a serviceable evening suit, she's outfitted in the latest London fashions. Not for her the dropped-waistline of a dress, no, she wears a tightly fitting mauve gown, cinched at the waist, and while it covers her legs down to her ankles when she turns, a significant swathe of dusky flesh is revealed.

I smirk inside my head because whenever Margot catches sight of so much skin on display, she positively shudders with disgust. Not content with having a criminal amongst her precious guests, there's also one who has no problem in showing what she's got, as one of the scurrilous newspapers might phrase it. Poor Margot. If she ever ventures south to London again, she'll have a terrible shock for everyone dresses now as though they're about to step onto a film set. The film stars of the day are the very people who determine what is and what isn't deemed fashionable, and so everything is too bold, too bright, too much, just waiting for the flashing bulbs of cameras to go off.

Miss Amelia Clarke wears matching mauve shoes with a heel at least three inches high on her feet. I admire her being able to totter about on such a narrow heel. I'm far happier with my sensible Mary-Janes, with the wide heel, and as I've discovered on more than one occasion in recent times, as good for the library as they are in a police station being questioned for crimes I didn't commit.

Miss Amelia Clarke hasn't travelled to Cragside alone. While she shimmers with blonde hair beneath the electric lights, moving to sit on one of the ebonised mahogany chairs before the fire, her friend and confidant bows low between a mass of tightly curled brown hair. I can see where she's tried to tame her mane with bows and slides which glitter amongst her hair, but it's entirely failed. I think she should leave it well alone, but of course, all the adult women film stars have immaculately waved hair.

Rebecca Barlow wears a dress of demure green chiffon. It has about it the hint of extravagance, but all carefully tempered down with a jacket of brown corduroy, I'd sooner expect to see while out walking or riding. I assume she's cold, which doesn't surprise me with the storm blowing outside the walls of the vast house, hammering against the expensive Morris and Company glass windows that would offer a view of the estate if it wasn't so dark. From the look of her, I know Rebecca Barlow to be a competent horsewoman and one who's been shoe-horned from her jodhpurs on pain of death for dinner. I know a moment of empathy for her. Lady Bradbury keeps a fine stable of excellent mounts. Miss Barlow has no doubt been enjoying riding throughout the day.

Rebecca nibbles on a fingernail as she sits in one of the other chairs facing the fire. A sign of nervousness? Or perhaps as simple as a jagged nail she's not had the time to tame. For the life of me, I can't determine why she's a friend of Miss Amelia Clarke. Two women couldn't have different temperaments unless they were purposefully being obtuse.

I don't look, but I suspect that Miss Barlow might still wear riding boots if I did catch a glimpse beneath her long trailing dress. Once more, I smirk, but for an entirely different reason.

And then, I'm forced to consider the next two guests of Margot and Edmund Bradbury. Again, these two are friends of my husband's, and I had thought, my friends as well. But being accused of murdering my poor, dear husband has lost me so many seemingly good friends that I can't think any of them were indeed my friends, to begin with. Certainly, as Miss Amelia Clarke does, I don't have a Miss Rebecca Barlow standing at my side to announce my innocence no matter the nature of the allegations. Not that I'm feeling sorry for myself about that. I know my innocence. What does it matter if others determine to think ill of me?

Reginald and Gwendoline, the Lord and Lady of Sunderland, are so similar, if it weren't for the dress Gwendoline wears and the trousers that Reginald has donned, it would be difficult to distinguish between them. They share almost the same hair colouring and angular jaw. Sometimes, I've even considered that Gwendoline has need of shaving to remove the fine hairs from her upper lip. My thoughts have become even less charitable towards the pair of them since my husband's murder and my arrest. Reginald, I believe, must only shave once a week or less frequently.

They share the same indeterminate black and grey hair, more like the coat of my beloved dog, Daisy, sadly killed alongside my poor, murdered husband. And more than once, I've had to refrain from reaching out and stroking the long mane of hair that cascades down Gwendoline's back. She wouldn't appreciate my thoughts on her hair. She'd take great offence at being referred to as a dog, but she should perhaps stop scenting the air in mimicry of a hound if she wishes to dispel the illusion.

She wears a sensible long brown skirt, a blouse of deep cream tucked into her waistline. Over it, she wears a matching jacket, and on her feet, slippers of the same colour. While the rest of the guests have been disturbed from their dinner preparations, it seems that Lady Sutherland has yet even to begin hers. I consider where she's been and what she's been doing. She reaches across the table and helps herself to the remaining sandwich before moving to another table, sitting in the shadow of the corner window and taking the first seat there.

Her husband, Reginald, is already in his dinner jacket and

white shirt. The bow tie he wears has been ripped aside so that it dangles down his chest, a splash of black against the crisp white of his shirt. Neither of them is particularly slim, and neither are they fat. Not for the first time, I consider whether they wear one another's clothes. I'm sure they would fit them both.

The remainder of the guests giving me evil glances are a small collection of Margot and Edmund Bradbury's acquaintances and professional colleagues. There's a small, squat man with a belly so vast, I think he might be broader than tall. He's entirely bald and has a soft, spongy looking face. When he speaks, it's more spit than sound. I've not yet seen him, even at the breakfast table, without a snifter of whisky close to his side, if not in his hand. He smokes with Hugh and coughs with Margot. He's altogether a disagreeable man, and not just because he, too, was a life-long friend of my husband. As a barrister, I could perhaps have expected him to speak for my innocence, but no such thing occurred.

If anything, he was quicker than most to lay the matter of my husband's death at my feet.

Mr Hector Alwinton is a bachelor, more through missed chances than through choice. My husband once assured me he was an attractive man when he was much younger. But in all the years I've known him, Mr Alwinton's belly has hung over his trousers, and he almost always drunk as well. He must, I assume, have his expensive clothes hand-made for him. The tailor must fear he won't ever have the cloth to cover him whenever he comes calling.

Hector Alwinton waddles to the other mahogany chair before the fire and squeezes his bulk into it.

Miss Lilian Braithwaite is a slip of a young girl and Edmund's personal secretary. She's dressed for dinner in a simple gown of pale orange. The colour should look garish on her. I could certainly never wear orange with my blonde hair, but it suits her. I consider what assistance she's had with her wardrobe. Lilian doesn't dress as though she has only her salary upon which to live. But, I know next to nothing about Lilian other than what

Edmund has told me. She meets my eyes and then veers towards Lady Sutherland, sitting close to the window. I note that with interest. I didn't think the two much liked one another. Lady Sutherland has always been a snob, and with little intelligence, is no doubt in awe of the university-educated young woman.

And last, but not least of the living, is Miss Olive Mabel. Miss Mabel is a woman of sixty-three years old and watches the goings-on around her through a perpetual squint. She's proud of her age and thinks nothing of announcing it alongside her name. She wears not clothes from the last decade, but possibly the last century. I almost expect her to have a bustle beneath her skirts. She wears a vibrant purple dress, covered in ruffs. And yet, for all its aged look, the clothing is new and shows little sign of wear. Another one who must have her own seamstress at her beck and call. Again, that's very last century. She's one of Lady Margot Bradbury's oldest friends.

Olive makes her way to the fire and stands there, for Hector and Amelia have the two chairs, and neither looks like giving them up, although it's evident Olive expects them to do just that.

Only then does Detective Inspector Aldcroft return to the room. He makes his way to the fire, forcing Miss Mabel to move aside. He turns from one guest to another, his sweeping gaze filled with a calmness I admire. That look seems to imply he judges no one there. Yet I know he judged me on discovering who I was. Perhaps this time, Aldcroft's decided to have more of an open mind about the culprit responsible for the dead body found on the rockery.

"Ladies and Gentlemen." Aldcroft possesses a commanding voice, a firmness that has every eye watching him. Even Miss Rebecca Barlow leaves off from chewing her nail to watch him. "As you know, we've now had two murders in the space of twenty-four hours. Both victims died horrible deaths. It's my responsibility to find the culprit, and to do so, I'll be interviewing everyone once more."

"And why is she here?" Lady Margot Bradbury almost spits with disgust, her painted finger extended in my direction.

"Lady Merryweather has been released without further charges. And of course, being away from the property while Mr Norman Harrington-Featherington was murdered means that she can't have played a part in that tragedy either."

"She's not welcome here," Lady Bradbury announces, arms folded defiantly in front of her, pushing up her chest. She looks like the female guard at Holloway prison in such a poise. Not that I'd ever dream of saying that. It's better if I never think of that terrible place again.

"Leave her alone, my dear," her husband tries to calm his wife, his fingers clasping and unclasping around his pipe. He's desperate to light it. I can tell that. But what are the options available to him? I can hear the rain drumming on the roof outside. And if he decides to stand in the garden alcove, where I know he prefers to smoke, he'll be faced with a view of the latest murder. Perhaps Edmund will take himself off to his study and open a window. Even then, I imagine Margot will scent the pipe smoke and raise her voice in outrage.

It surprises me that Edmund is once more prepared to argue with his wife over me. Margot's cold eyes sweep me. Then she turns aside, head raised, nose high in the air.

Chief Inspector Aldcroft pauses for a beat and then resumes. "While Lady Merryweather is no longer a person of interest in the murders of either of your guests, she must still remain here until I conclude my investigation."

I'm sure that's not true, but I welcome the words from the Detective Inspector, even though earlier in the day, I was as angry with him as Lady Margot Bradbury is now.

23

# Chapter 3

"**A**nd now, I'm afraid, I must interview all of you again. Lord Bradbury, may I make use of your study again for these interviews."

"Of course, of course," Lord Edmund Bradbury agrees gruffly. "Use it whenever you require. And I'll have Underhill inform the staff so that they know to take heed of any instructions you give. There's no need for them to seek my approval for every little thing." Lady Margot Bradbury stiffens at the words. I look down at my clasped hands. They remain white with cold, the large diamond engagement ring standing proud from my ring finger. With effort, I resist the temptation to twirl it with my thumb.

"Then, if you don't object, Lord Bradbury, I'll begin with you." With no further words, Detective Inspector Aldcroft walks to the inner hallway. I catch his eye as he turns to ensure Lord Bradbury is following him. There's something there, but I don't manage to grasp what he tries to tell me with just a look.

Lord Bradbury trails after Aldcroft, the two hounds following in their wake. It's an amusing sight. Silence settles between the remaining guests, Lady Margot's left hand almost around her neck, as though struggling to breathe. I consider who'll speak first.

I'm unsurprised when it's the rotund Mr Hector Alwinton.

"Well, it can't be me, as you all know," he pleads with the other members of our party from his place in front of the fire.

"And why is that?" Miss Rebecca Barlow surprises me by asking. She's sitting as close to the fire as it's possible to be, warming her knees and her hands. She doesn't even look at Hector when she replies, although he's so close to her. Miss Amelia Clarke seems unaware that anyone has spoken.

Hector's mouth opens and then snaps shut, only to open again. He leans forward, or as far as he can over his protruding belly, and then takes a deep breath. I watch it fill his chest, the buttons on his evening shirt, straining at this extra pressure on them.

"I, of course, would be unable to overpower anyone in my pitiful state." He motions down to his large stomach as he speaks. "And even if I could, I was with Lord and Lady Bradbury at the time of this second murder."

"And what time did the second murder take place?" Rebecca Barlow probes. There's no malice to her voice, but her intent is pointed. Perhaps the detective inspector should have asked her to assist him instead of me.

"I, well. Of course, it was sometime this afternoon. Since luncheon, when I last saw poor Mr Harrington-Featherington."

"When did everyone else last see Mr Harrington-Featherington?" Rebecca doesn't raise her head but asks the room in general. Her words sound almost bored.

"When did you last see Mr Harrington-Featherington?"

It's Lady Bradbury who spits the question at Rebecca. The two are like cats circling one another before pouncing. Now, this I might like to see.

"I last saw him after luncheon. I was, here, in the library, with Miss Amelia Clarke and Hugh Bradbury. And you?"

"Well," Margot splutters. "I really don't recall, but I was with my husband and Mr Hector Alwinton immediately after luncheon and until we were once more brought together and told of Mr Harrington-Featherington's death." How Margot speaks of the dead man assures me that my assumptions about her feelings towards him are correct. She didn't like him, and he didn't like her. Watching them share meals, sat next to one another in my home nearly a year ago was a sight to see.

"So, you were with Mr Hector Alwinton and Lord Edmund

Bradbury, and I was with Miss Amelia Clarke and Mr Hugh Bradbury. And, of course, Lady Ella Merryweather was at the police station. So who does that leave?"

Unknowingly, my eyes slide towards Lilian and Olive.

Lilian sits very neatly, one thin leg crossed over another. She seems insubstantial and entirely unable to kill another. Yet, I know better than to allow someone's appearance to influence me. The kindest looking people can be the roughest: the roughest, the kindest. If I hadn't known that before, then my incarceration at Holloway has reinforced the knowledge.

"I was out for a walk in the rain," Miss Lilian Braithwaite announces. "I like to walk in the rain. The house felt quite stuffy and hot."

"And you were alone?" I can't get a word in edgeways to ask the questions. I'm secretly relieved. Sooner they think I'm angry with the Detective Inspector than attempting to help him, the more likely they are not to watch their words as carefully as they should.

"I wasn't. I had the dogs with me."

"Then you were alone other than with two canines?" Rebecca retorts.

"I was, yes." Lilian confirms softly.

"And where did you walk?"

"To the old quarry, Cragend. It's a tricky walk in the wet. I fell and scuffed my hands." As though to prove the point, Lilian shows both of her hands. They have small cuts on the palm of them, where the implication must be pieces of gravel have pierced her skin.

"And you were gone all that time?"

"Yes. I returned when the Detective Inspector had already arrived."

"And you, Miss Olive Mabel?" Rebecca lifts her head from the perusal of the fire, and her eyes alight on Olive, who has moved back to the heat of the fire, now that Aldcroft has left the room.

"I was resting, in my bed-chamber," Olive states, her words ringing with finality.

26

"And you, Lord and Lady Sunderland? Where were you this afternoon?"

The two look affronted to be called to account by someone so beneath their notice. They share a look and then glower at Rebecca.

Rebecca ticks off on her fingers what she knows. "You weren't in the library, as I was in there with Hugh Bradbury and Amelia Clarke, and you weren't with Lord and Lady Bradbury and Hector Alwinton in the drawing-room, and you weren't with Olive Mabel or Lilian Braithwaite."

"No, we were in our bed-chamber as well. It was a late night and looked to be another one this evening." "I thought it better to catch up on my sleep." It's Reginald who speaks.

"And did you sleep?"

"I did, yes."

"All afternoon?"

"Yes. Why?" and his forehead furrows, eyes disappearing beneath his eyebrows.

"So you don't know what your wife was doing then? She might have slept, or she might not have done."

"Now," and Lord Sunderland looks bristly, like a hedgehog in his rage. I'm surprised he can show such anger. He's such a calm soul, usually.

"Calm down, dear," his wife consoles him. "I can assure you that I slept all afternoon as well. We're not used to drinking heavily and staying up so late talking with much loved friends about such shocking events. We had another dear friend to mourn, and we believed justice was going to be achieved for poor Lady Carver."

Those words make me doubt Lady Sunderland, although Rebecca seems to accept them quickly enough. I grimace, realising what Gwendoline implies with her statement. They were up all night talking about the fact I'd been led away in handcuffs. Again.

I've heard Lady Sunderland and Lady Bradbury have blazing rows before now. I remember one such occasion, very specifically from the house party we held last year, which resulted in my husband's death. I didn't hear all the words, but I witnessed Margot sulking away from the library and heard Lady Sunderland smash something into the fireplace. I later found one of my maids trying to remove pieces of broken glass from the grate. I was too late to witness what it was, but once more, I'm aware that these men and women might profess to be friends and allies, but I'm not sure of it. Not at all.

"So," Margot snarls in Rebecca's direction. "You have your answers. You must admit that it looks more and more likely that Lady Merryweather was responsible. She might not have been here physically, but perhaps she had someone else do the deed on her behalf. The Detective Inspector is a fool if he thinks she's not the guilty one. After all, she's killed before." Margot hisses as she speaks. The temptation to slap her face for such a shocking diatribe has me sitting on my hands, focusing on keeping my face expressionless. Abandoned on the table before me are the remains of the sandwiches and cold teapot.

What Margot has failed to appreciate is that I'd not even arrived at the house when Lady Carver was killed yesterday.

"I disagree," Rebecca sneers, showing more emotion than I expect from her. "It looks to me as though someone in this house is trying everything they can to send an innocent woman up for murder, again. I can see that the Detective Inspector is aware of that now. As he said, of us all, there's only Lady Merryweather who can't possibly be responsible for the murder of Norman." I'm astounded to hear someone defending me.

Before Margot can respond, Edmund returns to the library. Aldcroft hasn't taken long to ask his questions of the owner of Cragside.

"My dear, it's your turn now," Edmund Bradbury informs his wife. Arm clasped over the opposite arm, Margot stands and gives Rebecca such a cold stare, I expect the fire to gutter and go out.

"I'll ensure the Detective Inspector knows where I was and who I suspect." So spoken, Margot strides from the room, high heels clipping on the wooden floorboards. The sound echoes with the stone of the walls.

Edmund sinks into a comfortable looking chair to the far side of the room, closer to the bookcases. His face is ashen, the pipe clutched tightly, as though it's a life vest intended to keep him afloat.

"All these years," Edmund mutters softly. "All these years and nothing terrible has ever befallen this wonderful house built by my father. And now. Well now, two in two days, well, less than twenty-four hours. I'll never recover from such a tragedy." I think Edmund might be about to break into sobs, but somehow, he doesn't. His gaze lingers on the fire.

"Lady Bradbury informs me that you were with her and Hector, all afternoon, after luncheon, in the drawing-room."

Rebecca is a tenacious woman. She offers no empathy for Edmund's disturbed thoughts. I admire her.

"What? Yes, yes, of course, she was."

"So, she didn't leave the room to powder her nose or anything like that?" Rebecca presses. From Lilian's darting eyes, I can tell that she's not considered such a possibility. I have. All these people would have needed were a handful of minutes to kill Mr Harrington-Featherington. We don't know how long he'd been dead on the rockery before he was discovered. "No one has mentioned seeing him since luncheon."

"I'll not have you speak about my wife in such a way," Edmund doesn't explode, but the words are softly spoken and all the more menacing because of that.

"I'll speak how I like," Rebecca responds, her mouth suddenly twisted with fury. "I'm brought to a house where not one but two people are murdered, and I'm not allowed to leave it. I don't much care for who you are or what titles you have after your name. To me, you could all be the murderer. All of you." Her words escape on a shriek. My respect for her evaporates in the wake of her terror.

I expect Edmund to defend Margot further, but he deflates before me.

"You are, of course, right to say what you do. This is terrible. Just terrible. I do believe we might all have left the room at one point or another," Edmund admits.

"Come now, old boy, I didn't leave the drawing-room." Hector fills his voice with false humour. I detect a thread of fear, which I think is worthy of note.

"I know that I did," Edmund announces, as though not hearing Hector. "I thought I heard the dogs and came looking for them. But I must have misheard, as there was no sign of Lilian or the dogs. Of course, sound does echo strangely in the valley," Edmund concedes.

I try not to glance directly at Lilian at this admission. It means that she might have been closer than she'd first implied. I'm learning a great deal. I imagine more than the Detective Inspector. I can't see that Margot will even listen to his questions, let alone answer them truthfully. She's a woman eager to impress on everyone that she's a member of the gentry.

"Edmund," Margot's cry rings from the inner hall, the single word shrill.

"Yes, dear," Edmund calls.

"I need you," and we all hear a thudding noise as though something heavy hits the floor. It too strongly reminds me of the men carrying Norman's body through the house that, for a moment, I do worry that Margot might have fallen to her death.

# Chapter 4

"Oh goodness me," Detective Inspector Aldcroft's surprised voice is the next I hear.

"My Lord Bradbury. Lady Bradbury has fainted," he calls through the open doorway.

With alacrity, Edmund leaps to his feet. I make to follow, but then pause, suspicions aroused. Is this an attempt to hide something amongst the men and women who remain in the room? Is Margot's faint all an act to allow something to be secreted amongst their accomplices? After all, none of them knew why they'd been summoned to the library before they arrived. I slow my steps.

Already, I can hear Edmund speaking to Margot urgently, demanding to know what she's doing. Hector Alwinton huffs behind. He's wedged in his chair and comes loose with a popping sound I pretend not to hear. But none of the others stirs, not even Olive, and that surprises me, as she's always been Margot's especial friend.

"She does it all the time," Olive says softly, the words directed at me. I narrow my eyes, surprised by her admission, and then find a tight smile for my warming cheeks. "It's her heart or something. She's not been strong since her last illness."

"Illness?" I don't know about this. Olive nods vigorously. No one else is listening to us as we stand close to the warmth of the crackling logs in the fireplace.

"It was when you were, indisposed." Silently, I thank Olive for choosing such an innocuous-sounding phrase. "She spent almost the first six months in her bed. At one time, Edmund was convinced she'd never recover. I think he'd half-planned on his next bride." Olive's dark eyes gleam with scandal, the dull glow of the electric lamps and the fire doing little to dispel the blackness at their centre. Olive can tell I'm shocked by what she knows.

"Edmund will not remain long unwed should he be left behind after her passing." She informs me even more softly.

"What exactly was the matter with her?" I pitch my words as low as hers. The activities from the hallway drown out our conversation.

"I don't rightly know," Olive confides. "She won't speak about it, just calls it 'her little problem.'"

By now, Margot has made her way into the room, Edmund propping her up from the right-hand side. She does look wan, but I ignore that. Had she been pale and lifeless during the brief time I spent with her yesterday afternoon? It's just possible she might have been. Maybe Margot truly is unwell, and this isn't all an act?

Yet, for all Olive's words of foreboding, Edmund fusses around his wife. Even Detective Inspector Aldcroft has been pulled from Edmund's study to ensure Lady Bradbury receives the care she professes to need. Not that Aldcroft looks contrite. I try to catch his attention, only to be studiously ignored.

I'm looking forward to discovering what he's determined from the other houseguests when it's my turn to be interviewed.

A housemaid arrives, the one I saw earlier, dashing around outside in the streaming rain, flushed cheeked, carrying a thick plaid blanket, which is placed over Margot's knees, where she now sits in the chair that Hector has been forced to vacate before the fireplace.

"She really should be allowed to rest." I'm surprised that it's Hugh Bradbury who makes the demand. But he's up on his feet, face filled with worry. I would have expected Hugh and Margot to be enemies, not allies. After all, should Margot not be unwell and outlive her husband, it'll be Hugh who'll have command of her home and her wealth.

"She can rest, now I've spoken to her. Lord Bradbury, you may escort her to your bedchamber if you feel that's the best place for recovery." Aldcroft's concession is gallantly made. A flash of fury engulfs me. When I was being accused of murder and bundled off to the local police station, where was his understanding?

I note the look of horror on Margot's face. She might wish to be the centre of attention with her little show, but what she really wants is to sit there, being fussed by everyone. That way, she can keep a watchful eye on her guests, and no doubt, me most of all.

"Yes, of course," Edmund offers his support to Margot once more, as the housemaid snatches the blanket from where it falls to the ground as Edmund urges her to stand. Margot's face is a picture of unhappiness. With no sympathy at all, I watch Margot walk slowly from the room and towards the elevator that will take her upstairs from the other side of the door in the hallway. She looks back on reaching the door, and I meet her eyes. I hold myself steady. She can hate me all she wants, but hating me won't make me a murderer. No matter what she hopes to achieve.

"And now, Lord Sunderland, if you would." Detective Inspector Aldcroft is straight back to it. He's obstinate. When I spoke to my local solicitor, he lamented the Northumberland County Constabulary, especially the woeful lack of detectives.

"I know that Scotland Yard has many detectives, as does Newcastle Upon Tyne Police, but Northumberland has only five, and they're all self-taught men. They've had no training. I doubt they even know how to investigate something as serious as the murder of a member of the nobility. They have no one superior to them, to assist in such matters. There's much talk of a detective division being needed, but so far, it's all talk and no action."

I nodded along with the solicitor, appreciating his low opinions of the man who interviewed me, another of the detectives named Andrews. The two men did little but puff their chests at one another as I was asked questions, which my solicitor refused to allow me to answer, no matter how irate Andrews grew.

"Yes, yes, I'm coming," Reginald announces, struggling to his feet from the chair beside his wife, and recalling me to the here and now. He and his wife did not attempt to assist Margot. Neither did Rebecca or Lilian. The only ones who were at all solicitous were her husband and her husband's nephew, as well as Hector, and what good was he? Even then, if what Olive implies is true, Edmund is keen to have a new wife to replace his sick one, for it seems that Margot might not be recovered, even if she no longer spends her time in her bed.

With so many people gone from the room, it's possible to move around more freely without fear of tripping over hounds or feet. The two hounds have settled beside Lilian. I thought she liked them, having taken them for a walk that afternoon, but instead, she holds her head away from them as though they reek of the worst possible smell.

I stand and stride to the window where Gwendoline already sits close to the highly polished table. It's impossible to see anything beyond the small panes of glass that make up a much larger window. It's black beyond the elaborate glass because it's night. Somewhere below me, I know the precipice of the rockery descends into the valley. The river will be burbling nicely with all this extra water gushing down from the hills and surrounding heath. On a clear day, I'd be able to see the trees hugging the hillside opposite, perhaps even a glimpse of the twin lakes, but not today.

I'm not left alone for long. Lilian joins me. She clutches a book, the brown leather cover speaking of something from the library of Lord and Lady Bradbury. Many of the books here are bound in the exact same shade. I admire the commitment to a plan. I don't remember seeing her choose it, but then, I've been busy observing the interplay between Lord and Lady Bradbury. By the light of one of the converted cloisonne vase lamps, she might have been able to have her pick of any of the books.

"A sorry business," she squeaks. I've not really spoken to her in any great depth before. I've been aware that she has a soft voice and can easily be overlooked in any room. She's mouse-like, and yet, I also detect fierceness in her. I should like to know how she obtained the personal assistant position to Lord Bradbury. Perhaps there's more going on here than I thought, considering Olive's sly remarks about the state of Edmund and Margot's marriage.

"Indeed. Most upsetting, especially for those deemed guilty despite the absolute absence of evidence."

"Well, yes, of course," and she falters, looking down at her hands, where they clutch the book tightly. Maybe I should have been less martyred with my words.

"Tell me, have you been with Lord Bradbury for long?" I know she attended my house party, but there wasn't the time to speak with her then. Not with everything that subsequently happened.

"Just over eighteen months. I replaced the previous assistant who left to get married."

"And where are you from?"

"Kent, My Lady."

"And your particular specialism?" Edmund has had a long line of personal assistant's with a specialism he means to pursue with fierce determination.

"I'm a biologist. I'm here to assist with cataloguing every plant in the vast gardens."

I startle at that. If there were anyone here that I might consider spending their time bent double over specimens in the hothouse, formal gardens or even just on the sweep of the hillside that shoots skywards behind the house, it wouldn't be Lilian. Surely, I think, Edmund has no end of gardeners to assist with his project of cataloguing the many millions of species of plants and trees that thrive within the estate?

"A fascinating subject." I'm keen to keep the conversation going.

"Yes, it is," and now Lilian's face alights. "Lord Bradbury's predecessor spent a great deal of time and money on bringing exotic specimens to Cragside, but alas, not so much time on their records."

"And you've been cataloguing the gardens for all of those eighteen months?"

"Well," and now Lilian falters, eyes downcast. I can determine an actress when I see one. "For some of the time, Lady Bradbury was quite unwell, and I was called upon to assist her in keeping her correspondence and affairs in order."

"And you didn't enjoy that?" I decide to play the game. After all, this might inform me whether Margot Bradbury is truly unwell or not.

"Well, just because I'm a woman doesn't mean I wish to tend to someone who's ill. I came here to do a particular task. It's still unfinished. I blame Lady Bradbury for that." A faint flush touches Lilian's cheeks as she speaks. I watch her side-on. She isn't unattractive, but she's quite young, especially compared to Margot. Perhaps, after all this time, Edmund still hopes for an heir to his estate. I thought he'd long accepted that Hugh would inherit, but perhaps not. If Margot should die, Lilian could replace her. She might not have the money and the reputation. But she has something far better – a younger body and the means to get pregnant.

"So, what ailed Lady Bradbury?" I decide to press Lilian on this. I'm curious as to what felled Margot. She's long been formidable, allowing nothing, and certainly not her childlessness to stop her.

"I would say she had a crisis of conscience and nothing else." Lilian sneers as she speaks, nose bending almost to touch her lips.

"About what?"

"That, I don't know, but she would mumble in her sleep. Her letters were filled with apologies."

"And who did she write to?"

Lilian turns to face me, her eyes raking in my face. I consider what she sees before her. Does she note that I'm as old as Margot, without an heir as well, or does she merely see a foolish woman, desperate to determine who her friends and enemies genuinely are?

"She wrote to everyone, but some letters were almost flippant, others filled with an inner rage that was uncomfortable for me to write. I only wish I'd been able to read the many replies she received."

"So, she had you write her letters but was able to read her own."

"Yes. It was incredibly frustrating, like only hearing half of a whispered conversation. Even now, and as much as I despised the task set me, there are some things I'd dearly love to know the answer to."

"Such as?" I ask, but now her lips purse.

"It wouldn't be appropriate for me to discuss that with you?" and now there's hatred in her words, and her tone is icy.

I smile. I've seen this too many times in the past.

"You would do well to remember, Miss Braithwaite, that I'm an innocent woman. One not only wrongly accused but vilified for it as well. I didn't kill my husband. I couldn't have done so."

"Ah, but you could," Lilian hisses, surprising me with her vehemence on something that shouldn't concern her. "And while I might despise Lady Bradbury, she knows how you did it."

I laugh. The sound is brittle, as though glass shatters on the polished wooden floors.

"Lady Bradbury knows nothing. I took you to be a more intelligent woman than that," I stride from her side. I'm impressed by how calm I feel. Margot Bradbury knows how I killed my husband, does she? I think it is more likely that she knows how he was killed because she arranged it. There's more than just Edmund, who've been keen to move beyond the confines of their marriage. I'm only grateful that my husband was too enamoured of me to take a bite of Margot Bradbury, despite her best efforts otherwise.

# Chapter 5

The next time Detective Inspector Aldcroft appears, he summons Lady Gwendoline Sunderland. She stands, tottering even in her flat, sensible shoes, as though unable to support herself. She looks to her husband, but he's moved straight to the drinks tray on the side table behind the chairs that face the fire. Reginald splashes a considerable quantity of whisky into one of Lord and Lady Bradbury's cut-glasses. He swigs it as though a man unable to breathe without the fluid rushing down his throat.

Once more, I try and catch the eye of Detective Inspector Aldcroft, but he escorts Gwendoline away as though nothing has happened between the husband and wife. I wonder if either of these long-standing couples is happy with one another any more? It takes a great deal of effort to keep a marriage alive after decades, not years together. Perhaps only my husband and I managed that with some ease.

"Pour me one," I murmur to Reginald as I walk closer to him. He does so even though I'm not sure he heard the request. The measure I receive is less than half of his own. Does he subscribe to the idea that ladies shouldn't drink too much? I doubt it.

"What did he ask you?" I mutter to him. Reginald blinks, his eyelids moving so slowly I think he might be the next to topple over.

"About where I was and who I was with when the man was killed." His tone is one of wounded pride. It seems he doesn't like to be questioned about such things. I imagine he was as aggrieved when examined by the detective inspector investigating the events surrounding my husband's death. Of course, we were all together then, as well. The six couples, the heir-apparent, Amelia and Rebecca. Lilian, Hector, and so too was Mr Harrington-Featherington and Lady Carver. All of us, together, for the Christmas festivities, at our home in London. Not that they ended on a festive note.

It means that everyone here spoke about me, probably against me. Twice they've had me arrested for something I didn't do. I'm grateful for the mistake because it must have been a mistake that's seen Mr Harrington-Featherington murdered while I was in police custody. It seems they've perfected it to some sort of an art form.

I've decided it must have been a mistake – not the actual killing, but the time it was carried out. Maybe the murderer hoped to strike at the same time as Lady Carver was drowned? Or, perhaps it wasn't planned at all. It is possible that Mr Harrington-Featherington witnessed the first murder or suspected someone and had to die because of that? I'm eager to find one of the guests who look distinctly rattled at this turn of events.

Once more, my gaze sweeps the room from where I stand close to the window, but it's Reginald who speaks and draws my attention.

"Lady Merryweather, Ella." His tone surprises me.

"Reginald," I don't waver in the sharpness I've employed ever since my first arrest.

"I really must apologise to you. For everything." Reginald's words startle me. I swear I've never heard him apologise for anything in all the years I've known him. He's a man who will do anything not to have to apologise.

"For everything?" my voice has lowered. I confess he's knocked my careful composure with his heartfelt words.

"Yes, for everything. I was swept along with it all. I acknowledge when poor old Bertie was murdered, and there was all that hoo-ha, I genuinely could think of no one who would want him dead but you. That police bod, I forget his name, assured me that if a man should die in such a way, then it could only ever be the fault of the wife."

He speaks about Detective Inspector Davidson. How I detest that man and his ineffectual investigative skills. I blame him entirely for the fact that my husband's murderer is still at large. If he'd been less convinced of my guilt, even before he'd laid eyes on me, then I might not have feared my death on the end of a noose.

Detective Inspector Davidson is a tall, thin man with a constantly dripping nose and about as much vigour as a dead slug in the greenhouse. How he ever became a detective inspector, I do not know. I do know that he detests me as much as I hate him, for he's being investigated for such woeful performance following my release from prison. I hope they send him back to the beat. He can do much less harm plodding around the streets of Kensington than he can determining someone's guilt or innocence when corporal punishment is dependent on the verdict.

"And now you suspect someone else?" I ask the question, meeting his bullish eyes firmly.

"Yes, I do," he hisses at me, turning aside to splash more whisky into his empty glass. He holds the decanter open in one hand, his glass in the other. It wouldn't surprise me to see him drink directly from the decanter. He seems that on edge.

"Who do you suspect?" I'm whispering now, even as I try and watch those who observe us. Does Hugh know what Reginald and I speak about as his gaze sweeps over mine? Does he even care? Does he suspect?

"My wife, surely that's obvious to you."

"Gwendoline?" I blurt. I confess, he astounds me.

"Yes, my bitch of a wife. I believe she killed your husband over some long-held slight. Did you know that before you married Bertie, Gwendoline and he had a bit of thing going on?"

I do know this. As Bertie once regaled me with the tale, puffing on a cigarette after I'd beaten him at a fiercely contested game of chess. It was Gwendoline who believed there was more between them than he did.

"Yes, Bertie told me," I confirm.

"And did he tell you what she did after the engagement of you and Bertie was announced?"

Now, this I don't know.

"She went to his house, under the guise of offering her congratulations, and bloody well punched Bertie in the face. He had a black eye for nearly two weeks."

I feel my forehead furrow as he speaks. I remember that as well. We had to put off having our photographs taken while the bruising went down.

"He told me that came about through a game of cricket or rugby, something like that."

"Yes, well, he wouldn't have wanted anyone to know that Gwendoline was responsible. But she told me one night, years later, when she'd imbibed far too much sherry, what had happened. She was bitter about it that night. She told me I was nothing compared to Bertie. And she hated you."

"So why wait over twenty-five years to kill Bertie?" I demand to know.

"Margot." Reginald snaps.

"Margot?" This is getting confusing. One minute he speaks of his wife, the next of Lady Margot Bradbury, Edmund's wife.

"Yes, Gwendoline believed that Margot and Bertie were having an affair, and she was distraught. Why would Bertie risk it all with Margot Bradbury when he wouldn't do the same for her? I tell you, she's a jealous bitch."

Reginald's face has gone through all the shades, from white with unease to puce with rage as he speaks to me. I've had to move back to avoid his whisky-tipped spittle.

"And now she's killed Mr Norman Harrington-Featherington?" I don't believe that Gwendoline killed my husband, if she did, because of jealousy. But I'm intrigued to know how much thought Reginald has given the matter. What has he managed to convince himself about?

"Norman suspected there was more to Gwendoline and Bertie's relationship. I overheard him speaking about it one night at the Angel Club, and earlier today, before luncheon, they had a furious argument in the formal garden. I saw him stride away from her, his face clouded with fury, and she refused to speak to me when I asked her about it. I suspect he accused her of the murder of Lady Carver as well."

"Why? Was Lady Carver also having an affair with my husband?" Bertie would laugh to hear about all these women who thought he loved them.

"No, but Lady Carver and Gwendoline are long-time enemies. I suspect that Norman shared his concerns with Lady Carver."

Lady Carver and Mr Norman Harrington-Featherington? I can hardly imagine a more mismatched pairing, but they were often found in one another's company, so perhaps not. I had suspected that they shared a secret, but this wasn't the sort of secret I had in mind.

"Surely," I begin. "If Gwendoline needed to murder someone to protect her secret, she would have begun with the person spreading the rumours."

"So you don't believe me? I've told the Detective Inspector. He took my concerns seriously."

I shake my head.

"It isn't that I don't believe you, but I'm well aware of the need for proof, and also, the timing of events needs to make sense. It is, I admit, strange that the two dead people were so often found together. But whether it's because they shared a secret or not, I'm unsure."

I think Reginald will walk away from me then, disgusted by my more reasoned tone, but he doesn't.

"If proof is needed, then I'll find it. But I've told the Detective Inspector that I'm surely the next victim because I know the truth. That's why I told him, and also you as well. My wife can't kill all of us." His judder, when he says 'wife' assures me, he's very much disturbed by his such thoughts.

"But I thought you spent the afternoon together, in your

bedchamber? At least, that's what you said earlier. What's made you change your mind?"

"I was woken, at some point in the afternoon, by barking dogs, and she wasn't in the room."

"And you didn't think to say this earlier?"

"I was fearful," he confirms. "I suspect my wife of killing three people. I didn't wish to become the fourth." His hiss is too loud, and I'm aware of Rebecca's scrutiny.

"And now you've decided to inform me and the Detective Inspector of this as a means of staying alive?"

"Yes, the more who know, the better." Reginald nods vigorously.

"What will you do when the Detective Inspector finishes interviewing her?"

"He'll apprehend her for the crime of murder."

"With what proof? Have you found the murder weapon? Have you confirmed that she slipped away, and you witnessed her slicing open Mr Norman Harrington-Featherington's neck?"

Reginald looks stricken at my words and slugs the rest of his whisky before pouring more with shaking hands. I almost snatch the glass and decanter from him for fear both will tumble to the floor.

"Why do you think I'm drinking?" he hisses. Is he genuinely scared of his wife? I would never have thought it, for all she's often seemed the stronger of the two in their marriage.

"I hope the Detective Inspector will insist she be kept away from me? I'll not share a room with her this evening, and never again."

"Even if she's innocent?"

"She's not innocent." His words are firm when he speaks. I'm prepared to see what the Detective Inspector does next. Certainly, Gwendoline has been gone for longer than the other interviewees.

"I always thought Bertie must have been killed over a financial transaction that went wrong, or something like that. Not because women were fawning over him," I admit. While

Reginald is so convinced of his wife's guilt, I think it might be worthwhile prodding him for more information.

"Why? He was a whizz at managing his holdings effectively. He really was. And you must be aware of that, now that you've been allowed to inherit, as per the terms of his will. Bertie was a genius. I could wish I'd made such a success of my financial ambitions." By now, Reginald's eyes have lost their sharpness, and his jaw has slackened. He's drunk far more than he should have done. The decanter is nearly empty. Underhill will tut on seeing the good Scottish whisky depleted so quickly.

"So, why do you think I killed him then? If I did?" Reginald is so unhinged, I know he'll finally answer this question that has plagued me for the last year.

"You wanted his money and knew that if you divorced him, you'd get only a fraction and cause quite the scandal."

"What did I need his money for? I have my assets and always have." It feels dirty to me that people think I would kill a man I adored over some paltry banknotes and shares. Well, not paltry, but still, killing for money seems debasing.

"Ah, but you wanted more, always more. I've seen how you spend, and Gwendoline always listed your new acquisitions for me. I can't see how you could have gone on spending like that forever. All those motorcars and thoroughbred horses."

A soft chuckle leaves my lips. I finally take a sip of my whisky. It's good quality, but I don't like the stuff. I shake, even as it warms me from the inside. I should have asked for another pair of shoes. My feet are still cold despite the warm fire.

"I had the funds to pursue my twin loves of motorcars and horses. Bertie never paid for any of the motorcars, although he always enjoyed pretending they were his. I left him to his vices of saving and investing while I got on with earning a good enough stipend on what I had to invest as I saw fit, in vehicles and animals that pleased me."

I go to say more but abruptly, clamp down on my following comment, for Gwendoline has reappeared, with Aldcroft at her side. She's quivering with rage, whereas Aldcroft looks aggrieved. I take it the interview hasn't gone well.

"You bloody fool," Gwendoline rails at her husband from the doorway. I see then that Aldcroft has one hand held firmly around her upper arm. Without that act, I think Gwendoline would have rushed across the room and throttled her husband with her large hands. Perhaps she might have punched him as Reginald informs me Gwendoline once did to Bertie. I'd quite like to see such an attack.

"How could you?" Gwendoline continues angrily. "You always were a weaselly little man. I should never have married you."

Reginald's response surprises me. I expect him to cower behind me, but he doesn't. The whisky has given him strength.

"I should never have married you either. I should never have endured all the lovers you took during our marriage. You were brutal to me, and I have the scars to show it."

The eyes of every other guest in that room flick between the couple, and I'm amongst them. This is a fine performance from both of them.

"Come now, Lady Sunderland," Aldcroft interjects. "I'll be sending you to the police station at Rothbury to make a formal statement regarding recent events. One of the other detectives is already there. There's no need for matters to become heated here."

"To the police station?" Gwendoline gasps, her fury draining away in the face of such a statement.

"Yes. To formalise everything you've said and to have your fingerprints taken. We'll also be conducting a thorough search of your bedchamber here. You were, I believe, in the Owl suite?"

"You won't find anything?" she blurts. "And if you do, it'll be because that worm put it there. You should arrest him as well," she shrieks, using her left hand to point at her husband.

"I haven't arrested you yet, Lady Sunderland," Aldcroft continues. By now, two sergeants have appeared in their dark blue uniforms, eyes aglow at what's playing out in the library.

"Please take Lady Sunderland to Rothbury police station. She's to stay there but be treated well. Detective Andrews is to interview her about the statement she just made to me."

The two men lead Gwendoline away, although she tries to shrug aside the hand on her arm angrily. We all listen to the scuff of her shoes on the wooden floor and the more resounding clip of the police boots. The local solicitor also told me that the policemen are paid a stipend, a boot payment because they do so much walking around. Looking down at my feet, I think it strange that the men are given money for their boots, but no care is taken of their actual feet.

"And now, Mr Alwinton, if you please," and without offering anything further, Aldcroft walks back to the study as though nothing's happened, Hector falling in behind him. As soon as the men depart, a hub of conversation fills the room. With the eyes of everyone in the room on him, Reginald seems to grow taller, even as he refills his whisky.

"It was the correct thing to do," he announces and then turns away. I leave him to gaze out of the black window into the darkness of the terrible storm that continues to batter the many windows in the library. I'm sure we'd be warmer and more comfortable in the drawing-room with the hearth that's double the size of the one here, but of course, it's not comfort and warmth that the Detective Inspector wants any of us to feel.

"Can you imagine it?" It's Miss Amelia Clarke who gasps out the question. Her true feelings are difficult to determine. She sounds shocked, and yet there's a fleeting look of admiration on her bright, young face. She clasps Hugh's hand tightly, or perhaps he squeezes her hand tightly. It's not easy to tell the way their fingers are splayed together. Rebecca shakes her head. She's disgusted by Gwendoline and Reginald, but which one and for what reason, I'm unsure.

"Imagine what?" Hugh asks her. He seems very comfortable in the library, despite my earlier words. They sit together on a black leather sofa, although Hugh, with his legs spread wide, takes up far more room than Amelia, who sits, legs hooked, one over the other, in an elegant pose. It must be hurting her back to sit in such an upright way.

One of the housemaids has replenished the tea tray, and Amelia sips delicately from a fine bone china cup decorated with birds in flight. Amelia holds the saucer in a firm hand.

"Doing that to your wife? Where's his loyalty to her? For how long have they been married?"

"My dear," and Hugh's voice is much louder than her soft one. "No matter the length of a marriage, a man can't live with someone he suspects of terrible crimes, of murder. Could you sleep easily in your bed if you suspected me of killing someone?"

"Now, Hugh, dear." Her eyes are hard as she examines him. "We all know that many men have killed. The Great War might have been over for nearly two decades, but all those who fought in it killed someone." I'm impressed that she calls her fiancé out for his oversight. Of course, Hugh is too young to have fought in the war, but perhaps Amelia's father or older brothers did so. I've heard terrible stories of the nightmares experienced by our returning soldiers, of men who've taken their service revolver and ended their lives, or others, with it. It's shocking cruelty for some of them to have outlived their friends and comrades, left them behind, and not know where their bodies lay.

"Well, I do mean in normal circumstances, not during a bloody war," he harrumphs a little, clearly displeased to have been brought to task over such an issue. "All the same," Hugh continues. "I shouldn't like to share a bedchamber with someone I suspected of being a murderer or even capable of murder."

Olive interjects from her place beside the fire. She almost has her back to the others.

"It's best not to make such sweeping statements," she drawls slowly, almost as though half asleep. "The truth may see you made a fool of."

Hugh's mouth opens and closes twice before he shakes his head and reaches forward for his cup of tea. I'm surprised he's not on the whisky, but then, he's not just informed on his wife to the police.

Hector reappears very quickly. He strides into the room, as much as a man of his vast girth can, and hurries to join Reginald at the window. Reginald bows his head to listen to whatever it is that Hector wishes to share with him. I miss the Detective Inspector calling for Olive to account for her movements for the day. What, I consider through narrowed-eyes, are the two men discussing?

Bertie assured me many years ago that Hector was not always such a corpulent shape. It seems an injury at boarding school playing rugby robbed him of his physicality, and fine food and wine led to a sudden decline in the years before I knew him. I would pity him, but he seems to get along very well. The stairs at Cragside are a trial to him, but there's the elevator for when he's needed on the first floor.

Edmund reappears then. His eyes sweep the room, trying to determine what's happened in his absence as he quickly appreciates more than one person is missing.

"Lady Sunderland has been taken away for questioning at Rothbury police station," Rebecca informs him, loudly enough that Reginald hears. His shoulders stiffen at the implied criticism and the reminder of what his wife has allegedly done.

"Has she?" Edmund gasps, eyes wide with shock.

"Yes. Lord Sunderland shared some rather incriminating information with the Detective Inspector."

"And how is Lady Bradbury?" I ask to break the resultant strained silence, heavy with recrimination. Edmund's eyes focus on the grouping of Reginald and Hector. There's a perplexed expression on his furrowed forehead. What does he suspect? What does he know? Not for the first time, I wish I'd paid more attention to what everyone else was doing rather than being content with my husband, motorcars, and horses.

"Sleeping. She's been quite unwell. Her lady's maid is sitting with her, for now. I hope she'll sleep until the morning. It'll do her some good."

"I didn't know she was unwell?" Now is the time to check what Lilian and Olive told me about her.

"Yes, for some time now. It comes on in waves and lasts for differing amounts of time. She'll rally. She always does." Do I detect a hint of reproach in his words? I shake my head. I'm sure I must be imagining such things, and yet Olive glances at me, a smirk of triumph on her upturned lips that her gossipy words are true.

"Ella, a word if you please," Edmund indicates I should join him beside the windows in the library where Gwendoline was sitting. If it were daytime, these would look out towards the long sweeping drive and the lakes that hover, just out of sight, which power the electricity to the house. A fine invention. A very fine one indeed.

"What is it?" I demand. Having called me to his side, Edmund now won't meet my eyes but rather looks through the bleak windows.

"Margot," he eventually says but then pauses again.

"Margot, what?" I prompt him when the time between his words has stretched for over a minute.

"She's dying," he informs me, some semblance of sadness in his voice. "It's not well known and certainly not spoken about. Sometimes, I don't even think she remembers."

"How long does she have?"

"Months, a year if she's lucky, not much longer than that." His expression is morose. This, then, doesn't sound like she took to her bed with a guilty conscience when I was arrested, as Olive implied.

"I'm sorry for her and you."

"Don't be sorry for me," he swings his head to face me. His eyes are shadowed but perhaps not with grief. "I would sooner she was simply gone. It would be easier all round, now I know of her many infidelities. That woman has never been faithful to me." I've never seen Edmund so furious. "Did you know?" he challenges.

"I didn't know she was dying, no. And while I've heard some salacious remarks made about her in the past, I never gave them any credence. She always seemed so devoted to you."

"Devoted to my money, not to me. The bitch." Spittle flies from his mouth, landing on the window pane. I watch it slowly start to ooze down the glass, reflecting the lamplight from the interior of the room.

"You could just separate now," I suggest, unsure what else to say. I'm faced with another man who's discovered his marriage isn't all it's supposed to be. It's not lost on me that it should be the husband who has dalliances, not the women. How very modern Gwendoline and Margot seem to me at that moment. How very modern and also selfish.

"What, and add heartless bastard to the title of a cuckolded husband. I think not. No, I'll put up with her until she's dead. But I warn you; your husband is implicated in this whole mess as well."

"Are you sure?" I ask. I'm not angry with the question, but I'm unsure that Bertie did anything wrong.

"She's fawned over him for years. She always wanted him. She and that other bitch, Gwendoline, seem to have made it some sort of game to snag him from you."

I shake my head.

"Neither of them are Bertie's type. Despite what they both seem to think, he was more content with his accounts books than a fine female form."

But Edmund's shaking his head.

"I don't believe it. I saw him often with other women when you were out of London, buying your motorcars and your horses."

I don't doubt that Bertie might have been seen with other women. In fact, I know he was because he always told me.

"And were you, out with other women?" I turn and half glance over my shoulder towards Lilian. She's sitting quietly before one of the lamps, to all intents and purposes, reading the book she holds up before her.

"Now, Ella, I won't have you put it on my shoulders. It was Margot."

"And yet you already seem to have chosen her replacement." If Edmund looked furious before, now his face is purple with rage. He shakes before me. Edmund is a man under too much pressure. He might just explode with his fury.

"I have a lineage to produce to ensure this house and estate stay under the control of the Bradbury's."

"You have Hugh," I shrug nonchalantly. When I came here, I knew that these people I'm surrounded by were not the friends I'd always thought them to be. Now I'm discovering how 'other' they all were. Two marriages held together through bonds of desperation and not true companionship at all. I know that Bertie would have been horrified. He believed his friends were content in their unions.

"Hugh is my brother's son and not fit to claim this house. I'm not yet old and senile. The doctors have assured me I'm still perfectly capable of performing the act and begetting my own child."

I consider my own inheritance. Bertie and I had only one child, a much-loved son, but he died in infancy from a terrible condition, and we were never so blessed again. The loss of young Bertie was hard on both of us, but my husband never looked for another woman to give him a son. I think he blamed himself too much for what happened. I have a will ready in the event of my death, but while some people might think they know what it contains, I've never even informed the beneficiaries of what they will inherit. I think it's better that way. I feel safer as well. There was a great deal of debate when I was incarcerated, and people thought I'd hang for murdering my husband, but I never said a word about it. I trust my solicitor didn't speak about it either.

"Then I wish you luck with that, but I would attempt to keep your intentions a secret. Some here have already alluded to your plans."

I feel Edmund stiffen beside me, but I refuse to look at him. In the pooling reflection of the water dripping down the exterior window, I watch Olive return to the library and Amelia stand, Hugh's hand slow to release his grip. There's something between the two of them that doesn't quite ring true for me, although what it is, I just don't know.

"You have no right," Edmund hisses, still just as angry.

"Then don't ask my opinion because that's precisely what you were doing." I turn my back on him. All this talk of affairs and jealousy is making me uncomfortable. I loved my husband, and he loved me, and yet we seem to have surrounded ourselves with people who were unhappily wed and determined to do all they could to seek their own pleasure, no matter who they hurt in the process.

Again, I refuse to allow Edmund's words to soil my memory of Bertie. I don't believe he was ever disloyal to me. If he was, then I'm a terrible judge of character and need to stop pretending to be anything but that.

Amelia is gone for only minutes, and then Rebecca replaces her, but only after Amelia has whispered something into Rebecca's ear. Hugh watches on, clearly uneasy at whatever they plot. I consider what it is. Perhaps it's nothing more than an assurance that the Detective Inspector's questions are not too taxing. Maybe it's something more sinister.

I feel someone watching me and meet the gaze of Lilian as she pretends to her reading. But really, I know she's listening and watching, just as I am. I rub one cold foot down the back of my opposite leg. Lilian intrigues me, and yet so do all of the guests. Even the events that Reginald and Edmund have shared with me spark more than just my interest. They make me suspicious. What if the two men are colluding against their wives? Perhaps having their wives taken down for murder is preferable to getting a divorce or waiting for one of them to die?

Lilian appraises me, as I do her. I incline my head to her and then realise that Lilian's gaze is fixed firmly on Edmund rather than watching me. I sense something in her look, but it's not love or compassion. She's ambitious that one. I should have seen it when we first spoke.

But then she's pulled away from her reverie by Detective Inspector Aldcroft, and only when she returns are we allowed to partake of our dinner. By then, I'm almost faint with hunger, and I'm forced to ask one of the housemaids to run upstairs and fetch me a shawl and also some warm shoes. I simply can't go on as I am, even when Edmund is solicitous enough to allow me to sit with my back to the raging fire in the dining room.

We all eat quickly, conversation muted. I keep my eyes on the portraits that surround the room. Here are Edmund's ancestors in all their Victorian starched glory in heavy gold frames. I'm happy to rush away when I've eaten my fill. The detective inspector must finally share his findings with me, and only then can I bathe and retire for the evening.

# Chapter 6

## *The following morning*

I step outside. The rain has finally stopped, the drip of water pooling from the roof, a reminder of just how fierce the storm has been. The sky's a watery blue, soft clouds scudding overhead, and I huddle inside my good coat. I've managed to find my boots and so my feet are warm as I find myself on the very spot where Mr Harrington-Featherington had been found dead the evening before.

I'm not alone. Detective Inspector Aldcroft accompanies me. We don't speak. It feels as though we've spoken a great deal, late into the evening yesterday. I'd retired to a warm bed, and slept well. I don't think Aldcroft has been so lucky. He yawns, stifling it behind his hand, and I pretend not to see. The poor man. He must be exhausted, and now that he isn't apprehending me on the say so of these horrible people I once thought of as friends, I almost like him.

He's been led a merry dance by the inhabitants of the house yesterday. He's made arrests but none of them are the killer of Mr Norman Harrington-Featherington or Lady Beatrice Carver. Or so it appears. Still, Lady Gwendoline Sunderland has been kept at Rothbury police station, and under police guard. She's certainly not what she seems.

Despite the deluge of the night before, it's easy to see the spot where the body was found. A dark stain mars the grey stone. It's only a fraction of what must have bled from the man, but it's enough to see it, and to know that someone died here.

Belatedly, I notice that Aldcroft has turned, and is gazing back at the doorway out of which we've just walked. Last night, I'd used the main door, as had the police officers. This area had been marked as out of bounds while Aldcroft orchestrated a thorough search, despite the heavy rainfall and the darkness. He'd hoped, he told me last night, that the weapon might be found, or some other tell-tale sign, but there had been nothing. If the murderer had left something behind, then the wind had blown it clear, or the rain had sent it spiralling down the hill to the river below us. It was probably winding it's merry way down the stream, if it had ever existed in the first place.

I shuddered at the thought of the basin tank, where Lady Carver's body had been found. It would be fuller than normal as well.

"I can't see that anyone could have made their way out here, and not been seen." Detective Inspector Aldcroft face is lined in confusion.

"The library, and the study both look out on this spot, as does the garden alcove." I confirm.

"And the guests have made it clear that there were people in the library at the time. It would have been a terrible risk to take," he further muses, as though I've not spoken.

"The actions of someone desperate." I'm fast becoming convinced that while Lady Carver's death might have been planned well in advance, that of Mr Harrington-Featherington's has been opportunistic. Aldcroft has agreed with me when I'd mentioned it during our interview yesterday evening. While the remainder of the guests had been allowed into the drawing room following our dinner, they'd been watched by one of the police sergeants, essentially to ensure they weren't attacked but really to make sure none of them could try and kill anyone else, or tamper with any evidence they might have left somewhere, if they had been the killer.

"He was definitely killed here?" I ask, just to be certain.

"He must have been. The amount of blood. I can't see that

anyone could have killed him elsewhere and dragged his body here without being noticed. Yes, it was going dark, by the time we believe he was killed, but not enough to entirely mask what was happening."

"So the police surgeon is convinced the murder took place at dusk? At what 4pm?"

"Yes, based on what evidence he found, he is. Admittedly, it was a cold day so it's difficult to tell."

I walk to the edge of the rockery. From here, I can just glimpse the formal garden and greenhouses on the opposite bank of the burn.

"Surely, it would have been easier to push him over?" The fall's huge, and almost sheer. There's a path that winds down to the river, but it's treacherous. I've made the trek many times on previous visits to the estate, but it isn't for the faint of heart. It's impossible to admire the view. It's lethal to not watch your own feet.

Aldcroft stands beside me, peering down, his expression inscrutable, as he ponders my words.

"It would have made it more difficult to find the body, that's a certainty. Yes, we'd have known he was missing, but whether he was actually dead or not would have been a mystery. Not until we found him at some point in the future. It would have meant you'd have to have been considered a suspect." While he speaks with consideration, the words sting.

"Then I'll be grateful for the mistake," I try to jest, but my voice sounds edgy, even to my ears.

We're not alone. There are two constables searching through the shrubs and plants, and in the cracks between the hard-packed earth and the grey stones. They pretend not to listen, but I'm sure they hear everything. It's that sort of day, when sound travels in strange ways; the calm after the storm. I imagine those inside the huge house, with its mock Tudor design, are listening closely as well, especially the actual murderer or murderers. I'm yet to be unconvinced that there were two, or more of them, involved in what's happened in such a peaceful location.

"So," Aldcroft turns to me. "We have a number of suspects who while thinking they have an ally, actually don't. Miss Lilian Braithwaite is one of them, as are Lord and Lady Bradbury and Mr Hector Alwinton. They were all alone at one point or another yesterday afternoon, after luncheon and before the victim was found."

"I'm intrigued by the notion that Lord Bradbury heard dogs barking and came to let his hounds inside. Lilian is adamant she arrived back only just as the body was discovered."

Aldcroft nods, brooding.

"Yes. She might well have returned earlier. Slit our victims throat, and then scampered back along the road way. No one was looking for her. It was expected that she'd be a long time, because the dogs needed a good run, and it's a fair distance to Cragend quarry and back."

"But why?"

It always comes back to this. Why had Lady Carver and Mr Harrington-Featherington needed to die? What did they know, or suspect, that made someone so desperate that only their death could make them feel safe?

"There's been a great deal of speculation that this is all connected to your husband's death." There's sympathy in Aldcroft's voice. Not many ever show it. Most people believe me guilty. It's taken my clever solicitor to argue for my innocence, and to pick apart the terrible report that the London detective cobbled together, with all his supposed witnesses.

I turn, hearing the scuff of a boot over the stones, and see my driver, Williams. I've not seen him since he returned me to Cragside yesterday, but he seems well enough. That pleases me. I know that Williams isn't happy with his room in the servants wing. It's quite distant from the main body of the house.

Williams nods at me. He's dressed in his usual chauffeur garb. He looks smart but competent. I notice that he has flushed cheeks and mud along his boots and trouser bottoms. Where has he been?

"Detective Inspector," Williams voice is gruff. He has no

love for Aldcroft, and is unaware that we've reached an accommodation to help one another. I couldn't find him earlier to let him know everything that had transpired last evening, and yet I believe he knows enough for I suspect where he's been.

"I walked to Cragend quarry and back early this morning. I've taken all the different routes, past Slipper Lake, and along the carriage drive, and even through the many rock paths. I did find some evidence of dog prints on the higher path, but nowhere else, and yet, I discovered this," and Williams holds out what can only be the murder weapon, its edge sharp and glistening with menace as he holds it in a white handkerchief, "crammed down the side of one of the rock paths. I've marked it and can show you exactly where it was."

Aldcroft beckons one of his constables closer, as he peers at the sharp knife.

"Have you an evidence bag?" he asks them, and the youngster rushes to get one from a black bag, similar to a doctors bag, lying on the ground close to the garden alcove door.

"Put it in here," Aldcroft instructs Williams. "But first, hold it out so I can look closer at it."

Williams, watching me the entire time, does as he's asked. Aldcroft grunts softly.

"It seems as though there might be a fingerprint in the gore. I'll have someone look at it. Now, place it in here, carefully."

I watch the two men as the knife's lowered into a brown paper bag. Williams is entirely loyal to me. Aldcroft isn't, and yet I can determine that both men see this as yet another indication of my innocence, if more were needed.

"Explain what you think happened," Aldcroft asks my tall chauffeur.

I nod swiftly, to show that Williams should speak freely with the Detective Inspector. It warms me to know that he would have been circumspect if I'd implied it was necessary.

"I think the dogs were walked yesterday afternoon, but I don't believe they went as far as the quarry." I consider how Williams knows this, but servants often know everything that happens in a country house such as this. "While accepting that it rained a great deal last night, I don't accept that it would have entirely washed away paw prints, not when the animals have such sharp nails that dig into the ground."

"How far do you believe the dogs were walked?" Aldcroft queries. I'm pleased he considers Williams observations.

"No further than just past Slipper Lake." Williams speaks of a lake that Edmund's father constructed for fishing. It's half way to the top of the slope, a more gentle climb for a man in his older years.

"So far enough away that their howls might not have been heard. But, what of Miss Lilian Braithwaite? She said she walked them to Cragend quarry." I'm impressed that Aldcroft shares such insight with Williams. I consider then that they might have already spoken about what they think happened.

"She may well have done, but Miss Braithwaite returned by a different route to the dogs. I believe she tied them up, and left them while returning to the house to kill Mr Harrington-Featherington ."

Aldcroft's lower lip twists in thought, but he doesn't dismiss the suggestion.

"And what? She discarded the knife when rushing back to the dogs via a different route?"

"Possibly, yes. It's certainly a quicker route if you needed to run."

"And then, she returned more slowly, bringing the dogs as her alibi."

"But why would Lilian have wanted to kill Mr Harrington-Featherington ?" I muse. "I can't see that she could have been involved in my husband's murder, either. She didn't know either of us before our house party. Why then would she have felt the need to shoot him with a pistol?"

Williams is shaking his head, as perplexed as I am.

"I don't know the answer to those questions, but there's certainly something strange going on, even if she's not responsible for leaving the knife wedged down one of the stone steps. She didn't walk to Cragend quarry. Or rather, she didn't take the dogs all that way or there would be prints in the mulch."

"Couldn't she have taken a different route." I press. I know how many routes there are to Cragend. There's anything from a gentle walk to a more strenuous climb.

But Williams shakes his head.

"The paw prints simply stop. The dogs stopped there. They didn't go any further."

"My thanks," Aldcroft states. "Have you done any other investigating?" There's no malice in his voice, just weary acceptance that Williams is my ally and likely to do all he can to prove my innocence.

"I've spoken with the servants. They have some interesting stories about Lord and Lady Bradbury."

"And I'd like to hear them, but perhaps not here," Aldcroft admits, half an eye to Edmund Bradbury who's standing in his study, watching what's happening outside, his pipe in one hand, although it's not lit. "But, in the meantime, can you take one of my constables to look at where you found the knife. I need photographs of the spot, and a further search to determine if there's any other evidence."

"Of course," Williams half bows and then straightens, realising that Aldcroft's a police officer, and not a member of the landed gentry. There's no need to show such deference. A wry smirk quirks on his lips.

"Thank you, Williams," I call to him. He grins at me, the years leaving him in that instant, and I see him as I remember him from when I first employed him to help me with my motorcars. He shares the same passion for engines, oil and tyres that I do. He's not so enamoured of horses. He'd rather not stand in ripe horse manure.

# Chapter 7

When Williams and one of the constable's have crunched their footsteps over the gravel drive, Aldcroft turns to me.

"This is getting more and more complex. The answers aren't easy to find."

"They never are," I console him. "If it's always the easy solution, then we wouldn't need the police to interrogate people."

"Perhaps. But, what, there are only nine people staying as guests inside the house, and while I wouldn't dismiss the servants without questioning them first, it still seems preposterous that one of them would have killed Lady Carver or Mr Featherington-Harrington."

"But as we're discovering, there are a great many secrets amongst the guests. They aren't quite the upstanding individuals I always believed them to be."

Aldcroft shakes his head unhappily at my words.

"I've already apprehended two individuals, but I know that one of those decisions was incorrect, and the other, while correct, isn't related to the murders here. Not as far as Detective Andrews can determine. I feel no closer to a solution, and I can tell that you're just as puzzled."

I nod. I am indeed puzzled. Silence settles between us.

"Come. We'll see if this knife came from the kitchen," Aldcroft mutters.

"I can tell you that it did," I offer, preceding him inside the house through the garden alcove. "In this house, the kitchen is close to the dining room, and the study and library along the outer hallway. It would have been simple for someone to duck inside it and take the knife."

"Yes," Aldcroft agrees, his unease evident.

"But. There are many housemaids in the kitchen. It would involve taking a huge chance." Despite it all, I can't envisage someone taking the chance, unless they were desperate. Of course, if Norman's murder was a crime of opportunity, and not planned, that risk might have seemed insignificant.

"Not for someone they might expect to see in the kitchen, such as Lord or Lady Bradbury," Aldcroft contradicts me.

I swallow. Despite everything, I still found it difficult to suspect Edmund, even if I can happily believe it of Margot.

Once back inside the house, we walk the short distance to the kitchen, passing the butler's pantry on the way. I note the black telephone and the butler's desk, although Underhill's away from it at the moment. No doubt, he's directing his footmen somewhere else within the house.

From inside the kitchen, the smell of fresh baking bread makes my stomach growl with hunger, as I note the vast array of brown jars, glass jars and the huge hearth over which the cook presides.

There's also a large wooden table, various dishes and chopping boards evident on it, no doubt preparations for luncheon or dinner later, and of course, a block in which knife handles can be seen.

The cook, a tall woman, is busy giving out instructions to her assistants, back to Aldcroft and I. I listen to her, and then one of the younger woman notices us and gives a slight squeak. I anticipate the cook berating her, only she turns instead, her own eyes boggling at the sight of us.

"My Lady, Sir," her voice is much lighter when she speaks to us than when instructing her staff. It's lost the tone of command she uses when speaking to her subordinates.

"This is Mrs Underhill," I introduce her. I've known her for many years and in all that time, all I can see are a few furrows around her eyes and the odd speck of grey amongst her naturally blond hair to attest to her age.

"Lady Merryweather," she bobs a quick curtsey, and I shake my head at her. She knows better than to show me such deference when she's helped me on so many occasions in the past.

"This is Detective Inspector Aldcroft," I indicate the police detective. "We're wondering if you might be missing a knife?"

Her eyes shoot open at the question, but she's already nodding.

"I am yes, the good sharp one used for carving the meat. I've had the girls looking for it all morning. I know one of them must have mislaid it, but they all deny it."

"Alas," and now Aldcroft speaks. "I don't believe you'll find it anywhere."

Mrs Underhill looks uneasy.

"I don't understand," she murmurs, looking at me, not at Aldcroft. "Are you saying that one of my knives was used as a weapon?" The words come out half-strangled. I can already see one of the house maids quickly making a cup of tea from the huge brown teapot to thrust into Mrs Underhill's hands. There's also a stall behind her, and she sits heavily, all the life gone from her.

"Do the knives have dark brown handles? Wooden handles?" I ask, just to be sure.

"Yes, yes, look," and she indicates the table, and with a visible shudder, pulls another of the knives from the knife block I'd already seen.

Even that brief glance is enough to confirm that the knife is indeed from the kitchen.

"Do you know when you last saw the carving knife?"

"Not today," Mrs Underhill confirms, taking the mug of tea with shaking hands.

"And yesterday?" I don't want to press the point when she's already so upset, but it's necessary.

"I couldn't rightly say. I believe it was used in the morning, but not in the afternoon and evening. I assumed it was lost in the dish washer. It's happened before," she confirms. I can tell how distressed the questions are making her.

"And do you know if you had any unexpected guests yesterday afternoon?" I'm pleased Aldcroft asks the question, for all Mrs Underhill's eyes suddenly sharpen as she meets mine.

"You mean? From here? With my?" I understand her shock very well.

"I don't think I rightly remember, right now," she lifts the mug of tea as though to take a sip and then puts it back on the table once more, steadying the mug and her hand at the same time.

"Do you think I might be in danger?" she asks fearfully.

A lengthy silence follows. I risk looking at Aldcroft, anticipating him saying something reassuring, but he doesn't.

"At the moment, I can't guarantee that you're not," he eventually announces. "I'll have one of the constables placed here, with you, and this evening, there'll be a police presence in the servants quarters. But I do need to know who visited the kitchen yesterday afternoon?"

Now one of the maids comes forward. I recognise her as the girl from yesterday. She brought me tea and fetched my shoes for me.

"If you please, I know that Lady Bradbury came in to ask for tea. She should have rung the bell, but as she was passing, she popped her head around the door. And while she was here, she checked on the preparations for dinner as well." The young girl can be no older than eighteen or nineteen. I think she's brave to speak up as she does, and so does Mrs Underhill, who reaches for her hand and pats it.

"Now I remember," she muses. "After the tea was taken to the drawing room, Miss Olive Mabel turned up to ask for some honey to soothe a sore throat and then Miss Amelia Clarke came in to ask for a crust of bread as she was starving. Miss Lilian Braithwaite poked her head around the door as well. She was after some off-cuts to tempt the dogs with on their walk."

It's quite a list. I notice that Aldcroft has slipped his notebook clear from his pocket and is writing down the names of the visitors to the kitchen.

"And were you in the kitchen all afternoon?" he asks Mrs Underhill.

"No. I went for a walk about 2pm. I took an hour, before the rain and the darkness fell. I often do. I need to stretch my legs."

"And does someone else stay in the kitchen during that time?"

"There's usually someone in here, in case of problems. Can you remember?" she asks the young woman.

"I think the gamekeeper took his afternoon tea beside the hearth. It wasn't a warm day."

"Thank you," Aldcroft also makes a note of this, and then turns to me.

"Lady Merryweather, would you remain here while I go and make a telephone call and summon some additional police officers. I shan't be longer than five minutes."

"Of course," I confirm. Mrs Underhill looks relieved at his suggestion.

"Would you like some tea?" the maid asks me.

"Oh, yes please," I reply and pull out one of the wooden chairs to sit on, while I face Mrs Underhill and the other maids and servants in the room. I try not to glance at the dishwasher, or at the steps which led down into the depths of the under-kitchen. I suddenly sense a murderer could be hovering anywhere. I feel as uneasy as Mrs Underhill and the rest of the servants.

"This is terrible," Mrs Underhill mumbles. "Bad enough when Lady Carver was found dead, but this, well, I'm shaken."

"I think we all are," I reply softly.

"You know," and she fixes me with her firm eyes. "I didn't believe it when they said you'd killed your husband. You and Lord Merryweather were always so much in love, if you pardon me for saying such a thing. We could all tell. Me and Mr Underhill used to comment on it. So different from all the other guests we get in this house."

I feel a warm glow touch my cheeks at her words, and my lower lip trembles. In everything that has happened, almost everyone has forgotten that as well as being labelled a murderer, I've also lost my husband of twenty-five years. One of the reasons I'd accepted the invitation for the long weekend is because, since my release, I despise spending time in London. The house feels too empty without him, and without the scent of his shaving foam and thin tendrils of cigar smoke sneaking out from his study.

"It must be hard," Mrs Underhill offers me more sympathy than anyone else. She would know, she and the butler, Mr Underhill, have been married for well over thirty-years now.

"It has been," I confirm, trying not to notice that the maid's listening as carefully as Mrs Underhill. I don't like to show any emotion, but Mrs Underhill's kindness has caught me unawares.

"I can tell you it'll get better with time, but that's no real consolation. Time is a contrary beast."

"It is," I murmur, sipping from my hot, sweet tea.

"And now this? The maids have heard whispers they believe it might be related to what happened...before."

"Yes, there's been some talk of that. It seems that there are many secrets I'm unaware about."

"This house is built on secrets," Mrs Underhill confides in me. "Lord and Lady Bradbury are not often to be found in accord with one another. Lady Bradbury tends to spend much of her time at one of the other houses, when she's well enough, that is. A terrible thing for her, to be dying of such a malady."

"And what is the malady?"

"Cancer," Mrs Underhill confirms. "Women's cancer," she continues. "Terrible to die such a slow and painful death. It happened to my mother when I was a young un'. That's how I ended up coming here."

This is the first time a name has been given for Margot's condition, and I feel a flicker of pity for her. I've heard it's a painful death. I wouldn't wish that on anyone, stranger, friend or enemy.

"She often takes to her bed?" I prod.

"Yes, for days, if not weeks on end. The doctor is fair run-ragged with her demands, for all I know he can only treat the pain and not the malady."

"It all started, I believe, when I was apprehended."

Again, Mrs Underhill nods. The colour's returning to her face, and she even reaches across and helps herself to one of the sweet biscuits cooling on a rack.

"A little too much salt," she cautions another of the maids distractedly. Amongst all this, she isn't going to allow her assistants to get away with a salty biscuit. I admire her.

"Yes. To begin with, I thought it might be related. And even now, it's possible it was, but eventually, the doctor confirmed the diagnosis."

"I understand that Lord Bradbury may have set his sights on a younger woman."

Mrs Underhill gasps at the revelation, and shakes her head, eyes furious.

"I may think the pair of them far from compatible, but to hear such said horrifies me. She still has her life, and will do so for some time yet. It's terrible to consider a future without her. I'm quite shocked by Lord Bradbury in that regard, if that is true.."

I nod. I share her shock. I expect more from Edmund.

"And I take it Mr Hugh Bradbury is aware of this?"

"It seems he is, yes. One of the housemaids overheard Hugh and Lord Bradbury having a terrible argument only three nights ago. She came all of a quiver because it sounded quite violent, and I sent Mr Underhill along to ensure all was well. He returned with three broken glasses and a smashed decanter."

"Quite a violent argument then?"

"Yes, and the housemaid is adamant they've been cold towards one another ever since."

"There is a great deal going on at the moment, isn't there?" I continue. I've been offered a biscuit as well, and find I appreciate the slight saltiness against the sweetness.

"Delicious," I offer.

"Don't encourage her," Mrs Underhill speaks with a rare smile. "I'm trying to persuade Millicent to follow the recipe and not just go with what she feels like putting in the mixture."

"Well, perhaps not for everyone then, but I enjoyed it." And I have. I wink at poor Millicent, and her face flushes even redder at the praise than at the criticism.

"The household has been quiet for the last few months. This weekend has brought together all sorts of issues," Mrs Underhill continues to confide in me. I'm grateful that while she speaks, the shock of what she's been told is beginning to ebb away. I could only wish I'd been shown such care when incarcerated for the murder of my husband. It had been months later that anyone had thought to offer me condolences and show some sympathy.

"Do you know anything about Lord and Lady Sunderland?"

"I wasn't shocked by what's come to light, if that's what you mean," the cook offers with a knowing glint in her eye. "She and Lady Bradbury weren't the allies and friends they pretended to be."

"What about Miss Olive Mabel?" Olive is perplexing me. She seems such a gentle thing, and yet I detect iron in her resolve and something must have happened to her to bring that about.

"Poor Miss Mabel. Waited all those years to get married, and then her husband died within the year. A terrible tragedy." I rack my memories, but I can't remember Olive ever being married.

"Was she married before the Great War?" I muse.

"Yes. And she was an older bride even then. She fancied herself a spinster. She had money of her own, so why did she need a man? And then she met Theodore, and it was a love match. But a short lived one."

"So he lost his life fighting in the Great War?"

"No, he was dead before it began and she's never remarried."

"How did he die?"

"Phenomena, I believe. Poor thing. Not a way to go."

I consider why I don't know this. Have I always assumed that Olive was merely a veritable spinster or has it been kept from me? I wish I could determine the answer to that without speaking to Margot or Edmund.

And then Aldcroft reappears. His expression is pensive.

"They're sending some reinforcements from Morpeth police station. There just aren't enough police officers based at Rothbury, and I must allow the men some time to rest" he confirms. "We'll ensure that no one else gets murdered here."

"Thank you," Mrs Underhill murmurs, some verve back in her voice. Only before she can say anything else there's a commotion, and Aldcroft and I share a glance and then rush to the front door, which stands wide open.

One of the constables is remonstrating with a man on the grey-gravel drive. I can hear loud voices, although the words echo too much for me to decipher them.

I notice it's the constable who's been sent with Williams, and then I realise that it's actually Williams who's arguing wholeheartedly with someone. I can't determine what's made my chauffeur so very angry. Only then, the man Williams looks fit to punch, turns his head, and now I understand everything. What, I think, is Detective Inspector Davidson of Scotland Yard doing at Cragside?

# Chapter 8

"**A**rrest her," his voice rings out, the hated flat-tones of a man who's robbed me of nearly a year of my life shuddering through my body. Why is he here? How has he known to track me down in the furthest reaches of North Northumberland.

I can appreciate why Williams looks fit to punch him.

I shoulder my way through the crowd of gaggling servants, and lay a hand on Williams arm.

"Come away," I urge him. "Leave it to Aldcroft to sort out."

I can feel Williams quivering beneath my fingers. He's furious. I'm not far behind.

"Let's go for a walk. I could do with some fresh air," I announce, casting a desultory glance at the Detective Inspector who's made such assumptions about me with no evidence whatsoever.

"Arrest her," Davidson tries once more, daring to lay his hands on my arm as though he'll handcuff me. Williams thrusts himself between us, and slices down with the side of his hand, severing the connection and allowing me to escape. The Detective Inspector staggers at the force of the blow, but sadly, doesn't fall to the gravel drive.

There are two new police cars on the drive. I hardly think there can be any police cars owned by the Northumberland County Constabulary that aren't at Cragside.

In one, there are two smartly dressed officers, watching everything with mouths agape. In the other, the vehicle filthy from the winter roads, a man is stifling a yawn, while another labours to exit the car. They're the officers from London. The other car is perhaps from Morpeth, or has brought men to relieve the two local constables. I can't be sure.

"This way," I direct Williams. He comes unwillingly, not wishing to disobey my instructions but certainly keen to put one over on Davidson. I have to pull on his arm to bring him away.

"What's that, that plank doing here?" Williams seeks a word that won't be deemed too offensive.

"That bastard has clearly heard of my arrest and come to cause problems." I speak to remind him he need not mind his p's and q's with me. We've been through too much together already.

"He must have driven all night and all day to get here so quickly," Williams notes sourly. "Even after all this time, he still believes he can pin it on you, and he bloody well can't." Williams is shouting by the end of the sentence.

"Aldcroft is on my side, this time," I attempt to mollify, but I can't deny that Davidson's arrival hasn't upset me. Just like Mrs Underhill, I feel myself in need of a sweet mug of tea and another biscuit as well. Davidson's an unwelcome reminder of everything that has happened to me. I don't want it. I don't need it. I left London to get away from it all.

"Show me where you found the tracks in the mud," I think quickly, keen for something to distract the pair of us.

"I will, but you'll need a coat. There's a biting wind."

"Just get one from the motorcar," I suggest. "That'll do me well enough." I can't face going into the house to find my favourite blue coat and hat.

Quickly, Williams skirts around the three Wolseley's, and opens the back seat door. There's a box in there that contains everything we thought we might need should the weather turn against us in the north. There are blankets, packets of food, Ryvita crackers and biscuits, cheese as well. Items that won't mind being stuck in the car. There are bottles of water, as well as some basic tools, including a jack and Williams box of tools which seem to contain every size of spanner available. There's even a gallon of petrol, just in case. I've visited the wilds of Cragside too many times in the past not to be alert to the dangers of the isolated location, even if I've always come in the summer months with the promise of pale blue skies and bright sunshine.

Williams brings me one of the spare coats and I gratefully slip into it. All the while, I can still hear Davidson railing against Aldcroft, from my position beneath the arch that joins both parts of the house together, the main house and the place where the servants live, while allowing access to the carriage drive. I'm glad to be away from it. I'm even more pleased that Aldcroft doesn't call me back.

"It's steep to start with," Williams hints at an apology, as we walk through the arch, beneath the edifice of Cragside where it actually seems to be more rock than house. To the right, I'm more than aware of the steep path that leads up to one of the most frequently taken walking routes that might take me to Slipper Lake. Or, it might lead me anywhere on the estate. The options are endless once I've reached the top of the almost vertical climb.

"It'll do me good. Too much time sitting down over the last few days, and not all of it by my choice."

But Williams is correct to warn me. The gravel drive crunches under my feet and I gaze at the way he indicates. It is indeed steep, threading a path through plants and flowers that are hibernating for the coming winter. Everything looks stark and brutal, shimmering with the rain that's fallen during the night, the wind cutting me deep, despite the welcome warmth from the overcoat. Overhead, the sky remains a blazing blue, and as I catch a glimpse of the distant Tumbleton lake, I'm spellbound, once more, by the beauty of the place.

Edmund and Margot are lucky people to call this their home. Even if they don't appreciate that.

A carpet of pine needles covers the path. My knees are burning before I've made it so much as a third of the way up the sheer incline. Williams keeps pace with me. Slowly, the sound of Aldcroft and Davidson arguing fades away, only to return when we once more draw level with the house, although much higher up, looking down on the triangular roofs beneath which the servants labour in the kitchen, and sleep during the night.

"It seems Davidson is about as good at listening as he is investigating," Williams breaks the silence, his eyes nearly alight with humour. He's trying to cheer me, and I appreciate the effort it must cost him. I'm relieved to see his fury leave him, even if only for now.

The sorry argument is left behind, as I make my way higher and higher. There are elaborate rock paths that cut through the steep embankment, but they're all so wet, it's far better to follow this much wider path that gives access to the dreaded basin tank, as well as offering a path to the Slipper Lake, and beyond that, in the far distance, to Cragend quarry. For the more intrepid explorer, it's also the beginning of the path to the twin Nelly Moss lakes and even Blackburn Lake and the small set of rapids which must be flooded after the terrible storm.

The scent of the rich loam reaches my nostrils, and I pick out small patches of bright red mushrooms and even some white ones, hidden in the darker earth and beneath the reaching branches of the many trees overhead. Many of the trees are firs, all different sorts of them, their green foliage dull even in the brightness of the day. At the immediate side of many of the paths, the rhododendrons have been cut back, ready to bloom in the spring. And what a sight they'll be then. The blaze of pinks, reds and whites will be entrancing. Something to look forward to, should I ever return to the estate.

"It feels strange, doesn't it, to realise that these magnificent trees will be here for far longer than we will. We'll be bones and dust and they'll still stand tall and proud." I feel the cold air burn in my lungs. Every word has been spoken against a gasp. It's hard going. But I'm not about to stop, even though my knees ache and grow heavier with every step I take upwards. Water runs down the steepness of the path as well. If the weather turns any cooler, the path will be unpassable on one side. Not even the jagged gravel beneath my feet will make it possible to make the journey.

The wind rustles through the trees, causing them to sway slightly from side to side. I peer upwards, shielding my eyes from the glare of the sun, and immediately feel dizzy from the passing of the clouds, high overhead. It must be even windier up there, in the domain of the birds and those few aeroplanes that might fly overhead.

"Aye, well, trees are uncomplicated things. And for that reason, they get to enjoy life for far longer than a human being does." I'm surprised by Williams insightful comment. He's much more of a thinker than many might give him credit for. On our journeys in the motorcar we often indulge in long, in-depth discussions about all things engine and horse related. We both try to avoid mentioning politics. I despise them, and Williams has some very strong views about the way our country is being managed at the moment, and while I don't disagree with him, they do distract from the enjoyment of the open road.

By now, we've finally reached the flatter part of the steep hill, and Williams stretches his legs and arms. I hurry to keep up. It'll be easier going from here, as we turn right to follow the line of the path, only amongst the trees. I'm once more shocked by the sheer amount of effort it takes to reach this height, even as I catch sight of the formal gardens and clock tower through the tangle of stubborn leaves and fir filled branches on the far side of the Debdon Burn. For a second, the sun blazes on the vast collection of buildings and greenhouses. Over there, I assume, is where Lilian spends much of her time, categorising the vast array of plants.

I consider Lilian's alibi for Norman's murder. If she has, indeed, come back to the house earlier than implied on Saturday afternoon, she'd have had to make the trip up the steep hill quickly, and without being seen. There are no end of people who could have seen her, especially from the servants quarters, and even from the front of the house, had anyone been looking for her. Someone could equally have spotted her from the formal gardens. Yes, it might be stretching it a little, certainly they wouldn't see her in any great detail, just as a colour moving against the starkness of the estate donning its winter colours, but still it is a factor to consider. I think I should inform Aldcroft of that.

"Do you think Lilian is fit enough to have run up here?"

Williams tilts his head to one side and then another, as he considers his answer.

"I believe anyone could be, with enough emphasis on what they were doing. Had she killed Mr Harrington-Featherington then she'd have been running on adrenaline, and that could certainly have sped her steps up the hill. Mind. I don't think she came this way. I believe she went along the carriage drive and only descended this way when she returned to the house afterwards."

I've seen a few paw prints on my journey up the hill, where the gravel runs out and the earth of the estate becomes dominant. Now, in the deeper mud that hasn't been forced down the slope thanks to the deluge of running water, I see more and more of them. The dogs have clearly come this way, and recently.

I pause to look at the stillness of Slipper Lake. It's a scenic spot, and promises to become even more so in time. There are trees and plants everywhere, and even two winter-brown ducks having a vicious sounding argument in the middle of the pond, their cries echoing in the stillness of the day.

"They sound just like Davidson and Aldcroft," Williams offers. I laugh at that, the sound burbling from my open mouth. Williams is entirely correct to make the connection.

"They do, don't they," I offer when I can speak once more. Williams watches me with a smirk on his face. And then we veer downwards, the path filled with luscious grasses that are slippery and very wet. I'm grateful to have been wearing my knee-high walking boots when Davidson appeared, or I'd be miserable with wet feet by now, and no chance of drying them for some time.

"Just down here the paw prints stop," Williams is in front, and he stops, just where the path connects with another one.

I turn. We're a fair distance from the house itself, and all around us, it's incredibly silent. It feels as though we're the only people in the world, a fact reinforced by the startled gaze of a small deer that's wandered from the surrounding heath beyond the confines of Cragside.

I stare at the creature, and it stares right back. I hardly dare breathe. For a long minute nothing happens, and I'm struck by how easy it would be to reach out and stroke the animal. Only a loud cawing sound ripples through the air from one of the many pheasants found on the estate. The deer bends low and startles, rushing away, through the thick ferns that have turned the same shade of brown as its coat. It's entirely gone before I can breathe again.

Williams points down at the disturbed ground, but I've already seen what he means. Here, the myriad collection of paw prints stops, but also becomes more tangled, wrapping around one another.

"They stayed here for a while?" I ask him.

"It looks that way, yes. They must have been tied to something to ensure they didn't return before Lilian wanted them to appear."

"Yes. I suspect one of the trees." While I gaze down, Williams is meandering amongst the trees that surround the spot. There are any number to choose from. But they all seem slightly too far away, and there are no paw prints closer to the trees.

"Or perhaps a bone, or something. Maybe she kept them here with food, or they're just that well trained."

"I'm not sure. If they'd seen a deer, as we just have, they'd have been off, chasing it. After all, they are hunters, for all Lord Bradbury coos over them as though they're his children." I grimace at Williams words. He's correct in his statement. Lord Bradbury is besotted with his dogs.

"And there's no sign of them having made it to the quarry?"

"Not by any of the usual trackways, no. They might have gone via the carriage drive, which wouldn't have left any sign of their passing, but then, there'd be prints in the quarry itself."

"Show me where you found the knife," I ask him.

"It's this way. Watch your footing. These rocks are slippery. I imagine in the winter, no one comes this way. They probably drive up to Nelly's Moss Lakes and then back down to the house."

I do as he says, and watch where I'm placing my feet. I expect the distance to be close, but it isn't. He leads me down and down. I begin to appreciate just how steep the first hill I've walked up is, if it's this far down to the carriage drive.

I've walked around the grounds of Cragside in their entirety many times. I feel as though I know it quite well, as well as someone could who only visits once a year. If you live at Cragside, I imagine you can spend an entire lifetime finding some new dip or tree, or hidden cave. It's a truly rambling pile in the far north of Northumberland, out of sight even of the coast because it's so far inland. To see the distant coastline, where Lord Bradbury's other house lies, I would need to head towards Alnwick on the road that cuts through the heath. Not that Lord Bradbury's other home is truly that. It's a castle, and I should name it as such.

All the same, I love it on the estate. If not at the moment, when Detective Inspector Davidson has followed me from London, and two people have been murdered, seemingly right under my nose.

"Here," in front, Williams halts. I can decipher, just from looking, that the constable who followed him to the place, has taken pains to search through the undergrowth for any other lost item. The ferns that crowd the spot are bent back, and trampled upon. I can see where he's even dug his fingers around the flat rocks forming the steps on the path.

"How on earth did you find it?" I ask Williams, watching his reaction. His forehead is furrowed in thought as he looks back along the path we've just traversed to reach this isolated location.

"I confess, I was looking for it, so I was being careful to observe as much as I could. And, the murderer hadn't done a good job of hiding it. Equally, if I hadn't slipped here, and landed on my arse, I wouldn't have seen the flash of the bloodied blade."

He grins as he speaks, a rueful expression on his face, as he rubs his backside.

"I can't tell you how much it hurt. I bit my tongue in the process, and I've quite the headache."

"You poor thing. But I'm glad you found it," I console.

"Me too. So, as far as I can tell, our murderer, left the knife here. Now, the only person who wasn't accounted for was Miss Lilian Braithwaite, wasn't it?"

"I'm not sure, to be honest. They've all given themselves alibis, and that doesn't mean that anyone of them can be taken as rock-solid. We might do better to look at those who were able to access the kitchen during the afternoon. Mrs Underhill said Lady Bradbury, Olive, Lilian and Amelia all went into the kitchen, and those are just the people she remembers. She was also absent between about 2pm and 3pm."

"Well, I think we can rule out Miss Olive Mabel, can't we?" Williams asks, but I'm shaking my head.

"I wasn't there when the body was found, and neither were you. We don't know how long it took everyone to assemble, or even where they came from. I need to speak to Aldcroft about it, see if he has considered that."

A silence falls between us, as I get down on my hands and knees to seek beneath the ferns. I doubt I'll find anything, but I've come this far and so I'm determined to make some effort.

"Are you really trusting that copper?" Williams eventually demands from me. His words are flecked with fury once more. "He trussed you up like a pig and took you away without so much as a thought for whether you might actually have had anything to do with Lady Carver's murder."

"I know that, but he at least accepts my innocence now, and not just because I do have a rock-solid alibi for when Beatrice was killed, and equally, was in police custody when Norman was murdered. We'll truly know his worth when we get back to the house and discover if that snake, Davidson, is still there."

"If he is, I think you should leave, no matter what. He'll find you guilty of stealing the salt and pepper shakers if you're not careful."

I know Williams opinion of Davidson. I share it, in all honesty, but I don't want to leave.

"I don't think stealing salt and pepper shakers warrants being locked up," I smile, and then turn serious again. "Whatever is happening, is potentially connected with poor old Bertie's murder. I don't want to run away when I can finally clear my name, once and for all."

Mutiny crosses Williams face and I move to distract him.

"Tell me, honestly, did the servants and staff ever suggest any infidelity on the part of my husband. It seems that Lady Margot Bradbury and Lady Gwendoline Sunderland are convinced he was in love with both of them."

Williams surprises me by snorting, loudly, through his nose, his face incredulous.

"Your poor husband, and I do pity him there, was beset by women throwing themselves at him all the time. But I assure you, he only ever had eyes for you. Ask his manservant. The pair of them had to concoct no end of bizarre circumstances to avoid the women. Bertie, if you'll excuse my familiarity, had no idea why the women wanted him so badly." I shoot Williams a stern look as I clamber back to my feet, but he's unrepentant in his amusement.

"I'm amazed you were oblivious to it all," he resumes. "But then, you look at motorcars the way women eyed your husband."

I reach out and slap him on the shoulder for such impertinence, and then begin to laugh as well, a low chuckle that surprises.

"Poor Bertie. Don't tell me I ignored him."

"Far from it, but you had eyes for one thing, and he had eyes for you. I wouldn't listen to the crows. They didn't know Bertie. You did, and he knew you, and, again, if you'll excuse the familiarity, he loved you just the way you were."

Williams words surprise me by bringing a tear to my eye. I'm reminded again of the rawness of my grief and anger at the person who killed my husband. My throat is suddenly tight, and I peer at the view that surrounds me, anything to avoid the pity in Williams eyes.

"I'll show you the way back to the carriage drive." Williams offers me his arm, because here, the stone steps are green with lichen and slippery as well. I don't want to land on my arse, as Williams had done earlier. I'm feeling emotional bruised without having physical ones to match.

"Tell me," I say into the quiet, broken only by the distant sounds of water pouring over some sharp edge, and the soft tread of our shoes. "What do you remember of the day my husband died?"

I hear Williams sharp inhalation, and refuse to look at him. We've avoided this topic since being reunited on my release. Now, it seems, it's important I know everything that he does.

"Where to begin," he murmurs, no doubt to assure me that he'll begin his account, once he's pulled his thoughts together.

"At the beginning," I offer, sadly. My dreams are still tormented with the image of my husband's dead face. It isn't something I think anyone should ever have to happen upon.

"As you know, there was a house party similar to this one, taking place. For Christmas, on that occasion. Christmas day itself had passed, and the party were enjoying the long, slow advance to the New Year's Eve celebration."

Just his few words take me back to that period of my life. I realise that I've forgotten much of it, or at least, tried to forget it. Now, suddenly, the scent of the Christmas spices are in the air, and I can almost taste the luxurious fruit cake my cook, Mrs Brown, had conjured up for us, complete with pristine white icing, delicious marzipan and enough alcohol to sink any of us.

The days had been lazy, the evenings raucous with too much alcohol, silly games and high stakes gambling. The women, I recall, had been worse than the men.

"Everyone had been rubbing along well enough," Williams breaks into my reminiscing. "You had a car you wished to purchase. If you remember, the seller, had been playing you a merry game, and finally, he'd agreed a date for the purchase to take place. You and I left while it was still dark, to travel the distance to Kent."

I smile at that memory. It had been a bitterly cold day, although mercifully, the roads had been free of ice. As we'd driven south, I'd regretted my decision, hands cold, even amongst my blankets. I'd pitied Williams. He would have been just as cold.

"The sale went well." I remember that. Not that I'd driven the car since. I couldn't face it. If only I'd not gone after another bloody car, I would have seen much more that day.

"By the time we returned home, the New Year's Eve party was in full swing. You asked me to park the car and disappeared inside the house to change."

At this point, it was my maid who knew what had happened in more detail. I remember taking a hurried bath, listening to her soft words as she told me of the scandal I'd missed while gone. My husband, it seemed, had taken high umbrage with one of the guests, which one she wasn't sure, and had locked himself away in his study for the day, only appearing ready for dinner. As she'd spoken, Bertie had poked his head into the bedchamber, and come to plant a kiss on my forehead. He'd looked unsettled, even I'd known that, but the dinner gong had rung out and he'd hastened away, promising to speak to me about some important matter later on. I was never to know what that was.

By the time I'd arrived at the dinner table, a little breathless, but finally warm from my bath, the soup course had been served, and I ate it hastily, as Lord Reginald Sunderland droned on in my ear about something. I believe he'd asked me about my new purchase, but had quickly become distracted with a tale of someone else who'd purchased a car in haste and regretted it when it had been beset with problems.

I'd detected some unease amongst the guests, but I'd ascribed it to whatever had happened during my absence. I'd not wanted to draw attention to it. Bertie had looked handsome in his smart blue suit, with a dash of a red bowtie around his neck. He'd always appreciated colour in his formal clothes.

I'd caught his eye, and slightly rolled my eyes at Reginald's drone, and Bertie had looked away, laughter in his eyes, although not as much as I'd have liked to see. I'd looked forward to the meal ending so I could speak to him in private.

"I spent some time with the car, as you requested, going over it and making sure there were no paint chips or problems with the tyres. Then I returned to the house for some hot food in the kitchen."

Williams didn't need to eat in the kitchen. He could, by rights, have joined us for dinner, but he wasn't one who enjoyed speaking with the upper class and all their in-built prejudices. I'd long stopped torturing him by even extending the invitation. When Bertie and I weren't entertaining, Williams had been happy to join us, if only so we could both prevail upon my husband about cars and horses he should buy instead of investments in stocks and shares.

"The cook, as ever, was up to her eyeballs in preparing a fine desert for everyone, while her assistants were doing their best to keep out of her way. I must say, she had produced a fine meal that night. I was sitting back, luxuriating in the warmth of the kitchen and a full stomach, when one of the housemaids appeared, sobbing. It took some time to work out what was the matter with her, because she was terrified, but eventually, she managed to stammer that she'd seen something, in one of the bedchambers, Lady Carver's. She thought it was a ghost," Williams shakes his head at that. Some of the housemaids can be taken with flights of fancy.

"Anyway, I went to investigate, alongside Richardson, and we found nothing, although something distinctly un-ghostlike had left wet footprints all over the Turkish rug in the room."

I nod. I remember hearing about this. I also remember that Detective Inspector Davidson had dismissed the idea without even investigating it. Not so Williams and Richardson. And not so Lady Carver.

"Richardson and I conducted an examination of all the doors

and windows in the house, and sent the butler to inform Lady Carver of what had happened. When we returned to the location of the crime, Lady Carver was quite beside herself. She said something had been stolen from her room, although she was less than forthcoming about what that was."

Suddenly, it's as though I'm standing in the room, watching all this happen around me. We've just finished our meal. The ladies are rising to retire for a quick sherry, while the men smoke and drink port. All of us have been sitting around the table, no one has left, not even to visit the conveniences. Whoever has broken into Lady Carver's room, it hasn't been one of the guests, although if it has been at the hands of one the guests, that's never been confirmed.

Lady Carver has rushed to her bedchamber, face pale, hands all aflutter. Bertie has gone with her, a caution in his eyes that I should remain in the dining room with the rest of the guests.

Uneasy and stilted conversation has flowed, and gradually dropped away so that we all sit, or stand, in uncomfortable silence. I can tell that the rest of our house guests are keen to ensure they haven't been robbed here, in my home, on New Year's Eve, but everyone remains. Bertie has that sort of power over everyone.

"Lord Merryweather had been attempting to ascertain the details. He'd asked Lady Carver repeatedly what had been stolen, but she'd merely shaken her head, sobbing, and demanded the police be called to investigate what had happened. Richardson was tasked with telephoning them. Lord Merryweather."

"Oh, do call him Bertie," I remonstrate with him. Every time he says Lord Merryweather it's as though Williams speaks of someone else entirely.

"Bertie," he offers me an apologetic smile. "Wanted me to stay in the room, I could tell. I kept a careful watch on everything while Lady Carver flittered from the dressing table, to the wardrobe, and to the bedside cabinet. Neither of us could actually determine what she looked for. I assumed, wrongly, that she must have been robbed of her jewels but she wore

so many that evening, her neck aflame with them, that her jewellery box was entirely empty anyway."

"She had her maid with her, and the poor girl was coaxed into the room by Mrs Grainger, but she was useless. I had repeated my question to Lady Carver about what had been stolen, but she'd merely shaken her head and trembled. In the end, it was Mrs Grainger who managed to quiet Lady Carver. Another room was made available for your distraught guest, and she was taken away to lie down, Mrs Grainger sending for tea and toast to calm her. We never did discover what had been stolen from her, if anything."

My eyes narrow at this recollection, but I don't interrupt him.

"At that point, the police had arrived, Detective Inspector Davidson and a sergeant."

I nod again, my throat suddenly tight. Looking back on the sequence of events now, it's impossible not to think that whoever killed my husband had thought of everything. By having Lady Carver insist on the police being called, it meant they'd been there when Bertie was found, slumped on the chair in his study, a bullet shot through the exact centre of his forehead, as though a military execution. Our poor dog at his feet, lying over his feet.

"They wished to speak to Lady Carver, but she refused to leave her room, and so they examined the bedchamber as we had. I'd already noted where the window had been forced open, but the Detective Inspector," Williams sneers as he speaks. "Was determined that the thief couldn't have possibly entered the house by that means because of the height from the ground floor. He discounted the muddy footprints I'd found in the frost covered flower borders close to the house, and instead decided to focus on the servants entrance. He was determined to interview every single housemaid and footman to determine if they'd seen someone suspicious."

"Bertie had unwillingly allowed Davidson to do as he deemed fit, and retired to his study."

I recall now the distracted look on my husband's face when

he'd come to whisper in my ear about what had happened and what was going to happen. He'd asked me to stay with our house guests while he disappeared to his study. I'd allowed it, but had squeezed his fingers tightly, an unspoken demand that he return as soon as possible.

But, it had proved impossible to keep my half-sozzled guests in one place. Margot Bradbury had demanded to take to her bed, upset by the events. Olive had wondered away somewhere, and no one knew where. Hugh and Amelia had found the gramophone and had been dancing away as though nothing had happened, Rebecca choosing what they should dance to. Norman and Hector had been engrossed in a heated debate which had led to the pair of them walking from one room to another, shouting random words to one another. Reginald had stalked outside without his coat on, having shared a few harsh words with Gwendoline, who'd prowled from the dining room to who knew where. Edmund had been moodily sorting through a deck of cards. Lilian had been gazing out of the window, occasionally swaying in time to the music.

I'd remembered with remarkable clarity when everyone's whereabout at 11.45pm had needed to be ascertained. It was at that time that the twin pistol shots had ricocheted through the house, startling everyone from whatever task they'd been doing. We'd all run, confusion on our faces.

I'd looked desperately for Bertie, but with horror, I'd quickly realised he was the only one missing, other than Lady Carver and Margot Bradbury, who'd both allegedly been in their beds at the time of the shooting.

"I'd been speaking with the housemaids myself, calming them down so that they wouldn't embarrass themselves when speaking to that Davidson chappy. But, when I heard the gun shots, I'd rushed straight to the study, and well, we both know what I found." His voice fills with compassion.

I nod, trying not to see the image of my husband, head thrust back against his leather seat, his eyes forever staring, with what I'd thought was more than a hint of surprise on his face.

I'd collided with Williams making my way to the study. He'd held me back at the doorway, firmly and without malice, as I'd racked in everything before me. The scent of gunpowder had been strong in the air. I'd shuddered. I would have collapsed on realising Bertie was dead if Williams hadn't been supporting me.

Into that scene, Davidson had hustled, a look of contempt on his face which had quickly changed to one of intrigue when he'd seen Bertie and Daisy. Between one heart beat and the next, I'd been arrested and taken away to the local police station. I'd never seen Bertie again, but some things stuck in my mind, even from my brief scrutiny of the room.

"After Davidson led you away, and before he thought to order his sergeant to seal the room, I managed to slip inside and take a good look around."

"Tell me what you found?" the words are barely above a whisper.

Stillness falls between us. I risk glancing at Williams. He's stopped walking, the carriage drive in sight just below us between two lines of winter-dull greenery.

"The desk was clear, but I suspected it hadn't been. Bertie's pen was resting on it, with no lid on, and he was never a man to do something like that. There was even a splatter of ink on his forefinger, so I knew he'd been writing. The windows were all locked, and the door had been closed until I opened it." Williams shakes his head, eyes narrow as he thinks back to that moment.

"I stood behind Bertie, and bent down low, keen to see where he'd been looking in his final moments. It was impossible not to realise he'd been looking upwards, at someone standing close to him. He must have known who the murderer was. He must have been forced to look into their eyes as they shot him." Williams utters the words in complete misery.

"I noticed then that his desk drawer was open, just a little, the key in the lock."

I nod. Bertie had kept few details from me during our marriage, but he had his secrets. Didn't we all?

"I quickly closed it, and pocketed the key," Williams

announces, his words tremulous.

"Thank you."

He coughs to clear his throat.

"When I went back and looked through it, after they refused to release you, I discovered all the documents in there were concerned with financial matters. Some stock certificates, some share certificates ones as well. But there was one item that perplexed me."

I eye him, considering why he's never told me this before.

"What was it?" I prod when he seems unwilling to continue.

"A marriage certificate."

I feel my forehead furrow.

"And it wasn't the names on it that worried me, but rather the speckle of blood on the corner of the document. I believe he was looking at it when he died, and that he thrust it back inside the drawer so that it wouldn't be found."

"But who was the marriage between."

Now Williams meets my eyes, a glint in them at the news he has to share with me.

"A Mr Hugh Bradbury and a Lady Beatrice Carver, dated 14th May 1926."

"But, Hugh would have been, what no more than eighteen at the time, and Beatrice twice his age."

"I know," Williams nods, his lips tight in thought.

"Are they still married?" I gasp. I just can't envisage a young Hugh married to Lady Carver, but it certainly offers a whole world of new possibilities.

"I've found no evidence that they ever divorced," Williams confirms. I'm amazed by all he's accomplished in my absence.

"Hugh was never a suspect, neither was Lady Carver, in the murder of Bertie."

"No, because Davidson decided you were responsible even though your whereabouts at the time the gun was fired was ascertained beyond all reasonable doubt by those you were standing beside in the drawing room. Detective Inspector Davidson believed, and still believes, that you had someone else murder your husband on your behalf."

"Well, the thick-witted fool couldn't even accept that he'd probably been called to the house for no known reason other than to be there when Bertie was killed and so have me arrested." My words are sharp. I'm still astounded that Davidson holds the position he does. He seems at worst incompetent, and at best, criminally ineffectual at his job.

"Indeed," Williams confirms. "But what if Lady Carver's copy of the marriage certificate was what had been stolen from her room earlier in the evening?"

"And what if it was taken by Lord or Lady Bradbury, one of them determined that Lady Carver should never inherit all their wealth."

"What, indeed?"

"Although, well, that was before Lady Bradbury was struck down by her illness, wasn't it?" I look at Williams then, noted the rigidness of his chin, the tension that runs through his body. What had happened to me, still plagues him, I know it does. If there's one person more determined than I, to finally find the true culprit, it's Williams.

"Are they still married?" Williams asks once more. The words seem hard for him to say.

"So, what, you think Hugh could have killed Lady Carver to enable him to marry Amelia?"

"Or Amelia, or even Rebecca?" And now I understand. Williams holds Amelia in high regard. While she and Hugh might be engaged to be married, from afar, Williams is a little enamoured of her. It'll never amount to anything, he knows that, and I don't believe he truly wants her to notice him, but it does mean he holds her on a pedestal.

This puts a very different spin on what's happened to Lady Carver.

"But then why would Lilian be involved?" I ask, because it's Lilian's trail from the day before that he's been finding, and which he now shows me.

"I don't know," Williams admits. "Every time I think I've made a breakthrough, the complexity of some other element means it either can't be so, or what I thought I knew is simply wrong."

"I quite agree," I confirm. I'm shocked by how much I don't know about Bertie's murder. I can't help thinking that if I'd not been arrested immediately, the true murderer wouldn't have remained undiscovered for so long, and wouldn't have been able to kill again. If that's what has happened, that is.

Abruptly, the carriage drive appears before us. I turn to gaze back the way we've come. The hillside's strewn with the decay of coming winter, the brown of ferns, the grey of stones and the almost black soil that's muddy now.

"It's further than you realise," Williams offers. "You can't see the house from here, and in fact, can't see it for at least another five minutes, and that's if you walk quite quickly."

"So, whoever brought the knife here was fit enough to make it here, and back before their absence was noted."

"Or it was Lilian who did have a legitimate reason to be out here."

"Or," and I know I'm playing devil's advocate. "They had access to a bicycle, or some such. Are there even any bicycle's at the property?"

"Yes, the gardeners sometimes make use of them," Williams states.

"But I can't imagine Hector on a bicycle," I chuckle darkly at the thought of his rotund shape trying to power his way up the hill.

"No, I don't see it either. But that doesn't mean he didn't do it. Perhaps he had an accomplice as well."

I shake my head, indicating we should move on.

"It's all well and good speculating," I confer, "but all we have are suspicions and possibilities. What we need is some sort of proof of something."

"To get that, you need to force your police chappy to ensure everybody's alibis for the time of the murder are correct."

"Yes, I do, don't I?" I agree. "Then let's get this over and done with. Here's hoping that bloody Davidson has left by now." And together, minds abuzz with all we've discovered, we walk back to the house. Williams isn't the only one to walk quickly and check, using a wrist watch, just how quickly the house can be reached from so far away.

# Chapter 9

Of course, Davidson hasn't left. The police car's still sitting prominently at the front of the house.

Williams growls low in his throat as we both catch sight of the London police car with its two occupants.

"Give Aldcroft a chance. It's not his fault that Davidson has appeared, unwanted. He's causing even more problems for our Detective Inspector."

"We'll see," and Williams tone makes it clear he holds out little hope of that happening. "I'm going to check the car over," he states, offering to take the coat from me that I've worn on our walk. "I want to be sure it's in good working order should we need to hightail it out of here." The words conjure up an image of us disappearing along some Northumbrian road and into the darkness of night, and I smile.

"If we must, then we must," I assent. "But that's hardly proving my innocence, and that's what I intend to do first."

"And we will, if we can," he indorses, as I open the front door, and immediately remove my muddy boots. Once more, I place my stockinged feet on the cold tiles and shiver.

I can hear an argument emanating from Lord Bradbury's study and quickly realise that Davidson and Aldcroft are far from reconciled with one another. Taking advantage of Davidson's distraction, I run up the stairs as quickly as I can, keen to find some clean shoes to wear, and another jumper and jacket. The house is cold, or I'm cold from being outside.

I enter the bedroom assigned to me for the weekend. It's called the yellow bedroom and in the summer months, it's a bright and welcoming space. But not today, where the brief brightness of the day is slowly coming to an end. Eagerly, I open the wardrobe and pull out a thick woollen jumper, something most people would expect a shepherd or farmer to wear. Pulling it over my thin blouse, I immediately feel warmer, and then feel warmer again when I pull a corduroy jacket from the wardrobe as well.

For my feet, I choose another pair of leather boots. They're not knee high, like the ones I wore to trek through the estate, but should I need to go outside again, they'll ensure my feet are warm and dry. As soon as that's done, I again descend the stairs and return to the kitchen. I heard no one in the rooms to either side of mine, where Olive and Lilian have been staying. I must assume everyone is busy about their business. Whatever that might be.

Mrs Underhill is busy directing her trio of housemaids, while a constable watches on. He stands in the corner, away from the hive of activity. I'm impressed by his alertness. It would have been easy to have been distracted by the housemaids who come and go taking drinks and food to people and returning with the empty cups, mugs and glasses.

"How are you?" I ask Mrs Underhill, as she pours me a mug of tea from the huge brown teapot in the middle of the table. It isn't a dainty china thing, far from it. As I sip the scalding tea, I consider whether it's ever allowed to empty or if it's constantly topped up with tea leaves and boiling water.

"Better now I've gotten over the shock. Thank you, My Lady, for your concern." I shake my head to deny her thanks.

"It's been a terrible few days. We need to be mindful of one another, no matter who we think we are in this household." Mrs Underhill's eyes shine for a moment, and then she coughs to clear her throat.

"I've been thinking again about everything that's happened, and the housemaids and the footmen have been talking as well. And there's a consensus that events on Friday afternoon, just before Lady Carver's body was found, are very important."

I hide my smile that we're all busy playing detective now. The more minds considering what has happened, the better, as far as I can tell.

"So, Lady Carver was found just after darkness fell. She'd taken herself off for an early afternoon walk, and when she didn't return, a small search party was ordered, just in case she'd become lost on the paths. It's easy to do. I've worked here for forty years, but every year, when the early nights start to fall, I find myself turned around, and lost. And it's not as if anyone can hear you shouting for help out there."

I nod. I know the events Mrs Underhill speaks about. I'd not long arrived at Cragside when the terrible events of the weekend began to unfold. It had been a long, if enjoyable journey north. On Thursday evening, Williams and I had stopped in a delightful hotel in Harrogate, and had then set off as soon as daylight broke. I'd arrived last of all the guests, not by intention, but rather because it had taken longer than I thought it would. In the past, Bertie and I would have taken the train north. Far easier than driving. But I'd decided against the train. If I'd taken the train, I'd have struggled for an excuse to ensure Williams stayed at my side, and these days, I only feel safe when he's close by.

"If I recall correctly, you arrived at 3pm, or thereabouts, and I was asked to send along tea to the library, where you and Lord and Lady Bradbury were reacquainting yourselves with one another. Not, of course, that Lord Bradbury could be immediately found. The housemaid said, when she brought in the tea, that you could have cut the atmosphere with a knife between you and Lady Bradbury."

I grin in remembrance. I'd not been amused at the time, but now I understand the depths of Margot's hatred of me, it's funny to think of how she'd been forced to entertain me by her husband.

"I believe that Lord Bradbury arrived at about 3.15pm. I remember glancing at the clock when I heard the dogs barking. He'd been off for a walk with them, or rather, the gentlemen of the party had been out shooting. So, Lord Bradbury went out with Mr Alwinton, Hugh, Mr Harrington-Featherington and Lord Sunderland."

I notice that Mrs Underhill's happy to name Mr Bradbury as Hugh. I make a mental note to factor that in with what she tells me. It seems she has a soft spot for the heir to the estate.

"And while the gentlemen were out shooting, some of the women had gone for a carriage drive with our chauffeur while Lady Bradbury had remained at the house, and some, such as Lady Carver and Miss Clarke, had opted for a walk.

"So, Olive, Lilian, Gwendoline and Rebecca had chosen the carriage drive?" Mrs Underhill quickly adds in all the titles to my casual use of first names, and nods.

"I believe so, yes. I'm sure Detective Inspector Aldcroft knows all this, but you no doubt don't. In the end, Lord Bradbury returned before everyone else. I didn't see him enter the house, but as I said, I did hear the dogs, and when I left the kitchen to ask Mr Underhill for something, I noticed all the mud on the wooden floor close to the front door. I heard his voice coming from the library. As none of the other men had returned, it must have been him in the library. Or so I thought."

I accept the refill for my mug from Mrs Underhill as she watches her housemaids carefully, even while considering what she recalls. The electric lights are now on in the kitchen, meaning it's easy to see what everyone's doing, even down to the housemaid with the task of reloading the dishwasher. But Mrs Underhill hasn't finished speaking.

"Only then, one of the housemaids rushed into the kitchen, saying that Hugh had asked for some crumpets and tea because he'd become perishingly cold while out on the shoot. I asked the girl if she'd seen the other men, but she said, and it was Alice here," Mrs Underhill points to the young woman, who bows her head and nods at the same time to confirm it was her. I recognise her as the housemaid I saw rushing outside and then back into the house when I returned on Saturday evening. "That the three other men hadn't returned, and that she'd met Hugh on his way to bathe."

"So he'd gotten very cold then?" I reiterate.

"And also, very wet. One of the footmen, Billy over there, brought his clothes away and they were sopping. Hugh said he'd fallen into a muddy patch out on the heath."

Mrs Underhill eyes me meaningfully and I realise that she isn't about to shade the truth to keep him safe.

I nod in understanding and she continues.

"And he wasn't the only one. When the rest of shooting party returned, accompanied now by Miss Mabel and Miss Clarke, Mr Alwinton was also sopping wet and chilled to the bone, and when the women returned, Miss Braithwaite was the same. And, I can tell you, it hadn't rained in these parts for nearly six days until last night's terrible storm."

"As you know, when the alarm was raised for Lady Carver, the valet, the chauffeur and the boot boy were sent out to look for her, along with all six of the gardeners, who know this estate better than anyone."

"But only Lord Bradbury accompanied them," I interject then. Mrs Underhill nods again and flashes me a rare smile, as though I'm her student and have pleased her by paying attention.

"The other men all declined to venture outside. Lord Sunderland was struggling with a nasty blister he'd obtained on his heel. Hugh said he'd caught a chill and couldn't go out, whereas Mr Harrington-Featherington refused to. Mr Alwinton, of course, couldn't be expected to go out again."

"And none of the women were allowed to venture out, I recall."

"No, not even Miss Braithwaite who knows the estate as well as the gardeners and the gamekeeper."

"And it fell to Lord Bradbury and his valet to find her, floating in the basin tank," I finish for her.

She grimaces sadly.

"And that's when everyone decided to point the finger of blame at you."

I don't need a reminder of what happened next, but all the same, it flashes through my mind.

The gamekeeper had come racing back to the house,

95

breathlessly informing Underhill to contact the local police based at Rothbury, and in no time at all, we'd all known that Lady Carver was dead. I'd still been in the library with Margot Bradbury, and the other guests had slowly collected there as well as people had recovered from their afternoon of activity, taking baths or eating crumpets or whatever else they'd needed to do.

The conversation had filled with shock and sorrow. I'd been as horrified as everyone else, a deep sense of foreboding already making me wish I hadn't made the journey north.

Tea had been provided by Mrs Underhill, and stronger drinks had been handed out by the footman. And then, when Chief Inspector Aldcroft had arrived, I'd been denounced, widely, rudely and in front of everyone else.

First to state I was a murderer had been Margot Bradbury. Her words had astounded me. Of everyone in that room, she'd known exactly when I'd arrived and that I'd spent the afternoon with her. Norman Harrington-Featherington had been the second to point the finger at me, his words cold and filled with horror.

After that, they'd all taken it in turns to ensure Detective Inspector Aldcroft knew of my chequered past. They'd also laboured the point that it was impossible for anyone else to have perpetrated such a terrible crime from amongst a group who'd professed their innocence when my husband had been murdered. No matter what I'd said, no matter how often I'd asserted my innocence, Aldcroft had simply not listened, instead, having examined the body of Lady Carver, only to eager to have an arrest before the body was truly cold.

In no time at all, I'd been handcuffed and led away to the local police station at Rothbury and there I'd stayed until sense had finally prevailed.

It hadn't actually taken Detective Inspector Aldcroft that long to determine the timeline leading up to Lady Carver's death. A great deal had been made of my late arrival to the house party. Williams had been summoned and forced to explain everything about our journey north in minute detail, including such things as what time we'd begun our journey along the A1 from Scotch Corner and along the A697 from Morpeth, turning right at Longframlington to follow the narrow road leading to the entrance to the estate just before reaching Rothbury itself.

"They say she'd been dead for no more than two hours when she was discovered," I talk into the silence now that Mrs Underhill has finished speaking. I'm aware that the police constable is listening carefully.

"Poor woman. Drowned in that dark pit of inky water was no way to go."

"No, it wasn't." No matter what I'm learning about Lady Carver, it's impossible to feel no sympathy towards her. She must have been terrified.

"It must have been petrifying," Mrs Underhill judders. I've been trying very hard not to think about it. I like my water to be warm and rose scented.

I clear my throat.

"They do say that drowning is one of the better ways to go." I'm not sure who said that, but I've heard it spoken by many people. How they know, I can't possibly say. After all, no one has ever come back from the dead to explain.

"And they confirmed she was drowned. She wasn't dead before she entered the pond. They say she tried to fight it. Her long nails were thick with mud from the edges of the basin tank. The police surgeon established that. And we have Hugh with sodden clothes, Lilian and Hector as well," I finish. Mrs Underhill grunts in agreement of those facts. She doesn't look happy about it.

"If I recall, Lady Bradbury, Olive, Amelia and Lilian entered the kitchen yesterday afternoon, and might have had access to the knife."

"That's correct. But I went out at 2pm," Mrs Underhill reiterates.

"So really anyone could have come into the kitchen, although I believe it's significant that Lilian is included in both lists, as having been soaking wet on Friday, and in the kitchen on

Saturday."

Mrs Underhill purses her lips, deep in thought.

"I don't believe I saw Hugh or Mr Alwinton in the kitchen. They were both more likely to send either their valet, in Hugh's case, or the footman, in Mr Alwinton's, if they required anything from the kitchen. I do believe that Mr Alwinton has no bell in his own home for he's always ringing the one here, and running the housemaids and footmen ragged."

"Lady Merryweather. What are you doing in here?" I turn to meet the furious expression of Edmund Bradbury, his eyes roving from Mrs Underhill to me, as though not understanding what he's seeing. I'm unsure why he's quite so angry.

"I came for a warm in the heat of the kitchen. It's a cold day outside," I inform him. His harsh expression immediately softens.

"It is, yes," he agrees quickly. "Sorry, Ella. I've been listening to those two police detective inspectors argue for the last two hours. I'm quite exhausted by it all."

"I don't understand why Davidson is here." I can't keep the fury from my voice.

"I'm afraid, that it's my understanding that Lady Bradbury telephoned for him. She told him to come and arrest you. Interfering witch," he comments sourly, and despite everything that Mrs Underhill has said to protect her mistress, she nods along with his assertion. "Our local chap is doing much better than Davidson could ever do."

I twist my lips at the news of Margot's involvement. I can't say that I'm surprised by Edmund's admission.

"I believed her too ill to leave her room?" I retort, my temper biting.

"She had her lady's maid make the telephone call. I knew nothing about it or I'd have put a stop to it."

As angry as I am, I feel slightly better knowing that Detective Inspector Davidson hasn't been stalking me, just waiting to hear a whiff of scandal so that he can arrest me once more. I had considered the fact that he might even have gone so far as to alert the Northumberland County Constabulary of my arrival in the hope they'd let him know of anything suspicious occurring in the entire county while I was staying there.

And Edmund looks far angrier than even I am.

"And now my study has been taken up by an argument lasting all afternoon long, and while it rages, there's no forward momentum on finding out who the murderer was. For all I know, I ate my breakfast and my luncheon with someone who killed two people I invited to spend the weekend with me." I appreciate then that Edmund isn't only furious, he's terrified as well.

It makes me consider what he has to be so fearful about, but maybe it's little more than the fact that three people he knows have all had their lives ended under terrible circumstances, even as his wife's slowly dying from a terrible disease.

"Here, have a mug of tea," I thrust one into his hand and he takes it without even looking and sucks it like a drowning man.

From the hallway, there's a sudden crash of a door closing, raised voices and then the sharp tap of heels on wooden floorboards. Edmund meets my eyes, a wry smirk on his tight lips.

"Ah, silence is restored," he mutters, reaching for a thick slab of shortbread on the kitchen table. I don't think something quite so solid would be served to the weekend guests. No doubt, it's for the housemaids and footmen to indulge in when they have their dinner later. Or perhaps for the stable men and women, and the gardeners, who spend all their time outdoors. They will need such hearty fare.

"My apologies for monopolising your study this afternoon," Aldcroft appears in the doorway. I wonder how he knew where to find us and quickly realise he's come in need of mug of tea as well.

Alice, with a raised eyebrow from Mrs Underhill, is quick to pour from the tea pot and hand it to Aldcroft.

"Constable," he addresses the other police man in the kitchen. "Please keep watch on the front door. I don't want the Scotland

Yard detective inspector gaining access to the house. My thanks." The police constable hastens to do as he's bid, walking through the pantry to accomplish his task.

"I don't wish to speak ill of my colleagues," Aldcroft eventually sighs having supped his drink. "But Detective Inspector Davidson seems to have no concept of the need for evidence. I've sent him away, but I fear he'll return, and no doubt with my superior, as he threatens me. Of course, my Chief Constable, Captain Fullarton James, needs to consult the Standing Joint Committee of the County and I can't see them being willing to disturb their weekends by travelling to the police quarters at Morpeth, so we have time yet." As Aldcroft speaks, we all hear a motor engine spring to life outside, the deep rumble seeming to permeate the house. No one speaks until the sound has rumbled through the arch and then dissipated as the car follows the road towards Tumbleton Lake. Then Aldcroft spears me with a firm glance from his sharp eyes.

"I need to talk to you, Lady Merryweather," he informs me, his tone formal. Edmund makes to stand, words of denial on his lips.

I lay a cautionary hand on his arm.

"Of course," and I rise smoothly and follow Aldcroft back to the study.

For a minute, he stares out of the windows, his back to me, his view that of the stunning Debdon valley. I wonder what he's thinking.

"Davidson hates you," he begins. "He'll do anything to see you hang for murder, whether you committed the crime or not. And that means, that I need to redouble my efforts to clear your name." His words startle me. I know we've made an agreement to work together, but I'd not expected him to actually want to help me.

"Thank you," I lower my chin as I speak, fearing to meet his eyes lest I see pity or worse, sympathy in them.

"Now, what have you discovered?" he demands to know.

"I think, first, I should like to know the whereabouts of

everyone on Friday, when Lady Carver went missing. I wasn't here to hear all the alibis."

I think that Aldcroft might deny me, but he mutters an agreement.

"Take a seat and we'll work through everything I know about that day."

His eagerness to help me, brings a smile to my lips.

He reaches for a notebook in his breast pocket and flicks through the pages, no doubt looking for the information.

"Here, I have it all written down. I was careful to tie people down, but I've not yet had the opportunity to cross-reference everything. Now is a good time to begin. I'll tell you what I found out first, and then do the cross-referencing." He pauses, takes a sip from the mug of tea he's brought with him from the kitchen.

"It's believed that Lady Beatrice Carver was killed at some point between 2 pm, when she was seen to leave the house by Underhill, Miss Amelia Clarke, who was also going for a walk, and Lord Edmund Bradbury who'd been extolling Lady Beatrice Carver not to go alone for fear she'd become lost in the short time before the November sun began to set, and when her body was found."

"Lord Bradbury was overheard speaking to Lady Carver by Mr Hector Alwinton, Mr Hugh Bradbury and Lord Sunderland, who were all walking to the front door to join him on the shooting trip. Mr Norman Harrington-Featherington was late to join them."

"As the men were being driven in two of the estate vans. Miss Olive Mabel, Miss Lilian Braithwaite, Miss Rebecca Barlow and Lady Gwendoline Sunderland saw them, as they were also going for a drive. Miss Amelia Clarke spoke to Miss Rebecca Barlow and then headed to the rockery and down towards the iron bridge and the river. She wanted a shorter walk and intended to venture only as far as Tumbleton Lake and the stable complex."

"So, you can be firm on when everyone left the house, and they did so at almost the exact same time. So none of the guests could have possibly killed Lady Carver in those few short minutes as they wouldn't have been able to make it to the basin tank and back in good time."

Aldcroft meets my eyes and nods his assent.

"Agreed, and various of the house staff can confirm the arrangements; Underhill, the chauffeurs who drove the men and women, and the gamekeeper who was leading the party of men."

"So, only Lady Bradbury didn't venture out with the rest of the guests?"

"No, Lady Margot Bradbury remained behind, with her lady's maid, sitting in the library before the hearth which she'd banked high as she was feeling the cold."

"And did the lady's maid remain with Lady Bradbury?"

"No, she didn't. She was asked to leave the room on numerous occasions to bring a blanket, a book, Lady Margot Bradbury's reading glasses that she'd left in her bedchamber, and also her medication, which likewise, was upstairs."

"But none of those trips could have taken that long?"

"No, they couldn't. The lady's maid, a Miss Ada Mitchell, assured me she was gone at most for ten minutes at a time, and that was because she was complaining with her friend, Mrs Underhill, about Lady Bradbury's ill-temper and general manner at the time."

I look down at my hands, so that Aldcroft can't see my smile at poor Miss Ada Mitchell's complaint.

"So, then we move along to your arrival, which I'm reliably informed took place at 3 pm. Mrs Underhill confirms the time as does your man, Williams, and Underhill, and every housemaid who saw you arrive. It seems," and Aldcroft fixes me with a firm glance. "That the entire staff were either pleased to see you or looking forward to meeting the infamous Lady Merryweather."

"My fame does precede me, unfortunately," I confirm.

"At this point, you were welcomed to the house by Lady Bradbury, tea was brought for you to the library, and then nothing happened until 3.15pm when Lord Bradbury returned with two muddy dogs, and muddy boots. He'd walked back from the heath at the two Nelly Moss lakes via the Slipper Lake, and the paths that cut straight down from there, and therefore, entirely avoiding the basin tank." I can hear Underhill's complaint in the words and nod because that's also what Mrs Underhill has said to me.

"The three of you then took tea together, until 4.30pm when the alarm was first raised that Lady Carver had failed to return from her walk. At that point, Lord Bradbury went off to search for his missing guest, leaving you with Lady Bradbury in the library."

"Now," and he pauses again. "This is where it gets more complicated. Mr Hugh Bradbury returned not long after his uncle. This is corroborated by the shooting party who confirm that he left them at a little after 3.15pm. Lord Bradbury had left at 2.45pm, content that his guests were happily occupied and that he needed to return to greet you at 3pm." Aldcroft's nose is buried in his note book.

"Mr Hugh Bradbury's exact arrival at the house wasn't seen, or heard by anyone, but the housemaid, Alice heard him running a bath at about 3.45pm."

"So Hugh might have returned in less time than Lord Bradbury, then?" I don't want to cast doubt on my one ally, but I think it worth mentioning, all the same.

"Yes. Lord Bradbury may have taken longer on his walk, but only by a few minutes."

"Hugh's clothes were so wet they had to be sent to the laundry maid to clean them." I add this because I want Aldcroft to know I've been finding out information as well. I watch him add a note in his notebook.

"The majority of the guests returned back at just after 4 pm. They came together, bringing back the two vans and the car which was driven by the chauffeur. It consisted of Mr Hector Alwinton, Mr Norman Harrington-Featherington, Lord Reginald Sunderland, Miss Olive Mabel, Miss Lilian Braithwaite, Miss Rebecca Barlow and Lady Gwendoline Sunderland. But, Mr Hector Alwinton and Miss Lilian Braithwaite were also wet, and they arrived slightly later than the others, by as much as ten minutes. It all gets quite muddled," Aldcroft apologises. "And, their chauffeur came back as a passenger in the van with Miss Olive Mabel, Miss Rebecca Barlow and Lady Sunderland as Miss Lilian Braithwaite had determined to drive herself back."

I startle at this as I'd not known of this divergence.

"Ten minutes?" I demand. It's a significant gap in time, especially as they had a car.

"Yes, the chauffeur who should have been driving the car complained it was filthy and needed washing thoroughly."

"And Lilian and Hector are the ones who both came back cold and shivering."

"Yes, they did."

Silence falls between us. "This is indeed significant. But ten minutes is still not a huge amount of time to have killed someone."

"And that's not the end of it either. Miss Lilian Braithwaite was absent earlier as well. The two groups met up at the top lake, by the boathouse, and Miss Braithwaite excused herself as she needed to have a moment's privacy." We both know what that meant. "But she was gone for at least twenty minutes, right after Lord Bradbury had arranged to return to the house to greet you. No one knows for sure how long she was absent. It seems she wasn't missed until she returned. I asked Miss Olive Mabel and Mr Norman Harrington-Featherington about the time lapse and they were both quite unsure about it. Mr Hector Alwinton is determined it was no more than ten minutes."

"Ah." I can see why this is causing the detective inspector problems.

"Do you think they could have done it together?" I can't see what reason Hector and Lilian, or Lilian and Edmund had to kill Lady Carver, but nothing can be dismissed without careful thought.

"I don't have enough information to say either way," Aldcroft pronounces unhappily.

"And what of Miss Amelia Clarke?"

"She didn't return until 4.25pm, just before the alarm was

raised by Lady Carver's maid."

I sit back in the chair, trying to think my way through this tangled web of times and events.

"And of course, there's then the problem of what everyone was doing after they returned to the house. For those who arrived back at 4pm, there was more than enough time to make it to the basin tank and back to the house. Not everyone joined the gathering in the library."

"No they didn't," I agree. It's difficult to remember who had been in there. Lilian and Hector hadn't been, of that I was sure because they'd been getting changed. Hugh had finally arrived at about 4.20pm, and Amelia had joined him, face flushed from a walk in the bitter air, so I was happy to accept that she had returned at 4.25pm. Lord and Lady Sunderland had only made an appearance once Lady Carver's body had been discovered.

"I have it here, and from Lady Bradbury who must have an exceptionally good memory, that Mr Hugh Bradbury arrived by 4.15pm, and that Miss Amelia Clarke joined you at 4.30pm, or just about then. It was just before Lord Bradbury was informed of his missing guest."

"She also appraised me that you only left the room, once, at about 3.50pm for no more than five minutes and that Miss Olive Mabel and Miss Rebecca Barlow joined the party at 4.45pm. Mr Hector Alwinton and Miss Lilian Braithwaite didn't arrive until closer to 5pm, Mr Norman Harrington-Featherington made his appearance at some time between those two sets of people."

"So, only Lord and Lady Sunderland were entirely absent after their excursions."

"Yes, and Lord Bradbury, as well, although he was accompanied the entire time he was searching for Lady Carver by the gamekeeper. They didn't let each other out of their sight because they both know how easy it is to get lost in the grounds."

"And Lady Carver was found at about 5pm?"

"Yes, so it seems, and the police were telephoned for at 5.15pm after the gamekeeper ran back to the house, on Lord Bradbury's instructions."

"So, we have Lilian, Lord Bradbury, Hector, Amelia and Lord and Lady Sunderland who could be responsible?" I try to summarise.

"And Mr Hugh Bradbury."

I shake my head. It's too many people. It feels as though it's impossible to reach any sort of conclusion with so many potential suspects.

"I find it interesting that it was Norman who was killed next. He was always with someone so he couldn't possibly have killed Lady Carver." I muse.

"Yes, it's curious. He must have seen something, or suspected something about the killing that the murderer needed to ensure he didn't share with the police." Aldcroft agrees.

"Or he knew something about my husband's murder, and someone decided to take advantage of an opportunity to kill him."

"Why? What have you learned about your husband's death?" Aldcroft is intrigued by my conclusion, I can tell because he fixes me with his piercing eyes.

"I've learned that Lady Beatrice Carver and Mr Hugh Bradbury were married in 1926. I don't know if they're still married. My husband was clutching the marriage certificate when he was found dead."

"Married?" Aldcroft squeaks, no doubt thinking the same as me.

"Yes, despite the difference in age, they were married. I also know that Lord Bradbury plans to marry Miss Lilian Braithwaite once his wife is dead, and that Lady Bradbury is dying from cancer."

Aldcroft grunts as he writes more notes, turning to a fresh page to do so.

"So now we have a plethora of suspects with motivation, as well as the means and the time. You believe that the three murders must all be connected in some way."

"I can't help but think that, but then, what if that's the conclusion we're supposed to reach? I find it a confusing mess.

There are many people hoping to gain. Lady Margot Bradbury wants me punished for murdering my husband, even if I didn't. Lady Beatrice Carver may have potentially been murdered by Miss Amelia Clarke who's just found out her intended is already married, and if that's the case, she's lost the huge country estate she thought would one day be hers. We have no record of a divorce and such things always cause so much scandal. But then, Mr Hugh Bradbury and Lady Carver have managed to keep their scandalous marriage a secret so perhaps that shouldn't surprise me."

"I'll speak to the prime suspects once more, and in that number I count Miss Lilian Braithwaite, Mr Hector Alwinton, Lord Bradbury, Hugh Bradbury and Miss Amelia Clarke. And while I do that, I'll leave you to see what else you can discover. I note, and I can't say I approve, that your driver, Williams, is also knee-deep in all this. Tell him to be wary."

"You have sharp eyes, Detective Inspector," I speak coldly. Earlier, I believed that Aldcroft had been grateful for Williams interest in the murder of Mr Harrington-Featherington.

"I do, yes. And that's how I know you aren't involved, at least not here. So, Lady Merryweather," and he adopts a similarly formal tone to my own. "Be careful what you think about me. At the moment, I'm helping you and I'll do all I can for Williams, but he must stay on the correct side of the law." I stand then, trying to decipher just what Williams has been up to. Perhaps, I realise, it's better if I don't know.

I incline my head and close the library door with a soft snap. I appreciate that as Aldcroft asks more and more questions, the mood of the party is going to worsen and people might just begin to say things they shouldn't. That can only be for the good.

# Chapter 10

I make my way up the sweeping wooden staircase to the drawing room. As I go, I notice the beautiful statue of the slave woman and shudder at the shackles around hands and feet. Such a travesty. I don't approve and never have. I wish Edmund would have the statue removed but he says it's a reminder of terrible crimes, and so it stays. I've checked the library but no one's in there, not even Edmund. From the kitchen, I hear the murmur of people busy at their tasks and from outside, I can hear male voices calling one to another. They aren't the voices of the house guests.

I pause to stare out of the staircase window at the last of the daylight. The gardens and grounds are coated in the browns, oranges and yellows of autumn. Despite the coming night, the colours are bright enough to cheer.

No sooner have I stepped foot on the first floor hallway than I hear angry voices drifting towards me, coming from the drawing room. I hasten my steps. I don't want to miss whatever's happening in my absence.

On entering the drawing room, I expect, as always, to have my vision filled with the enormous marble fireplace that dominates the entire room, detracting even from the beautiful chandelier that glimmers overhead. It's doing its best to drive back the shadows of the grey day. But instead, my eyes fasten on Rebecca and Amelia.

Amelia's back is to me but I can tell how furious she is from the set of her slim shoulders. And Rebecca's face is thunderous.

Lilian stands to one side, a hand covering her open mouth, while Hector's gaze flashes between the two women, unsure what to do. Of Hugh, Edmund and Reginald, there's no sign.

"You bitch," Rebecca screams at Amelia. I notice Rebecca's holding out something towards Amelia and I move so that I can get a better glimpse of it. It seems to be a silk scarf of palest pink. Not at all something I can imagine Rebecca wearing.

"You said it was mine, and now look what you've done to it." As she speaks, Rebecca lifts her left hand to reveal the tear down the middle of the scarf. "It's ruined."

"I never said it was yours, and even if I did, I haven't ripped it like that. I didn't even know you'd brought it with you."

"Yes you did. I was wearing it on the train journey."

"No you weren't. I would remember if you were wearing something that made you look half-dead. Whoever did rip it has done you a favour. At least you can't wear it anymore."

"Why you." And Rebecca launches herself at Amelia. I'm too slow to step between them, but Hector tries, only to be slapped sharply around the face by Rebecca. Even though she looks shocked at her action, she merely moves position and again lunges at Amelia. The sharp slap of her hand hitting Amelia stuns everyone. Rebecca looks from her hand to Amelia's rapidly reddening cheek and then away again as though surprised at what she's done.

That might have been it, but Amelia reacts by reaching out and pulling on Rebecca's carefully coifed hair. She yanks a handful of chestnut hair away with her hand, as Rebecca shrieks in pain. I eye the two women aghast, watching their chests heave as they fight for breath and some composure.

But their fight is far from at an end. Rebecca's hand bunches, and before I can consider stopping her, she's landed a perfect blow on Amelia's cheek, to go with the red mark. Amelia staggers backwards, caught off guard by the force of the punch. I share a quick look with Hector. He moves to help Amelia while I'm left with the growling Rebecca.

I grip her hand, where it waits to take another punch and at the same time, force her to look at me, and not at Amelia.

I notice then that while she always looks immaculate, Rebecca has old chicken pox scars running down the left side of her face, from below her hair line, down her face and around her ear. They aren't horrific, far from it, but it's clear she wears her long hair to cover them, and has heaped enough powder on them that until now, I've not appreciated she has them.

"Leave me alone," she growls but the fierceness is already draining from her voice. I suspect that at any moment she'll be sobbing with remorse for what she's done.

I guide her to one of the settees close to the huge marble fireplace, a beautiful creation covered in red fabric, faded around the armrests. She slumps into it, looking down at her curled hand as though she can't believe what's happened.

I risk turning, to see Hector and Amelia speaking in a furious undertone to one another, the words too quiet for me to hear. I haven't realised the two would have such intimate details to share with one another.

And of course, Hugh chooses that moment to enter the room. He's wearing a smart suit of brown corduroy and looks very much the part of a gentleman in the countryside. He's carrying his pipe and his eyes flash with shock as they flicker between the two women.

"What's happened now?" he demands, directing the question to me as though it's my fault.

"An argument. A fight," I correct. "I arrived when it was already well underway." I feel stung into adding. I'm growing irate with the assumption that where there's violence I must be the one to blame.

"Amelia," Hugh barks to his fiancee, although he doesn't make a move to ensure she's well, despite the two bright red marks on her face.

"She," Amelia heaves, remaining close to Hector, for all she points at Rebecca. "Slapped me and punched me."

I watch Hugh close his eyes momentarily, as though seeking calmness.

"Why?" he demands to know.

"That stupid silk scarf. She accused me of ripping it."

"And did you?"

I can't quite believe what I'm hearing. Hugh speaks to the two women as though they're small children, caught brawling over the same toy.

"I did not," outrage infuses Amelia's words. I get a good look at her then and wince in sympathy. She's going to have a black eye and a bruise on her cheek as well. Her eye's already purpling, while her cheek looks so red it's as though she's been burned.

I eye Rebecca, and also grimace in sympathy.

Where she's been hiding her chicken pox scars, a large swathe of hair is missing, exposing her scalp. It's going to hurt as well. Indeed, Rebecca has silent tears falling down her cheeks, although I notice, she doesn't attempt to interject in the conversation taking place between Hugh and Amelia.

"Then I suggest Rebecca apologise to you, and you apologise to Rebecca and we forget about this unfortunate incident. There are more important matters at hand."

Amelia raises sullen eyes towards Rebecca.

"I apologise," she mutters.

"I do as well," Rebecca replies quickly. Neither of them quite made eye contact with the other.

"Now, ladies, and Hector, if you'll excuse me, I've been summoned to speak to the pestilent detective inspector once more." And with that Hugh gives a brief dip of his head, and strides away.

I watch him walk away, through the arch and into the gallery, not wanting to witness whatever happens between the two women. I thought them inseparable friends, but it appears that there's a great deal of jealousy there as well. And not from Rebecca. I can't understand it. After all, Amelia is the one about to marry the heir of Lord Bradbury. She'll be wealthy beyond anything she's ever experienced before, and yet she's jealous of Rebecca.

I search Rebecca's hand, looking to see if she wears a ring, and is engaged to be married herself, perhaps to someone with greater wealth than Hugh, but there's nothing.

Hector slumps to the other settee, and a sullen silence falls between the four of us. In the distance, I can hear the creak of the lift moving between the floors, from outside the kitchen, to outside the gallery. No doubt, Lady Bradbury is using it, or perhaps one of the house staff, moving heavy equipment around. I can also detect the murmur of conversation coming from close by. Maybe some of the staff are gossiping on their staircase.

I search for some way to begin questioning these three members of the weekend party, but with no one speaking I know to be careful with how I phrase my questions. I really want to know if Hugh's still married, or rather, has been married, and if Amelia is aware. But that seems too incendiary a conversation to attempt when both women were still recovering from their violent argument.

Hector eventually breaks the silence.

"That police inspector chappy from London has no love for you, Lady Merryweather."

I incline my head. "No, he thinks I'm guilty of murdering my husband, and in his eyes, that's enough to have me hung. It seems that Scotland Yard don't believe having any evidence is necessary. It doesn't help that Lady Bradbury had him summoned here as soon as Lady Carver was murdered."

"Ah," understanding flashes on Hector's face as if that answers the question he hasn't yet asked.

"And what sort of evidence do you think is needed." I've not seen Lilian enter the room, but her question intrigues me. Is she trying to decide whether she's left herself exposed in some way having committed the murder, or is she merely curious?

"I think that finding the murder weapon is always a big help, especially if fingerprints can be taken from it. But of course, there also needs to be motive and means. And so, in the case of poor Mr Harrington-Featherington, I have no means to have killed him. And as of yet, no motive either."

I keep a careful guard on her face. She settles in a wooden chair close to the table on which sits a chess set. She's distant from everyone else, although her face looks towards the hearth where heather and peat burn, so as not to stain the priceless marble of the elaborate fire place. She's dressed warmly and sensibly, in a smart jacket and matching brown skirt, walking shoes on her feet. All in all, she looks as brown as the ferns outside. It would be easy for her to blend into the surroundings, if that's what she had in mind.

"And the same for Lady Carver, I take it?"

I'm intrigued that Lilian wishes to press the point.

"Yes. I hadn't yet arrived when she was most likely killed, and even then, my whereabouts can be confirmed by two people, one of them being Lady Bradbury herself." Margot's determination to have me strung up for murder is all the more bizarre because she's one of the people who can confirm I was in the library throughout the afternoon.

"So, if I was a suspect, the police would say that I had the means because I have no alibi for when Norman was killed, and equally, Hector and I returned to the house later than the rest of the party when Lady Carver was murdered."

"Yes," I agree, not feeling the urge to go into any greater detail. I'm nosey enough to see if she mentions the state of her clothing.

"Now, wait a moment," Hector interjects, roused from his stupor by the question.

"It's true, Hector. You need to be aware of that. We have only one another to prove what we were doing, and they might think that we would vouch for one another." Lilian shrugs a slim shoulder, even as her hands rest on her crossed knees. She's very cool and calm under pressure, I notice. Hector is certainly not.

"Well, I object to that. I really do. There was nothing untoward. You drove the car into a ditch and we both got wet trying to release it."

"Ah," and her lips split into a grim looking smile. "We know that, but no one else does."

Amelia joins the conversation then, her words slightly

muffled because of her swelling lip.

"So, I would be a suspect because I was walking on my own?"

"Absolutely," Lilian interjects. "You don't even have another person to vouch for you. Although, you didn't arrive back at the house in a state, as I did, and Hector as well. But still, you were alone."

"So what would be my motive?" Amelia retorts, as unhappy as Hector to be considered a suspect.

"I believe, and Lady Merryweather would need to back me up on this, that the fact your fiancé was married to the dead woman might give you more than enough motive." The words are spoken with sweet saccharine, and the effect they have on Amelia is immediate.

"He was not," she leaps to her feet, in the process, upsetting a side table placed close to the settee. Hector hastens to right it.

"I can assure you he was," Lilian's enjoying imparting this piece of information. But, there's no denying that Amelia had been unaware. Her face immediately drains of all colour, and I think she might well lash out at Lilian now. I've seen how well the two friends can fight already.

I hasten to check the other members of our small group, and realise with a start that Rebecca must have known about the marriage. I believe Hector knew as well. Neither of them look at all shocked by the revelation. This is all most curious.

"I'll ask him," Amelia makes to march from the drawing room, but then must remember that Hugh isn't in his bedchamber, but rather speaking to the detective inspector.

"He's not," she whispers, wrapping her arms around her waist.

"He was," I confirm. "Whether he still is, I don't know, but perhaps Lilian does. She seems to be very well informed."

Lilian glowers at me, as though I've stolen her greatest treasure.

"I don't know that. You'll have to ask Hugh and Lady Carver. Ah wait," and now she's back on firmer ground. "You can't because someone drowned her. Was it you?"

"Stop it," Hector's voice is filled with loathing for Lilian's obvious enjoyment in goading Amelia. "Leave the poor woman alone. This has evidently been a huge shock to her."

"What has?" Edmund Bradbury asks, walking into the drawing room from the gallery, determination on his face. I don't think he has any intention of stopping, but must have realised the dishevelled state of Amelia and Rebecca.

"We were discussing means and motivation for the murders. I told her of Hugh's marriage to Lady Carver."

"What?" Edmund repeats, his eyebrows furrowing so that it seems he has one long, dark eyebrow and not too separate ones.

"You knew? Hugh married Lady Carver when he was little more than a child. If that's not a reason to murder her, then I don't know what is." Lilian is fairly spitting needles with her ire.

"Have you not heard of divorce," I retort. "It tends to be less final than murdering someone."

"Hugh wasn't married to Lady Carver," Edmund imparts. "Not anymore. It was all a silly misunderstanding, dealt with long ago."

"How?" Lilian goads.

"Through the normal channels. An annulment, not a divorce. Silly boy," Edmund continues. I'm aware of someone walking along the gallery, and imagine that Hugh's about to unwittingly arrive at this discussion about him.

"And was Lady Carver happy about that?"

"Well, she was still Lady Carver, as you keep saying, so she must have been." Edmund's face flickers with annoyance. I think Lilian needs to be careful, or she'll be getting her notice, not marrying him when Margot dies.

"Who was still Lady Carver?" Olive asks, as she emerges from the gallery. She's wearing a day dress of myriad colours, the fashion at least thirty years out of date, a jacket covering her arms, and she carries a bag which I suspect contains either a blanket, or her knitting. I'm thinking her knitting. It isn't as though there's a lack of blankets in the drawing room.

"Lady Carver was married to Hugh," Lilian explains with no tact at all.

"Really?" Olive's raised eyebrows reveals her shock.

"It was annulled," Edmund is quick to interject, casting a meaningful glance at Lilian. She entirely ignores him.

"Yes, so Hugh, or Amelia could have quite easily murdered her. After all, she stood in the way of their happiness."

Edmund growls, low in his throat at Lilian's persistence. I suspect he might take her to one side and ask her to kindly stop talking about his heir in such a way. Only then Hugh does appear, his eyes downcast, to walk directly to the whisky decanter, without seeming to notice he isn't alone in the drawing room.

He splashes a very large measure into a cut-crystal glass and swallows it back in almost one gulp. Only then does he become aware of everyone else within the room.

"What?" he queries. "That damn detective inspector is like a dog with a bone."

"And what's he doing? Asking you about your marriage to Lady Carver?" Again, it's Lilian who spits the words. She really is a furious creature, I note to myself. Not at all the demure scholar and biologist she pretends to be.

Hugh's eyes shoot straight to Amelia's, as though about to deny the whole thing, but really, what point is there now that everyone knows about it.

"The union has been annulled," he offers hotly. "Almost immediately, wasn't it uncle?"

"Yes, it was, as I keep telling them."

"On whose instructions?" I interject. This, of course, hasn't yet been determined.

"Mine," Edmund speaks firmly. "I found out about it and had it annulled immediately." Lilian's mouth opens as though to speak, but Edmund gets there first.

"It was all done in a pleasant and very secretive way. No one knew of the marriage, and no one knew of the annulment. And as you can see, it hardly impacted my friendship with Lady Carver, or Hugh." I nod, as though satisfied with the answer. But I'm not. I have my suspicions and now I have even more. Had

Lady Carver and Hugh still held a flame for one another? Had they continued their affair in secret? Had they perhaps hoped to marry again in the future? Had Amelia actually known about the marriage? My mind fills with the many possibilities.

"Lilian, the detective inspector wishes to see you next," Hugh belatedly informs her. Lilian opens her mouth to protest at the news, scowling at Hugh. I believe she might refuse to leave, but then she huffs dramatically, shoulders her way roughly past Edmund and the chair he stands beside, instead of going around it. She proceeds to stamp down the gallery so that we can all hear when she reaches the wooden staircase because the steps are somehow even louder even though she's much further away.

I notice Edmund's wince of unhappiness and feel no sympathy for him. He's made his bed and he needs to lie in it.

"Now you all know my secret, there's no need for quite such shocked stares," Hugh flounces, returning to the decanter to refill his whisky.

"I'll have one of those, please," Amelia squeaks. Her face is turning green and black before my very eyes,

I look around the drawing room. Edmund and Amelia still need to be questioned once more by Aldcroft. Hector as well. Rebecca, Olive and myself are the part of the party that aren't currently under suspicion. Out of the thirteen of us at this weekend party, two are dead, one is already under arrest and Margot Bradbury is dying anyway. I can't help thinking that the chances of the rest of us leaving here intact are quite slim.

"Ella, a word, if you don't mind," Edmund says to me. I meet his eyes, and go to his side, but he moves on, leaving the drawing room and making his way to the billiard room next door. I notice the size of the billiard table, once more marvelling at just how huge it is. Bright electric lights glitter above it, making the coloured balls shimmer as though it's the summer. I lean across to pick up one of the red balls, observing how similar it is to my lipstick and nails.

"What's he banging on about?"

"Who?" I ask, forgetting for a moment.

"That Detective Inspector. He has all sorts of questions for me. Does he suspect me?" There's strain in his voice. I carefully place the red ball back on the green baize, and fix him with a firm stare.

"I think, unlike that fool in London, that Aldcroft suspects everyone because there's enough suspicion to think any one of us could have killed Norman Harrington-Featherington, well, apart from me. And really, the same goes for Lady Beatrice Carver's death. Your wife muddied the waters there by demanding I was arrested, even though there was no proof. Perhaps if not for her interference, Norman might still be alive."

I expect Edmund to loudly deny my complaint, but he doesn't. He merely shakes his head sadly from side to side.

"I've not been the kindest to her, in recent years, but there's no need for her to turn on you with such ferocity. I'm sorry for that."

"It's not for you to apologise," I retort. "Lady Bradbury is clearly unhappy, and determined to take down as many with her as she can."

"Perhaps. She fears her death, and the knowledge that there's only Hugh to inherit, and at the same time, doesn't want him to have the estate either. Her thinking is quite confused. She's better when there's nothing important to tax her mind. It saddens me."

"But not enough to have stayed faithful."

"Yes, well," and Edmund deflates before my eyes. "We all do stupid things when driven by lust. But, I didn't kill Lady Carver or Norman, or Bertie, either, for that matter."

"And do you suspect who might have done?" I'm sure he hasn't brought me here to offer denials.

"I do, as it happens, have my suspicions. I've shared them with the detective inspector. I'm wary of saying anything else for fear I might be the next one to be killed. He didn't dismiss my fears, but advised that he already has more police officers being summoned. At this rate, there'll be more police than there are guests."

"Yes, well the opportunistic nature of Norman's death is

unnerving, and with one of the kitchen knives as well."

"But you believe me innocent?" Edmund has the audacity to ask. I hold his eyes with mine.

"I do," I eventually relent. "I can't see why you would be concerned about Lady Carver marrying Hugh. Other than it might mean your family line ends with him as Lady Carver would have been too old to provide an heir."

"Yes, well, it wasn't that which made me push for an annulment. More that Lord Carver had only been in his grave for a handful of weeks and it was all done in rather indecent haste, especially when there was no problem of an unexpected pregnancy to contend with. Boys will be boys, and Hugh was quite young and dashing at that age. All the same, Beatrice, Lady Carver was embarrassed by the whole thing when she'd had time to not be quite so furious with me."

"So it all ended well then."

"Yes, I suppose. But I've had to keep a close eye on Hugh ever since. My brother allowed the boy far too much freedom growing up. And you. Why is the detective inspector allowing you such freedom?"

"I think, dear friend, that of everyone here, I'm the one least likely to have killed again, and equally, I really didn't have the time to kill Lady Carver. He also shares my conviction that it's all connected with the murder of Bertie, and as my name has finally been cleared for that crime, I can't really be suspected at all."

"Yes, that does make sense," Edmund admits. "But he's only looking at the party members. What of the staff? What of someone on the estate that we know nothing about?"

"A fair point," I concede. "But still, if you have your suspicions, why would you suggest that?"

Edmund looks uneasy.

"I just don't like the idea that someone here was responsible for killing my guests. I've made terrible decisions in the past about who to be friendly with, but this would truly show me to be the worst judge of character."

"I think, Edmund, dear, that it would show us all to be terrible judges of character. I shouldn't worry about that." A tired smile touches his cheeks and he mutters in agreement, "perhaps," as he rubs his hand through his thick hair.

"I just want it to be all over."

"Me too," I concur. Silence hangs between us, and I revel in it, only for a scream to echo through the house.

# Chapter 11

"Where did that come from?" Edmund's shocked eyes round on me.

"It wasn't the drawing room," I'm already preparing to run to some new disaster.

"Was it Margot's bedchamber?" I demand.

"I don't know," he admits. "The bedrooms are on that side of the house." He moves to the drawing room. I hasten to follow him, noting as I go, that no one's missing from the drawing room. All the people I've been talking to are in various stages of getting to their feet, eyes wide with terror. Rebecca is whimpering even more. Edmund and I shoot past them all, along the painting laden gallery, to be faced with a long hall, with bedrooms off to the left hand side. I'd rush to open all of the doors only a shocked housemaid stands far along the hallway, trembling from head to toe, eyes wide and pointing.

I hear the crash of Aldcroft boots as he takes the wooden stairs two at a time, and rushes to find the source of the noise, but my eyes are fixed on what's so upset the young housemaid.

And what a horror it is.

Lady Margot Bradbury lies on the floor of the elevator, mouth agape, eyes forever staring. It's clear what's happened. The housemaid has opened the elevator to load a basket filled with sheets and towels to take to the laundry, but as she's pulled back the door, she's discovered the lift was already full.

"Let me through," Aldcroft instructs, and he pulls up, mouth agape, to stare down at Margot. She'd been dressed for the day, but now her skirt is up over her knees, revealing her stockinged thighs, and one of her pink Mary-Jane shoes has come free as well.

There's a pool of blood beside her. I swallow back my nausea.

I'd hoped to never see something like this again, but just as with my husband, Margot has been shot, just above her two eyes.

Edmund shudders beside me, a strange half gulp/shriek coming from his mouth and then he begins to scream. There's no other word for it. He falls to his knees, reaching out to touch the still form of his wife, and I choke on my own sorrow.

Despite the events of the last few days, Margot has been my friend in another life. I hate to see the ruin of her life.

"Don't touch," Aldcroft words are surprisingly soft. "We need to examine her." One of the police constables is there as well, hovering at the back of the group.

"Telephone for the police surgeon," Aldcroft calls to him quickly. "And everyone else, please gather in the drawing room until I come and speak to you."

My gaze seeks out Lilian. Surely, she's been with Aldcroft when Margot was killed, but then, there's no guarantee of when Margot has been shot. We weren't summoned here by the gunshot but rather by the maid's discovery of the body. I note Aldcroft arrives without Lilian. But how, I think, has someone managed to shoot Margot without anyone else hearing? If the step of Aldcroft's boots on the stairs can be heard throughout the house, then surely a gun being fired would as well.

I pull on Edmund's arm. I need to get him away from Margot before he disturbs the crime scene. And it seems that no one else, and certainly not Lilian, is prepared to show him any compassion.

Quickly, I scan the group, noting who's there, and who isn't. It's something I'm having to learn to do.

Underhill arrives, no doubt as a result of the constable using the telephone, and leads the distraught housemaid aside, as I force Edmund to stand, and walk away with me. He keeps turning his eyes, as though he can't believe what he's seeing. I understand that far too well. I even know better than to urge him to caution. That image, of his wife lying forever staring, will never leave him, even if they've long since fallen out of love.

Hector greets us in the drawing room, glass of whisky to hand, and thrusts one into Edmund's lifeless hand. I guide Edmund to the settee, just in front of the huge ceiling-high fireplace, force him to sit and then allow him his drink. I look around for one of the many blankets to cover him with. He's already starting to shake. The shock will be immense, even for a man such as him.

Olive watches him with compassion in her eyes, from where she's settled opposite him. Lilian is nowhere to be seen, which doesn't surprise, and Lord Sunderland finally puts in an appearance. His hair is sleep-ruffled, and I appreciate that he's been woken by the scream. Amelia and Rebecca are holding on to one another, Amelia whimpers softly, while Rebecca looks calmer now, their argument entirely forgotten about, as they huddle on one of the other settees.

I look for Hugh, but he isn't there. I can't recall if he'd been by the lift or not? I make sure I'll tell Aldcroft that Hugh and Lilian aren't in the drawing room, as he's demanded from everyone. I'd like to find them, but I can't leave Edmund. He's murmuring to himself, over and over again.

"It's my fault. It's all my fault." I look to Hector and note his perplexed expression.

"It's not your fault," he tries, but I shake my head. Edmund's in such a state, it's wiser to just let him speak. He won't hear what we say, not for a long time, maybe months in the future, when he finally came to terms with what's happened.

I hear the unmistakable sound of a billiard ball hitting another one, and stand quickly, leaving Edmund with Hector, to walk into the next door. There, I find Hugh and Lilian, on opposite sides of the table, fury on the face of Hugh, while Lilian's gloating.

"What's going on in here?"

"Nothing. I'm just speaking to the ex-heir of the Bradbury

estate. Edmund is free to marry me now and I'll provide him with an heir."

"And you're discussing this already? Lady Margot isn't even cold yet."

"No, but she's most certainly very dead," Lilian crows. "And I'm pleased. She's been malingering for well over a year now. The doctor gave her a few months, and she's certainly had more than those."

Hugh's face is incandescent with rage. I'm unsure whether it's because of Lilian's vision for the future, or because she's speaking of his aunt so callously.

I'm relieved that Edmund can't hear her. I'll have to approach him in the future about his intentions. Whether he loves Lilian, or was merely caught up in the idea of an heir for his estate, I don't believe he'll be any happier marrying her than he has been with Margot.

"Don't speak about my aunt like that, you damn bitch." The final word rings through the room, and I wince at the raw edge to Hugh's grief. Not that Lilian seems to notice.

"We should all be in the drawing room," I announce, keen to end this argument which is turning ever more bitter.

"I'm happy here," Lilian calls to me in a sing-song voice, but Hugh stalks past me, eager to be away from her. I hear him speaking to his uncle in the room next door. He sounds heartbroken, his voice rumbling, and catching and then rumbling once more.

"I'll stay with you, as Aldcroft wants everyone to be with someone else. That's why he's asked us to gather in the drawing room."

"Why? Does he expect someone else to be murdered?" Lilian taunts. Her eyes have taken on the glint of crazed fear and ambition combined. I find in that moment, that no matter what I've thought of her before, she's truly an evil young woman, blinded by her ambitions.

"I imagine he has some concern that might happen. It wouldn't be a complete surprise, would it? Not when there have been three murders in as many days."

"But he suspects me of being the murderer, so I should be fine." Her words are edged with anger.

"I think he suspects us all," I calmly retort. From the other room, I can hear the murmur of conversation, and I'm eager to be a part of it. Not stuck here, with Lilian.

"Well, he doesn't suspect you anymore, does he? Although, now you mention it, you could have shot Margot? She did hanker after your husband. Maybe you killed her for that, hoping that the other two murders would provide you with all the cover you needed to get away with murdering someone else. Your husband, and his lover, both dead at your hands, and both shot. Probably with the same pistol."

I feel no anger at those words. After all, she's probably just thinking what the others are starting to realise, but her words do make me consider the sequence of events.

Three people, all murdered in different ways. There's an assumption they must be related to Bertie's death, but only Margot has died in a similar way. Perhaps Lilian is correct to question the assumption.

"Lady Merryweather, Miss Braithwaite, might I encourage you to join us in the drawing room." Aldcroft voice is filled with resolve. I hasten to obey. I'm pleased to be away from Lilian and the anger and fury that leaks from her as though a scent.

Stepping back into the drawing room, I see that Hugh is sitting beside his uncle, offering him support, while Amelia has been drawn to Hugh's side. The three of them look beleaguered, and I confess, at that moment, I don't believe any of them can be guilty of killing Margot. Either that, or I need to think they're all implicated, so united are they in their grief. Only Rebecca sits alone, and now that something has happened to distract her from her torn hair, she seems overly calm.

Thinking of the five people Aldcroft and I have decided might be prime suspects, that leaves only Lilian and Hector. I already have my suspicions about Lilian, and I'm wary of tainting what I suspect I know with a growing dislike of her. And Hector? He's always seemed such a genuinely pleasant individual. But, he had been late to return to the house on Friday, arriving with Lilian.

I can't think why she'd have murdered my husband, but there's surely a reason. I wish I knew if she'd been with Aldcroft when Margot was found? Not that it means she didn't kill Margot. Margot had been dead for some time. I'm sure of it.

Does that potentially only leave Hector as a suspect?

I examine him. From the billiard room next door, I can hear Aldcroft speaking to Lilian, demanding that she returns to the drawing room with the remainder of the party. I wish him luck with that.

The constable sent running for the telephone, reappears, breathing heavily, his eyes flicking from one side of the room to the other.

"He's through there," and I point the young man to the billiard room where Aldcroft remains.

"Thank you, My Lady." He huffs the words to me, and then walks more slowly into the billiard room.

No one speaks, not one of us pretending we aren't listening to Lilian's increasingly shrill refusal to comply with Aldcroft's requests. A shiver of crockery, and two housemaids appear with trays laden with a tea and coffee pot, fine cups as well. Mrs Underhill is proving her worth to the household once more.

It's been a long day already, and I doubt I'll be getting some sleep anytime soon. I gratefully take the offered cup and add a generous lump of sugar to it. I'm not one for cloying sweetness, but right now, I need it. Hector takes his tea, drinks half of it, and then turns to the decanter, and adds a vast quantity of whisky to the china cup.

Olive sits and sips demurely while Rebecca hurries to and fro, making tea for Amelia and Hugh. Edmund refuses to have any. Lord Sunderland sits in one of the two armchairs. His long body doesn't seem to fit the chair, but he seems unaware. Every face in the drawing room echoes my shock at what's happening to us.

We're due to leave Cragside the following day, but I can't see we'll be allowed to, not until someone has been arrested for the murders. For the first time in a long time, I'm desperate to return to my home. I should very much like to check beneath my bed, and in the wardrobes, and then lock the door and sleep for at least twenty-four hours.

Aldcroft reappears in the archway that leads to the billiard room, but without his constable. His face is black with fury.

"The police surgeon is on the way. It might take some time as he's travelling from Newcastle. My constable will remain with Miss Lilian Braithwaite next door, and I'll again need to interview everyone about this recent tragedy. My Lord Bradbury, Mr Bradbury, you have my sympathies for your loss."

Hugh nods, but Edmund doesn't speak, not even to blame himself once more

Aldcroft sighs heavily. He looks weary and I'm unsurprised. He was called to a suspicious death at Cragside estate and now there have been three such deaths, all of them, seemingly, murder.

"If any of you have anything to tell me about this collection of terrible tragedies, I would be willing to hear it. Not who you suspect, and why you suspect them, but rather cold, hard facts. Without those, it'll be impossible to convict anyone for these crimes, and three people will have died without recourse to justice. Now, My Lord, can you tell me, were there guns kept in the house?"

"Yes, there are," Hugh answers when Edmund doesn't even seem to hear the question. "There are four hunting rifles, and also my uncle's pistol from the Great War."

"And where are these kept?" Aldcroft's making notes once more in his small note book. I imagine he might soon run out of sheets.

"The rifles were kept with the gamekeeper. My uncle's pistol was stored in his study."

"In his study?" Aldcroft reiterates.

"Yes, in his study. The room you've been using to interview us all."

The news of this hangs heavy in the air. It seems unlikely that one of the hunting rifles has been used in the confined space of the elevator, but it also means that someone has brazenly taken the pistol, potentially even while Aldcroft was in the room with them.

"Who knew of the pistol?" Aldcroft persists.

"I did, and my aunt, and no doubt Lilian," Hugh sneers as he adds her name to the list. "It's no great secret that my uncle kept his war-time pistol. I think nearly everyone did."

"And the household staff?"

"I imagine Underhill knew of it, and perhaps the footmen. I really don't know. You would need to ask them."

"Do you remember when you last saw the pistol?" This is clearly directed at Edmund. I think he won't answer, but then his head lifts and he fixes Aldcroft with his firm eyes.

"I saw it only yesterday morning. It was in my locked drawer on the desk. I always keep it there. I went into the drawer to check on it after Norman's shocking death. I had to be sure the gun hadn't been used. And then I locked the drawer again, and have never let the keys out of my sight since. I also removed all the bullets, and asked the gamekeeper to hide them away with the rifles so it couldn't be used, unless someone knew to bring their own bullets."

Edmund's words are hoarse. I believe his grief will drag him down and down, until he has nowhere else to go. I pity him. I know what it is to grieve with no end in sight. People said time was a great healer, but I have so far failed to think anything but sorrow as the days, weeks and months between my time now and my husband's murder merely grew longer and longer.

"I'll need to see the pistol, please. And if you don't object, I'll have it examined to ensure it wasn't the murder weapon. It's possible to match the bullets with the pistol that fired them."

Edmund grunts his agreement, and fidgets with his pocket to pull forth a small bunch of keys.

"Here, take them. It's the copper-coloured key."

Aldcroft takes the keys without speaking.

"As soon as we have more details, I'll be speaking to you all once more. But in the meantime, and as shocking as all this is, I have to continue my investigation. Lady Merryweather, will you escort me to the study please. Everyone else, remain in the drawing room. I'll have a constable stay with you to ensure your safety, as much as that's possible."

No one thinks to argue with the instruction. I consider the wisdom of Aldcroft pulling me away from the room when it might be beneficial to hear the discussions taking place, but we need to discuss what we already know.

I follow him down the stairs without speaking and enter the study. Outside, it's pitch black. Night has fallen early. I can only see that it will slow down his investigation. From the kitchen, I can smell something that makes my stomach growl. I've been nothing but hungry since I arrived in Northumberland.

Aldcroft is already fiddling with the keys to remove Edmund's gun from the drawer. I listen to the sound of keys being manipulated, my gaze fixed out of the window behind his shoulder. I feel exhausted, entirely worn-out. I hadn't come to Cragside to be involved in more murders. I'd come here to assess which of my alleged friends killed my husband, and that number is dwindling by the hour.

Aldcroft sighs, and I meet his eye.

"What?" I ask, but in my heart, I already know.

# Chapter 12

"It's not here."

"The pistol?" I exclaim, moving to his side. We both stare into Edmund's untidy desk, filled with papers and smoking paraphernalia, as well as broken pen tips and half empty bottles of ink, one on its side slowly leaking into a piece of paper where the cork has come lose. I snatch up the ink, and the paper, and place them on the immaculate deep-mahogany desk, and then riffle through the remaining items. I'm much less careful than Aldcroft has been, and eventually, frustrated, I move the leaking ink-pot aside and take everything from the desk drawer.

I note bills and letters out of the corner of my eye, all neatly typed, some of them showing they've been paid, but I'm entirely engrossed in looking for something, which is patently not there.

Aldcroft has fallen to his knees, and examines the lock, one eye closed.

"I don't think it's been tampered with," he announces. And now I look at the small bronze lock. There's no signs of it being forced, either where the key fitted, or above or below it, if someone has thrust something small and thin into the lock to allow it to open wide, I'm sure it would have left some sort of mark.

"So, Edmund is our main suspect?" But Aldcroft's already denying my words.

"I don't believe he is, no. But I think the murderer wants us to believe it's him. Not that it helps us, a great deal. I need to find out if the gamekeeper has the key and the bullets still. I also need to know who had access to this room because I feel as though I've barely left it, so I'm perplexed as to how someone could have come in here, stolen the pistol and then killed Lady Bradbury."

"Unless it was Lady Bradbury herself." I've been toying with the thought that she's perhaps decided to end her life. The Lady Bradbury I've known all these years would never have done such a thing, but over the last few days, I've begun to appreciate how miserable she is. Death was coming for her and she couldn't stop it. Perhaps a woman such as her, would sooner make the decision herself.

"But why in the elevator?" Aldcroft asks me. I wrinkle my forehead in thought.

"Maybe she didn't do it there. Perhaps someone moved her to that location, removed the pistol and was content to make it look as though she'd been murdered."

Aldcroft shakes his head. "I just don't know if that's possible," but he doesn't dismiss it out of hand. "We'll see what the police surgeon determines when he arrives. Perhaps I should have found a room for him, had I known he'd be visiting quite so frequently." I grimace, not sure if he means it humorously or if he's merely stating a fact.

"What have you learned from Lilian and Hugh Bradbury?" I remind him of why we're talking as his eyes seem to lose focus.

"Ah, yes, well. Miss Lilian Braithwaite isn't a pleasant young woman, for all she looks like one. Every question I ask her results in an acerbic response. She might have fooled Edmund into thinking it was love between them, but on her part, it most assuredly isn't." I goggle at his harsh words and he offers me a shrug of his shoulders. "At least, that's what I believe having pressed her on it a few items. I don't believe she and Hector were together in the car on the way back to the house. I believe one or other of them collected the other from somewhere on the estate. I need to speak with Hector and see what he says, for Lilian is sticking to her story."

"I've yet to determine her true motive, but I believe it's

131

all wrapped up in her desire to marry Lord Bradbury. She can't actually account for where she was before Mr Norman Harrington-Featherington was killed. I imagine there'll be some doubt when we know the details of Lady Bradbury's murder, if it is murder, as well. She remains one of my prime suspects."

The news doesn't surprise me. I've been thinking much the same about Lilian.

"Mr Hugh Bradbury, on the other hand, is no longer one of my prime suspects. He confirms he and Lady Carver were indeed no longer married. He was free to marry Amelia. He had his uncle's agreement for the match, as well as the permission of Amelia's mother, her father having died during the Great War."

"But did he have the means?" I press him.

"I believe he didn't. He and Miss Amelia Clarke were together the entire afternoon during which Mr Norman Harrington-Featherington was murdered. Yes, they could both be responsible, but if they are, if must be at the auspices of Miss Amelia Clarke and not Mr Hugh Bradbury. He's a gentle soul. He can't even hack it as a solicitor, or so he informs me. He didn't enjoy reading the terrible crimes he might have had to defend and so he decided not to continue with his training, much to his father's disgust."

Aldcroft pauses, and meets my eyes. "It's not for the faint of heart. It takes a certain type of man to defend the indefensible. I've found that only those who seem to have no compassion, and are entirely mercenary, are able to do so. I'll not ask you your opinion on the matter. I'm sure it would not be a good one." A small smile plays around my tight lips. Indeed, I don't have the best opinion of solicitors, or police officers, if I'm honest with myself.

"After we've finished speaking, I'll ask Lord Bradbury to attend me in the study. But first, I'll have the gamekeeper summoned. I'm curious to know what he has to say."

As he speaks, Aldcroft rings the bell and in no time, Underhill appears. I furrow my brow at the sight of him, but of course, all of Aldcroft police constables have been given tasks. There's one in the kitchen, one with Lady Bradbury's body, one with Lilian and another with the surviving guests.

"Ah, apologies, but would you be able to summon the gamekeeper. I need to ask him about the pistol." The butler bows deeply, his face a mask behind which he hides his true feelings about what's happening at Cragside. It must pain him. Underhill has been a part of the fixtures and fittings at the estate since he was a young boy.

"Of course, Sir," and he leaves the room, closing the door softly behind him.

"What will you ask the man?" I prompt.

"I'll ask him as much as I can. I have him on my list to speak to. One of the constables has confirmed the details from Friday with him, but there are one or two elements I wish to clarify."

"Then I should leave," I turn to do just that.

"No, I should prefer it if you stayed," Aldcroft comments. "I believe it will help." I nod, but I'm unsure why my presence is necessary. Of course, I know the gamekeeper from all the times I've joined the shooting parties at Cragside, although I confess, I much prefer fishing in Slipper Lake. I find it far more relaxing than listening to guns going 'pop' all around me.

"Tell me, what did you learn upstairs?"

"Amelia and Rebecca have a strained relationship. They had a huge, and physical argument, but were clutching one another tightly as soon as Margot's body was discovered. Lilian was quite foul to Hector, so if they were perhaps both involved in these murders, then Hector might be worth badgering. Lilian is forged from steel. I assure you, Hector isn't." Aldcroft grunts as he listens to my words. "There's a huge amount of speculation about what's been happening here. But I confess, I both suspect everyone, and believe that not one of them could be responsible. They all seem so, well, normal," I end with a sigh of frustration.

Aldcroft grunts sympathetically. "That's the problem with police work. Everyone seems incapable of committing these terrible crimes. It's not as though a face reveals a great deal. And that is why, of course, we need to have evidence that can be used against perpetrators. Without it, it's merely preconceptions that make people convict."

"So, in my case, there was a preconception that a wife must be responsible for her husband's death." Aldcroft bites his lip, his expression keen.

"Yes, and vice versa. If a wife was killed, the prime suspect would always be the husband, and alas, often is."

"And yet, you dismiss Edmund as being responsible?"

"I do, yes. Lord Bradbury isn't the sort of man to kill his wife, even if he was thinking of divorcing her, before he discovered she was terminally ill." While I'm pleased that Edmund isn't at the top of Aldcroft's list of suspects, I'm not convinced by his reasoning. I'm about to argue with him when there's a knock on the door, and the gamekeeper appears at Aldcroft's command to 'come in', his hat held in his hand.

He's a tall man, and he bends his head even though the doorway is plenty tall enough for him. I imagine that in his estate cottage, that isn't the case, and so he's become used to ducking his head. He wears his spotless outdoor boots, and brings with him a shiver of the cold night that's fallen. His clothes are equally as well cared for. I expect nothing less from him. He's known as a firm, if fair man, and one of the things he prides himself on, is not looking like the sort of man who spends his time on his hands and knees going through the undergrowth. I greet him when he glances at me in surprise.

"Please, good man, take a seat," Aldcroft indicates the chairs opposite the desk, and I settle into the one the gamekeeper doesn't take.

"This is Lady Merryweather, I'm sure you two know one another." The gamekeeper gives his assent.

"Aye, sir, we do's."

"And your name is?"

"Patrick, Patrick Cooper."

"And how long have you worked at the estate?"

"I was born here."

"So, you must know all there is to know about Cragside then?"

Aldcroft is being surprisingly jolly.

"Aye, I've watched it change from a hunting lodge to a fine house, and the estate, well, I can hardly tell you everything that's happened to it."

I suppress a smile at Patrick's words. He knows the place better than Edmund does. He knows everything about Cragside.

"And how long have you been the gamekeeper?"

Alcroft's making no notes, but instead leans forwards, elbows on the desk, listening intently.

"Nine years this coming new year. I took over from my father when he was no longer able to manage the steep slope without huffing and puffing. My Lord was good about it. My father yet lives and he helps out with what he can still do, but normally, he sits by the fire and keeps his old bones warm."

"Lord Bradbury informs me you have the rifles for safekeeping."

"Yes, and the bullets from his pistol. There's a storage place where anything dangerous is kept safe and secure. I wouldn't want anyone getting their hands on the rifles, or the bullets. They're used as sparingly as possible."

"And can you tell me, are the rifles still in that place? And the bullets?"

Patrick nods slowly, his eyes narrowing. "So, it's true then? There's been a shooting?"

"Yes, Lady Bradbury. I'm sorry to have to inform you of that." But Patrick gives no visible sign of being distressed by the information.

"Well, I assure you. The bullets are still where I left them, and I have the other key for My Lord's desk drawer, here on the rest of my keys." Patrick fiddles with something at his neck, and I'm surprised when he pulls forth a strong looking chain with keys attached to the bottom of it. "I never take it off. I know the importance of ensuring everything is well guarded."

"And I take it that you have no cause to have shot Lady Bradbury."

"No, sir, no. I donnae have a reason to shoot anyone. I don't much like shooting anything, anyway. Not even the horses that need putting out of their misery."

"Could you show me where the rifles are kept?"

"Aye, sir. Aye. But if I do, then you'll know my secret place as well." Patrick's tone has become combative.

"Yes, but I'm a police officer. I can be trusted with that knowledge."

"Well, if you say so. But I'll need to hear it from Lord Bradbury as well. Just to be sure."

"Lord Bradbury is mourning the death of his wife."

"That's as may be, but I still need him to give his agreement. There's none know but me and my father."

I think Aldcroft might be angered by the response, but instead he readily agrees.

"I'll ask Lord Bradbury for permission, as soon as we're done here. Now, can you tell me if any one else has access to a pistol, bullets or a rifle on the estate?"

"Not on the estate, no. But there might be those who fought in the war that still have their pistols in the local village. And of course, some of the more distant farmers will have their own pistols as well, if not rifles. There's often people out shooting during the season."

Aldcroft grunts his agreement. I think he might have run out of questions, but it seems not.

"Tell me, if you could, do you know Miss Lilian Braithwaite?"

"Miss Braithwaite? I did, yes. I often come upon her on the estate. She likes to walk the dogs and of course, she's cataloguing the species of plants that grow here. It seems to be a thankless task. I would swear she's not covered more than a third of the estate in the time she's been here."

"How does she actually know what the trees and plants are?"

I can hardly see why this is relevant, but Patrick appears only too happy to answer.

"Well now, there's an old diary kept by the first Lady Bradbury which contains the names of many of the plants and trees, and of course, the estate books as well, which show what money was spent on what. Alas, there's no map, and some of the plants have found their way into new places. She also takes cuttings and says she has books in the library which she consults. When that doesn't work, I believe she consults Kew Gardens. Of course," Patrick adds. "She can ask my father as well. He has a surprisingly good memory sometimes. He can remember when different parts of the estate were planted and Underhill is also a good man to ask questions about the history of the estate."

"So, Miss Braithwaite often consults your father?"

"Aye, she does. She takes him a snifter of strong brandy, and he's content to speak with her until he falls asleep."

"My thanks," Aldcroft suddenly sits back in his chair. "I think I'll speak to Lord Bradbury and then I'll check your secure storage with you."

"Aye, Sir. As soon as I have My Lord's say-so, I can show you. But, I can assure you. No one knows where it is, let alone how to access it. And my keys have never left me, so my key can't have been used to open My Lord's desk drawer. I sleep with it around my neck, and I'm a very light sleeper. I have to be because my old father sometimes wakes in the night, confused, and I must help him find his bed once more or risk losing him on the estate. It wouldn't be the first time he'd wandered to the formal gardens."

Aldcroft nods with understanding.

"Tell me, as someone who's lived here all their life, who do you think killed Lady Carver? And how do you think they did it?"

"Well, the basin tank is a dangerous beast. It's so deep and there's hardly anything to warn people it's even there. I mean, it's not in a well-trodden part of the estate, but all the same, I think it needs more of a fence around it. We've had to fish drowned deer from it before now," Patrick shakes his head at the memory.

"And so, you think Lady Carver might have slipped in to the tank without realising it was there."

"Well, I couldn't say that, but it wouldn't surprise me. I do think," and Patrick offers this without prompting. "That if someone wanted to drown her, it would have been just as easily accomplished in any of the lakes, and with much less peril for their own lives. What, for instance, if they'd not been able to get out. The sides are mighty slick. That's why the deer can't get out."

I'm intrigued by Patrick's words. I've not truly considered the scenario he's been considering.

"I'll consult the police surgeon," Aldcroft confirms before standing.

"Lady Merryweather, please stay here with Mr Cooper and I'll speak with Lord Bradbury."

# Chapter 13

Aldcroft leaves the room quickly, casting a meaningful look my way. I have no idea what it means. And then I realise. Perhaps he needs me to ask about visitors to the kitchen while Mr Cooper was in there.

"Tell me. Mrs Underhill says you sat in the kitchen while she took her walk, yesterday afternoon. Is that correct?"

"Oh aye. It was cold and I needed a warm. They always have something tasty to eat. It's a treat, to sit there and watch all the coming and goings."

"Are you aware that the weapon which killed Mr Norman Harrington-Featherington was a knife taken from the kitchen?"

"Yes, I heard that, but I can assure you, no one, other than the staff, came in and out of that room while I was in there. With Mrs Underhill gone for an hour, the housemaids all take their ease a little. I'd have remembered if we'd been forced to stand and bow or curtsey."

"Thank you," I murmur. I decide it's probably good if there's no one else to add to our list of potential suspects.

"So, the Detective Inspector has decided you didn't kill the poor woman then?" Patrick Cooper speaks with some surprise.

"Yes. He's realised I can't have done it."

"Well, I'm astounded. I never think these police people really knew what they're doing. Certainly, that other one, from London, was sniffing around my work shop looking for some means to incriminate you."

"Well, that one I have little respect for," I announce, my tone firm. "He just wants to find me guilty of something so he can get his career back in good order. And when was he in the gamekeeper's workshop?"

"Yesterday afternoon, My Lady. Before I came up to the house. Why do you ask?"

"Because he should have been on his way back to London, not nosing around on the estate."

"Like the Detective Inspector here, I think he was looking for all the rifles and pistols. I had to ask him to leave. I didn't like to be so firm with him, him being a detective inspector and all. I didn't trust him not to find something I was guilty of doing."

"I don't blame you," I commiserate with him. "He makes snap decisions and sticks with them, even when the evidence proves to the contrary."

"And then he wandered off. I'm not sure he left the estate before it went dark." Now I look at Patrick Cooper in consternation.

"He didn't leave until then?"

"No. He had his drivers sitting around waiting for him, lingering at the stable block, no doubt making sure they stayed out of sight from the main house. I noticed the car when I walked to the house, and back again."

"And what was Detective Inspector Davidson doing?"

"I only caught sight of him once or twice. The car more often. I was busy, checking the inventory after the shoot on Friday. I like everything to be in order for the next time we go out. The first time I saw the Detective Inspector after our discussion, I didn't think much of it, but when he was still there when I locked up the workshop as night fell, I did notice it."

I open my mouth to ask another question, but the door opens once more and Aldcroft walks in, Lord Bradbury behind him. I almost don't recognise Edmund. He seems shrunken as he rubs his hands together, one over another.

"Ah, Mr Cooper, I admire your loyalty, but of course, you must show Detective Inspector Aldcroft the gun cabinet. It's important he knows that everything is where it should be."

"My Lord," Patrick lowers his head.

"You've not lost your key, have you?"

"No, My Lord, I have it here. You know, I never let it out of my sight."

"Thank you. Thank you," and Edmund moves behind his desk and settles onto the chair there. He worries at his lip with his yellowed teeth.

"Did you hear about Lady Bradbury," his voice breaks as he speaks Margot's name.

"I did, My Lord, I did. A fine woman. She'll be missed." Cooper's words lack all empathy and yet they're sympathetic. Edmund responds well to the words.

"She was, wasn't she? A travesty. I never thought what it would be like without her, no matter the fact she was ill."

"Aye, My Lord, you never do. It's always a shock, no matter how prepared you think you are." I hold myself still, convinced that Edmund has forgotten he and Patrick aren't alone in the room.

Silence fills the room and then Patrick stands.

"Well, My Lord, excuse me, and I'll show the Detective Inspector what he needs to see."

"Yes, of course. Sorry to keep you," Edmund apologises, but makes no attempt to move.

I catch Aldcroft's eye and he bids me stay while he follows Patrick to the gamekeeper's workshop. It'll take them at least ten minutes to reach it, walking along the road to the stables, beneath the two arches that connect the two halves of the house; the side in which Lord and Lady Bradbury live or lived, and the side in which the servants are housed.

I wait silently. Edmund doesn't speak again. Yet the silence isn't as uncomfortable as it might have been. We've known each other for a long time. We've always been good friends, even before I married Bertie.

"I can't believe she's gone," Edmund eventually mutters. "I know she said she was dying, and that she was often unwell, but all the same, I keep expecting to see her walking in the room, or hear her voice haranguing one of the housemaids."

"The first few days are very hard," I console.

He mumbles something incoherent, his expression mournful.

"But why?" he moans, the cry heartfelt.

"That's what we need to find out. Do you know of anyone who might have wanted her dead?" My thoughts immediately turn to Lilian but I'm aware enough of my feelings that it's just because I'm learning to despise her.

"No, no one. She was a good woman. I just can't see that she could have cultivated an enemy who wished to kill her when she was dying anyway." I think that a fair point, but in the back of mind, I can hear Lilian telling me of all the letters she's written, and Edmund's admission that Margot summoned Detective Inspector Davidson from London. The letters must have been going somewhere and Margot certainly despised me.

Still, this is a conundrum, I can see that. After all, there seems no point in killing a dying woman. Whatever it was that's brought about her murder, it needs to be something immediate that had to be stopped. And that means that she must have known something about one of the murders? Surely?

"Did she speak to you about her suspicions as to who killed Lady Carver and Mr Harrington-Featherington?"

"Only in so much as to implicate you, even when you were at Rothbury police station."

"So, she was so convinced it was me, that she didn't even allow her thoughts to consider someone else."

"No." I feel cruel pressurising him for an answer, but if Margot didn't know anything about the murders, I have to reconsider why she's been killed. Was it possible there was something else taking place here as well? I can't contemplate that two separate people decided to use the weekend retreat as an excuse to kill people. It would be too much of a coincidence.

"Then it's perplexing, to say the least," I admit, watching him carefully. I'm unsure what to say to him. I can offer him all sorts of trite sentences; time's a great healer; it will get better; one day it won't hurt as much as it does now, but they were all words others have said to me, and continue to do so. I can categorically state that such words offer nothing to the shocked individual trying to come to terms with the death of someone they were close to.

"I'm sorry, Edmund." I infuse my voice with all the warmth I can summon. It pains me to see him enduring everything I have. I'm just grateful that he hasn't been arrested, as I was by now.

"I know you are, despite everything she said to you, and despite the bitchiness of her and Gwendoline. You're a good woman, Ella. I hope that one day, you might find happiness again. I know I never will."

This is too good an opening to ignore.

"You'll not remarry?" the words sting my lips as I speak them and yet I'm determined to have an answer, all the same.

"I thought I would, but now, how can I? Everyone will think I killed Margot to open the door for Lilian, or even that Lilian killed her. I won't have such scandal surrounding this family. Hugh will inherit, and he'll have a child who'll inherit after him. As much as I love this estate and never want to see it broken apart, I'll not remarry. I simply can't."

I watch Edmund, weighing the words he speaks. They seem heartfelt.

A tentative knock on the door and Underhill appears.

"My Lord, I'm sorry to disturb you but that Detective Inspector is back. Not *our* Detective Inspector. The other one."

"What?" I gasp, already half out of my chair, but Edmund waves his hand, bidding me to stay where I am.

"Bring him to the study. I'll hear what he has to say."

"He should be in London," I rail.

"He should be, yes, but he's not. Best to hear what he has to say this time."

I'm angry by Davidson's return to Cragside, and by the knowledge, offered by Patrick Cooper, that he's been sniffing around the place even when Aldcroft had ordered him to leave. Even now, he seems to be able to slip in unnoticed. He must, I think, have either been waiting for Aldcroft to leave, or used one of the other entrances to the estate in an attempt to avoid him.

There's once more a knock on the door, and Davidson appears as Underhill holds the door open for him.

"My Lord," he begins, not seeing me, but focusing instead on Edmund. "I really must insist that you allow me to apprehend Lady Merryweather. There's new evidence that links her to the murders. She's playing that local chap for a fool."

Only now, fully in the room, does Davidson emit a small gasp on seeing me.

"My Lord, I must speak with you in private," he tries to recover, his face showing not his horror at being caught out, but a firm conviction that he'll have his way.

"Detective Inspector Davidson, you barge into my house, at this time of the night, when I'm mourning the loss of my wife, and make these vile accusations about Lady Merryweather. I demand you tell me what this evidence is."

"My Lord," he all but squeaks. I almost feel sorry for him, but not for long.

"I have evidence that she arrived before she said she did on Friday afternoon. Her motorcar was seen entering the estate at 2pm."

"Who by?" Edmund asks, his voice deceptively civil.

Davidson fixes me with his triumphant eyes and swivels back to Edmund.

"I'm not at liberty to share that information. We've seen how she's killed not once, but three times and I won't put the life of someone else at risk."

"Then are you sure you've checked your source, and double-checked it. I'm unsure if you know this, but I have an identical car to that of Lady Merryweather, and I sent my chauffeur to collect some items from Rothbury on Friday after luncheon. I think you'll find that he returned at 2pm."

"What?" Davidson's confidence drops away just as his mouth falls open.

"Yes, I can assure you of that. If you merely asked the locals if they saw a black Rolls Royce Phantom 2, then they'd have been correct in informing you that they did. Did you ask them if they saw Lady Merryweather in the motorcar? If they noticed the registration plate on the motorcar? If it was her chauffeur driving? By which entrance the motorcar entered the estate?"

Despite Edmund's trauma, I'm enjoying his dismissal of the Detective Inspector's theory. For the first time since Bertie's death, I actually feel supported by my long-time friend.

"My Lord, I must be allowed to apprehend her? Return her to London."

"I think not. You've presented no new evidence to me, and I'd also question who you've been speaking to about the murders. Detective Inspector Aldcroft ordered you back to London. As I've heard nothing from the Chief Constable of the Northumberland County Constabulary, I must assume you've failed to convince him as well."

Davidson's face curdles at the words

"The Chief Constable of the Northumberland County Constabulary is not my superior, and has no right to tell me what to do."

"No, but you're in his jurisdiction, and that does count for something. If you want, I'll telephone your superior at London, and inform them of your inappropriate conduct. I'm sure they'll have something to say while you're under investigation for bungling the enquiry into the death of my life-long friend Lord Bertie Merryweather." Edmund's becoming increasingly calm as he speaks. I know it's a bad sign. Edmund has quite the temper, but it isn't a fiery temper. No, it's colder than ice and twice as deadly.

"My Lord, I suspect your affinity for the suspect is hampering your ability to think rationally." Davidson stands tall before Lord Bradbury.

I grimace at those words.

"You're questioning my ability to see clearly when you're entirely blinkered? I think not, Detective Inspector Davidson. Now, leave my property and my estate. I'll have one of my men ensure you're gone."

And with that, Edmund rings the bell and so quickly that I know Underhill has been listening at the door, he swings the door wide and inclines his head.

"Get the steward and two of the footmen. They'll escort Detective Inspector Davidson and ensure he leaves the grounds of Cragside."

"Very well, My Lord," and while Davidson fumes, casting malicious looks my way, Edmund sits behind his desk, chest heaving. He's grieving and now he's found something to channel his sorrow that doesn't involve him thinking of Margot.

Quickly, we hear the sound of heavy boots coming along the wooden corridor, the walls lined with delicate tiles.

"If you would, please," the steward, a stalwart man in his mid-forties manages to be both courteous and implacable at the same time.

"When it's found that she," and Davidson spits the word at me. "Was the culprit, you'll be a laughing stock. I'll have you brought up for impeding justice," Davidson roars, before turning on his heel and leaving, surrounded by the three men. Underhill remains, and leans in to close the door.

"Thank you," Edmund announces, quickly collapsing back into his chair.

"Tea," I say quickly, and Underhill nods and closes the door.

"Thank you," I say into the silence.

"It should have been said long ago," Edmund growls. His hands are clenched tightly together on the desk before him. "If the right culprit had been apprehended, then Margot might still be here," and a harsh sob erupts from him. I sit, shocked by such a show of grief.

"We'll find the culprits now," I confirm, when he has control of himself. As I speak, a knock on the door heralds the arrival of the tea on a tray brought by the housemaid, Alice, and the return of an irate looking Aldcroft, with Patrick Cooper just visible behind him.

"My Lord," Aldcroft speaks quickly. "I must apologise and beg use of the telephone," he requests, all without seeing Edmund's dismay, so caught up in his own problems.

"Of course," I speak for Edmund because he's incapable.

The housemaid moves to quickly lay out the tea things, and with a swift bob, leaves the room. I know that news of Edmund's grief will be quickly spread throughout the house. I don't think it's necessarily a bad thing. If the staff appreciate how much Lady Bradbury will be mourned, they might think better of their lord. Especially after the flirtation with Lilian, which everyone seems aware of, no matter who I speak to about it.

Aldcroft leaves quickly, but Patrick Cooper lingers in the doorway.

"What did you find?" I ask him, while Edmund turns his chair aside so that we see only the back of his black hair, with tendrils of grey flashing beneath the lamp light.

"The rifles haven't been fired. The bullets were where I left them."

"So, whoever used the pistol knew to bring bullets with them?"

"Yes, or it was actually a different pistol, and Lord Bradbury's pistol has merely been mislaid."

"I haven't considered that," I comment, standing and pouring the tea. I walk behind the desk and hand one cup to Edmund, his eyes clouded with tears, although he's doing his best to control himself.

"Tea?" I ask Patrick.

"No, My Lady, but thank you. I wanted to ask My Lord if he still wants me to keep the key? The Detective Inspector has suggested that the key to the drawer in the desk should be handed to him, for safe keeping."

"Yes, do that," Edmund's words are soft, but audible.

"Aye, My Lord. I will," and Patrick inclines his head and leaves Edmund and I alone. I drink from my fine china cup, savouring the bite of heat, while I seek some sort of clarity.

Detective Inspector Davidson's reappearance is unwelcome and speaks of a man who's desperate to salvage his career. I decide I need to speak to Aldcroft about it.

Margot's death is a tragedy but equally, it might have been a kindness.

What has happened to Lady Carver and Mr Norman Harrington-Featherington defies any sort of logic.

And, if it's all linked to Bertie's death, I'm unsure how.

A further knock on the door, and Aldcroft enters, his face clouded with fury.

"I've reported him to my superiors, and they'll contact London, and also send someone to ensure he makes it home, on this occasion."

"My thanks," Edmund offers, his back still to us. I have something I need to say, and appreciating I lack all tact I simply say it.

"Tell me, does Detective Inspector Davidson have an alibi for any of these murders? That man is so desperate, he might well have determined on any means to have me hang for a crime I didn't commit."

I expect Aldcroft to repudiate my words, but instead he smiles at me, appreciation on his face.

"Very good, My Lady. I'll telephone back and see if my superiors can find out where Davidson was from Friday afternoon until today. If there's anything untoward, I'll have him arrested, immediately."

I continue to sip my tea as Aldcroft disappears. I doubt Davidson is to blame, but it feels good to repay his dogmatic thinking by having him questioned just as closely as I have been. And if his superiors don't find any means of punishing him, then I'll appoint my solicitor, Rogerson, to find some means of prosecuting him. Combined with the investigation into how my husband's death has been examined, Davidson won't be a police officer for much longer.

Aldcroft doesn't reappear for some time. I'm aware of activity beyond the closed door of the study. People are coming and going up the stairs, I imagine the police surgeon has arrived. I stay with Edmund. It seems inhuman to leave him alone with his grief. It also feels safer in the small room than returning to the drawing room. I can only imagine what's happening up there. Lilian will no doubt be behaving in her usual manner. I almost look forward to Edmund informing her that their relationship is over.

I ring for more tea, and smile at Alice when she curtseys and brings biscuits as well as a fresh pot. And still Aldcroft stays away. I know it's getting late. Outside the windows of the study, I glimpse some small lights coming from the distant formal garden and the houses there, the only light in the darkness. I'm also aware it must be nearly time for dinner.

I imagine Aldcroft is caught up with some police business.

A knock on the door recalls me to the here and now, and Aldcroft finally reappears. I try to catch his eye, but his focus is on Edmund. I brace myself to hear some terrible news.

"My Lord," Aldcroft announces.

"Yes?" Edmund sounds sleepy, despite the vast quantity of tea he's drunk. He's been quiet for so long, I wonder if he's been asleep, his back to me.

"We've discovered the pistol," Aldcroft announces.

"Where?" I ask, but Aldcroft shakes his head at me, his eyes fixed on Edmund. Slowly, Edmund rotates his chair. In the glow from the electric lights, Edmund looks almost skeletal. He certainly doesn't look well.

"In your wife's hand." I gasp at the revelation, hand going to my throat. I might have considered Margot killed herself, but to have it confirmed, is shocking.

"So, she did kill herself?" But Aldcroft looks pained.

"If she did, it wasn't in the elevator. Her body has been moved, and placed there. I've examined her room, and can find no evidence that she died there. I've also examined the Turkish bath suite, the Bradbury rooms and indeed, every room in the house. But, none of them show any signs that a woman died from a gunshot wound there."

"So, she died somewhere, that wasn't the elevator, but you don't know where. But equally, why would someone have moved her?"

"The police surgeon and I are agreed that they moved her so that they could make it appear as though she was killed by someone else, someone here." I admire Aldcroft then for finally meeting my appalled expression.

"So, they think I killed her, do they?" I was speaking of the ubiquitous 'they.'

"Yes, My Lady, that's what my constable tells me they've been discussing in your absence."

I shake my head furiously. "But I was with you, or with them, how could I have done so?"

"My Lady," Aldcroft breaks into my angry retort. "I am, once more, aware that you couldn't be the suspect. And that's not the only news I have to share from the police surgeon, he also informs me that he doesn't believe Lady Carver was murdered after all, despite his initial findings."

Now, this catches my attention, and my complaints about my alleged friends are forgotten. I sit forward, eager to hear the reasoning behind such a re-evaluation.

"Our chap believes that if she'd been murdered, there'd be signs of violence on her body, a mark around her neck, or on her body, but there's nothing. Not even a blow to the head. He postulates that alas, Lady Carver, entered the pool for some reason, or perhaps slipped and fell in. We don't have her shoes to determine if that might have happened, and then she simply drowned, unable to lever herself out of the water despite her efforts to the contrary, which account for her mud encrusted nails."

I shudder. Having heard Patrick Cooper speak about his demand that there be greater protection for the unwary traveller around the deep and dark basin tank, I consider that Lady Carver has been most unfortunate. The gamekeeper spoke about the deer that drowned in there, and no doubt, there have been other animals as well.

"But, if she wasn't murdered, and my wife killed herself, then there is only the murder of Mr Norman Harrington-Featherington to solve."

"Indeed, My Lord, you're correct in that summation. Although, we do need to know why Lady Bradbury's body was moved, and where she met her end." I admire Aldcroft for his tact then.

"And, if Lady Carver wasn't murdered, then Norman can't have been murdered to cover up whatever he knew about who the murderer was." I'm warming to my subject. If Lady Carver has merely succumbed to an unfortunate accident, then that changes a great deal. It changes everything.

"And so, what, we must reassess everything we know about events on Friday afternoon and Saturday afternoon?"

"It would seem so, yes. My police surgeon has consulted two other medical professionals. He didn't share his findings with them first, but asked for an opinion, and they both agreed with him. Lady Carver wasn't murdered, although there may still be charges to face for how she did die."

Edmund nods along with Aldcroft words, his eyes fixed on mine.

"So, did Norman die because of what he knew about Bertie's murder then? And why was my wife's body moved, if she took her own life? And how did she get hold of the pistol and bullets for it?"

"I wish I knew, My Lord. I'll continue with my investigations."

"Yes, you must." Edmund continues to look deeply unhappy.

"Where did Lady Bradbury like to go?" I ask Edmund. "I mean, where was her favourite place on the estate? Surely, if she took her own life, she'd have done so there."

Edmund flinches at my words. I regret my choice of words.

"Lady Bradbury was happiest in the greenhouse at this time of year. She enjoyed watching the plants in a warmer location than walking through the estate."

"Then, Aldcroft, you need to search the greenhouse in the formal gardens."

"But someone would need to carry her back here, or bring her in a car?" Edmund complains as I make the statement.

"Yes, they would, but it seems that might have been what

happened," I stop him from saying Aldcroft can't do as I suggested.

"And if not there, then the stables. She was a keen horsewoman when she was younger. Did Lady Bradbury have a horse she liked to ride above all others?"

"Yes, yes," Edmund is adamant as he speaks. "Of late, she hasn't been able to ride at all, but she's been taking carriage drives with one of the stable hands so she can at least see her horse."

"It would have been easier to get her here from the stables than the greenhouse," Aldcroft announces.

"Quicker, not easier. It still remains to determine how she was brought back into the house. The elevator only goes from the ground floor to the first floor. Someone would have needed to get her inside."

"If we find where her accident befell her," Aldcroft states, "we can then determine the rest."

"But it's dark?" I groan as I realise it'll be impossible to continue the investigation this evening.

"It is, but we have strong torches. I don't plan on giving up for the evening. If you would both kindly remain within the house. If you want to join the others in the drawing room, that would also be acceptable."

Edmund makes no effort to move, and so I stay as well. It would be time for dinner soon. I hope that nothing fancy has been planned. I don't want to sit in a room with people that are suspects in this strange pattern of events.

"I'll return as soon as I can," Aldcroft announces, and then leaves once more.

I reach for a book on Edmund's desk, and also click on a reading light beside me, without which I can't see the words. I'm unsurprised to find it's a practical tome on estate management. It's hardly interesting and yet I don't want to do more than that and risk upsetting Edmund.

In no time at all, and despite the vast quantity of tea I've drunk that day, I quickly find my eyes rolling. Despite my best attempt to stay awake, I fall asleep. The next thing I know, there's angry shouting, and angrier footsteps coming from the hall. I startle upright, immediately noticing that Edmund's no longer sitting in his chair, and wrench open the door into the hallway.

I'm not prepared for the sight that greets me.

Aldcroft, his face furious, is in a full blown argument with Mr Hector Alwinton. Hector is busy jabbing his rotund finger into Aldcroft chest, even as Aldcroft's tries to place a pair of handcuffs over Hugh's hands. Edmund's remonstrating as well, while Amelia shrieks from the wooden staircase, where she and Rebecca watch Hugh being arrested.

I can't believe I'd slept through so much that's clearly gone before this scene.

"Now, Sir, if you simply allow me to take Mr Bradbury away, without all this interference, I'll not have to have you handcuffed as well." I can tell that Aldcroft's seeking to restore some peace to this infraction.

"You can't take him away from here," Hector's remonstrating, face flushed and sweating.

"I am the police, and I can do what must be done. I must question Mr Bradbury under caution, and I'll not do that here," Aldcroft continues.

"Hector," Edmund bellows. "You must let him do what must be done. I'm sorry Hugh. Please, go with the Detective Inspector, answer his questions, and then, hopefully, you'll be free to return soon."

Of everyone there, Hugh actually looks the most composed of them all.

"Hector. It's fine," Hugh tries to convince the other man. "I'm sure it's just a misunderstanding, nothing else." Hector slowly backs away from Aldcroft, but he doesn't look happy about it. Unable to ask Aldcroft what he's discovered, I watch, astonished, as Hugh's led through the front door. Just then, I catch sight of Lilian, from further up the staircase, and what a smile she has on her haughty face. I know then that Lilian's enjoying all of this far too much, and that only increases my suspicions of her.

# Chapter 14

We assemble for a meal in the dining room, as soon as Hugh's been driven away in yet another police car. Amelia doesn't wish to join us, but Rebecca convinces her of the need to eat. I feel a moment of sorrow for Mrs Underhill and her housemaids, who've spent so long preparing a meal, fit for weekend guests. Only then, a warming stew's placed before us all, and I realise that rather than crafting any sort of delicate meal, she's opted for something that will easily keep, and be served at all times of the day.

I devour my serving of the venison stew, savouring the fresh vegetables and the thick meaty gravy. Others, I realise, and Edmund most of all, hardly taste the food, but I savour the warmth and the comfort of it. I'm so hungry. Tea and biscuits just aren't enough to keep me going all day. I realise we didn't have luncheon, and breakfast is a long time ago.

My eyes settle on the stained glass panels in the fireplace nook which represent the four seasons. I'd certainly appreciate not being here for the winter. I linger on the coloured dresses the women wear in the images, designed by William Morris. I can't help think that they'd have cold feet, no matter the weather, and no matter how long their flowing gowns are.

I listen carefully to the conversation, and eventually manage to determine what's led to Hugh's arrest.

Lady Margot Bradbury hasn't met her death in the greenhouse, despite Edmund's belief that she would have gone there. Instead, a deep gouge has been found in the stable where her favourite horse is housed. A bullet has been pulled from the wall. There were some splashes of blood on the floor, hidden beneath the horse's hay, but what's pointed the finger of suspicion at Hugh is that he's been seen by three separate people, walking to the stables that morning, and hasn't been seen returning.

Margot had been driven to the stables by one of the grooms. When they'd gone to take her back, she couldn't be found. Although the groom had asked the stablemaster and the stable hand, neither of them had seen her. And eventually, he'd decided that someone else must have escorted his mistress back to the house. And indeed, someone must have done, for she's been murdered there, in a place that's always comforted her in the past.

As much as Margot has offended me over recent days, I know she adored her horse. She wouldn't have wanted to frighten it by discharging a pistol. And so, Margot has been murdered as well.

Yet, I'm not convinced that Hugh has killed her. There's simply no need for him to have done so. If anything, if Edmund intended to marry Lilian, then the sooner Margot was dead, the worse it would be for him.

I want to question the other members of the party, but feel unable to while Edmund's sitting amongst us, his face slack with sorrow, drinking rather than eating. It's a relief when he excuses himself as soon as we've withdrawn to the drawing room, and conversation burbles up without me even having to say anything.

Amelia is first, eager to defend her fiancé now that his uncle has gone.

"I know what you're all thinking. But he couldn't have done it. I just know it."

"Why? Was he with you?" Lilian's quick to retort, her tongue whip sharp, as I've come to expect. I doubt that Edmund has made his recently discovered feelings towards her clear yet. She must still think she'll be the lady of Cragside estate. I consider why she's once more able to mingle with the rest of the guests.

She was so stubborn after Margot's body was discovered, that in my heart, I'd hoped she might have been arrested and removed from the house.

"No, he wasn't with me." Amelia replies, eyes red from all the crying.

"He was with me for much of the morning," Hector confirms, fixing a glowering gaze on Lilian.

"But not all of the morning," Lilian presses.

"No, not all of the morning. But certainly, he was gone for too short a time to kill his aunt, and place her in the elevator."

"Why? Do you know how long it would take to do something like that?" Lilian's taunts are flung to wound. I find her questioning interesting. She's given the matter far too much thought.

"I can assure you he was gone for no longer than thirty minutes, and it would take at least ten to get to the stables, and another ten to get back, if he were alone. How, I ask you, was he to transport his aunt's body?"

"I'm quite sure it could be done." Lilian isn't giving up.

"But," and I interject because I've had enough of listening to the shrew. "There's no motive for him to kill his aunt."

"Of course there is," Lilian snaps. "She must have seen him kill Lady Carver, or even Mr Harrington-Featherington." She stands, back rigid, in front of the huge and elaborate marble fireplace. Above her head, the skylight shows the clear, black sky overhead. I just bite back on my comment that Lady Carver hasn't actually been murdered. Aldcroft hasn't made that announcement yet. So far, only Edmund and I know the truth of Lady Carver's death.

"And why did he kill Lady Carver?" I challenge.

"Why, because he married her and didn't want anyone else to know."

"But the marriage has long since been annulled. There's no reason, not anymore."

"Then, it must be because she was making demands on him. Perhaps she wanted paying to keep quiet, and we all know that Hugh has no money of his own."

I laugh. I can't help myself. Lilian's eyes blaze with fury at my response.

"Tell me, Miss Braithwaite, why are you so determined to advocate this chain of events? You've stuck to this argument for some time now, refusing to consider anything else."

"Because it's what happened," she retorts. "Must I spell it out. I saw him knock her unconscious and lower her into the water."

Amelia gasps, her hand going to her mouth. I fear she might fall over as she absorbs Lilian's words.

I shake my head in astonishment.

"I doubt Lady Carver would have allowed herself to be lowered into the water without a fight," Olive dismisses Lilian's claim.

"But that's not what happened, is it?" I look to Hector. He can't take his eyes from Lilian's triumphant smirk.

"No," he says, as though the words are wrenched from. "No, that isn't what happened. Not at all."

"Why, you," Lilian rounds on Hector. Her face is hectic with colour, clashing terribly with the orange blouse she wears over a dour, brown skirt. No one has changed for dinner. We all wear our day clothes. The time for pomp and ceremony is long past.

"What? You and your lies. I'll not have them directed at young Hugh. He did nothing wrong."

"I'll tell them what you did," she spits. She looks fevered. Fevered and ugly, angry red marks on her cheeks, her chin wobbling with rage.

"Then you must do so, for I no longer care. I'll not have you frame Hugh for something he didn't do."

This has my interest now.

"Then I'll tell them what you did. Hector is the one who broke into Lady Carver's room at Lord and Lady Merryweather's."

Hector's cheeks shade to a deep plum colour. He looks down, perhaps hoping to find his feet, but his stomach gets in the way.

"Did you?" I insist.

"Yes, I did. It was me."

"Why?" I ask, but Hector raises his head, fixes me with his eyes and holds his lips tightly together.

"I'll not tell you that," he counters. "But neither will I be blackmailed by Lilian about it any further. And, I will say that she and I didn't spend all our time together on Friday afternoon. She forced me to give her an alibi and now I refute everything I said. We might have returned to the house together, but we weren't together for at least an hour on Friday afternoon. She could have been up to anything."

A loud hiss fills the room. I don't turn away from Hector. It's evident Lilian is the one making the noise.

"And what did you do during that hour?" I enquire.

"I amused myself by walking along the flume." His wobbling chin is held up, daring me to argue with him.

"So, what, you spent an hour walking through the mud and over the difficult terrain from the flume to Nelly's Moss lake?"

"No, I walked so far along it from the lake. I didn't risk it all the way, and even then, I slipped into the stream and that was why I came home shivering and freezing. What Lilian did to get so wet is beyond me." I hold his gaze. I find I want to believe him.

Now, I peruse Lilian. It isn't far from the Nelly Moss Lakes to the basin tank. Not for someone as fit as Lilian. I know that I can walk it in about twenty minutes at the most. Despite the police surgeon suggesting Lady Carver hasn't been murdered, Lilian has certainly been up to something in that hour she's forced Hector to give her. There's a reason she'd wanted a firm alibi for when she eventually returned to the house.

What had Lilian been up to? I wish Aldcroft were still at the house. He should have been here to hear all this.

"It's no concern of anyone in this room what I was doing."

"Ah, but it is." Olive surprises me by the iron in her usually frail voice. "You either tell us, or we'll call one of the constables in, and have you apprehended as well."

I think, for a long few seconds, that Lilian will crumble under such words, but slowly, her confidence returns.

"You must do what you think is best. I assure you I won't be telling anyone what I was up to during that time." Lilian sits down in a chair, and focuses on the fire. Olive looks from Hector to me, and I nod.

"Constable," I call to the young man standing outside the drawing room, in the gallery. At least he can't have been bored with the vast art collection on display there. It might have given him a headache to be faced with so much upon which to feast his eyes. The sound of his boots scampering over the wooden floor assures me he's coming, and at a trot.

"My Lady." He appears in the archway, all puffed up, worry on his young face.

"We have information that Miss Lilian Braithwaite and Mr Hector Alwinton gave one another false alibis. Mr Alwinton has explained what he was doing, but Miss Braithwaite refuses to tell us anything. We request that she be questioned by the Detective Inspector."

A wave of emotions floods the young man's face. He has short-cropped hair, and a snubbed nose. He looks about ten years old. I certainly believe that police officers are getting younger and younger. But, he has his wits about him.

"Detective Inspector Aldcroft isn't here at this time, but I'll have her escorted to her room, until he returns. One moment," the constable moves outside again. I hear him speaking to someone, no doubt one of the housemaids, before returning.

"Just one moment and I'll be relieved by another of the constables."

"Very good," I confirm, unwilling to take my eyes from Lilian. I wouldn't put it past her to lash out at Hector. Or to try and make her escape.

It's almost as though no one dares breathe in the room. Amelia glowers at Lilian, Rebecca holds her hand tightly with both of hers. Hector is still flooded with embarrassment, whereas Olive looks as though she might be the next one to physically harm Lilian. Reginald has his hand on her arm, and I don't doubt that if she does make a move towards Lilian, he'll restrain her.

I'm shocked by how few of us there are now. While I didn't actually see Lady Carver over the course of the weekend, this house party should have consisted of Lord and Lady Bradbury, and nine guests. There are only six of us remaining, seven if we include Edmund, but he's taken to his bedchamber after dinner. It's an extremely high rate of attrition, reminding me of the terrible reports of survivors in the trenches during the Great War.

We all hear heavy steps along the great hallway, and a hurried conversation taking place between two of the police constables, before the first man reappears.

"Miss Braithwaite, if you will," he has a pleasant voice. While I thought him too young to be a police officer, Lilian, being of a similar age, quickly bows her head and goes with him from the drawing room, and towards the gallery. The bedrooms are to the far end of the gallery. She walks, shoulders back, chin up high. I'm tempted to swipe the smirk from her face, but I don't.

After she's gone, an uneasy silence fills the room.

"What did you break into Lady Carver's room at my home?" I turn to Hector.

He swallows heavily, his Adams apple bobbing against the strain of his tight collar.

"She had something of mine that I needed, and she wouldn't return it to me."

"So, more secrets?" I bite angrily.

"Yes, more secrets. There are secrets everywhere, Lady Merryweather, but you were always so blinded by your horses and your motorcars to truly pay enough attention. Unlike your husband. He was a man who enjoyed knowing others peoples secrets."

I'm not alone in gasping in horror at the sharpened words.

"Lord Merryweather had information on all us locked away in his safe, all of us. Even you?" this he directs at Olive. Olive physically recoils.

"And what was it that Lady Carver had that was yours?"

"Some documents regarding my involvement in a court case. If she'd presented them to Lord Merryweather, as she assured me her intentions were, I'd have been embarrassed and no doubt lost Bertie's good opinion. I assure you, I didn't kill him, and I didn't harm Lady Carver either. I wouldn't do such a thing." While Hector speaks with outrage, I'm not truly convinced by it.

"And you, Olive, what did Lord Merryweather know about you?"

"I don't know," she holds her two hands out, and shrugs her shawl covered shoulders. "I do so little, I can hardly see that anything would be worthy of being held over me."

Hector laughs, the sound as pleasant as rocks falling down a steep hill.

"You pretend to your innocence, but we all know the truth. You and your husband were never actually married, were you? You lived with him despite never having exchanged wedding vows."

Rebecca's eyes flicker from Hector to Olive and I can see the astonishment on her face. Truly, I'm shocked as well. Before the Great War, it would have been beyond scandalous to live with a man without being wed, especially for someone in our echelon of society.

"Ah, well," and Olive smiles sadly. "I don't truly think of it as scandalous anymore. And I doubt that anyone would."

Again, no one speaks. I'm struggling to understand just what Hector's saying, and why he felt the need to do as Lilian demanded from him. Was there, I consider, more to it than even that?

"And so, it seems to come down to this, once more. Who was responsible for my husband's death?"

No one meets my gaze. Rather than suspecting me, perhaps they actually all suspect one another.

I allow the stillness to grow uncomfortable. Perhaps, even after all this time, one of them will say something that gives them away. I can only hope they might. If there are any more deaths, or arrests, there'll be only half of the party left. I can only imagine the scandal in the national newspapers when it comes to light.

Amelia, surprises me by being the first to speak.

"I suspected Lady Carver of being responsible." Her voice is small. "I thought the robbery in her room was all a means to draw attention away from her."

"And was that the only reason you suspected her?" Reginald asks. He's not spoken for so long, his words startle me.

"No, I confess it wasn't. I could tell her feelings towards Hugh were more than just friendly, but I didn't know they'd ever been married."

"So, there was more than a little jealousy as well, that made you suspect her?" Amelia nods quickly. Her eyes focused on her hands. Her face is a welter of bruises, her red-rimmed eyes make her appear even more unappealing.

"Yes, some jealousy. I knew he was too good for me, and yet he asked me to marry him all the same. I was eager to ensure we married and I didn't want anyone to distract him."

"Thank you." I offer. It feels only right when she's opened herself to ridicule by such honesty.

"You know he loves you," Rebecca reassures her eagerly. "Hugh would do anything for you."

"I confess, I believed my wife was involved," Reginald is the next to speak. His words aren't a surprise, not after what we've learned about her.

"And I thought it must be Lady Carver as well," Hector speaks quickly. "That woman had altogether too many secrets and Bertie hoarded them all. She had far too many dodgy political dealings," he confirms, as though that explained everything.

"And you Rebecca? Who did you suspect?"

She shudders at the question.

"I thought it must be Norman. He'd behaved most strangely on the evening of the murder. He was nervous, I could tell he was. I caught him rushing in from the garden. He smelt strangely. I thought he must be drinking out there, but if he was, it was no alcohol I've ever smelt before. Still, it had a strange tang, something I knew I recognised, but which I've never been able to name."

"But why would he have killed my husband?"

"I think for the same reason everyone else was uneasy around him. Your husband must have known something about Norman that could have caused him problems."

"If Bertie knew all this information, then where is it now?" I huff. "To worry so many of you, he must have had evidence which he could use against you? His word would surely not be enough to cause problems?"

"I saw some documents," Hector announces. "He held them in his desk drawer, and also, I believe in a bank safe."

I rack my memory. I do remember mention of a bank safe amongst Bertie's personal effects but I've no idea it contained anything more than deeds to his properties. I need to contact my solicitor, to determine if there's indeed proof, as Hector seems to believe.

I'm about to ask yet another question, when Edmund reappears. He looks terrible.

"Why is Lilian locked in her room with a constable outside the door?" he queries. His eyes are blood shot. Either he's been drinking, or, and I suspect this is the truth, he's been woken from a very short sleep.

"Her alibi for Lady Carver is no longer viable," Hector admits.

"In what way?"

"She wasn't with me, as I said she was." Edmund flashes me a quick look, before settling into a chair.

"So, now everything begins to fall apart. What will we hear next? That Lilian had been seen with one of the kitchen knives? That she was in the stables with Margot?" His eyes are hard when he looks at me and I flinch. It's exactly what happened to me, and yet no one else says anything else about Lilian. It's not a house of cards that means to declaim her as a murder.

"No, it's just the one alibi that's questionable," I confirm, pleased that Edmund makes no reference to Aldcroft's claim that Lady Carver wasn't actually murdered. "Unless, of course, you have something to add?" Unlike Lilian, I don't ask to wound, but rather out of curiosity.

Edmund stays still for a heartbeat before shaking his head.

"No, I know nothing further. I didn't see Lilian with a knife, or anywhere near my wife."

"Tell me, Edmund, what did Bertie know about you? Everyone here, even Olive, has been forced to admit to some frivolity or transgression that came to his attention. What was yours? If not Lilian?"

I think Edmund might ignore me, but he doesn't.

"I have financial problems. The house is mortgaged up to the hilt. Lady Bradbury had her little habits, you see, and because I'd fallen out of love with her a long time ago, I indulged them when I shouldn't."

"What sort of habits?" Amelia challenges, her voice rich with outrage. She thinks herself marrying into a family where she need never concern herself with worries about money again. It seems she might have been wrong.

"Gambling. She had a terrible affliction for it. She persisted, even when I removed all those from her company who encouraged her in such a reckless endeavour."

"What did she gamble on?"

"The horse races, of course. She adored the thrill of it all, but she was, alas, not very competent with her gambling. She always lost more than she gained."

"And Bertie would have held this against you?" Reginald queries. I can hear the disbelief in his voice.

"I doubt it, he tried to help me, but I was uncomfortable with him knowing, and with the knowledge that someone was speaking to him about it all. I asked him, none to politely, to butt out and leave it well alone."

"So, Bertie didn't threaten to share the information he had?"

"No, he threatened to speak to Margot about it, and then he offered to help me out. His pity was the worst of all because he genuinely meant it."

This seems understandable. I really do pity Edmund now, although for a second, I suspect that he might have more to gain from the life insurance if Margot died a violent death.

"And Rebecca? What did Lord Merryweather know about you

that you needed to keep quiet." Rebecca smiles but it isn't pleasant.

"Why Lady Merryweather, he knew nothing about me. I am who I say I am, and I have no money to get into any scrapes. I don't have a secret marriage, either." Yet, for all her words, I'm not at all convinced by her proclamation of innocence.

"And what did he know about you?" Reginald turns his cool gaze on me.

"My husband knew everything there was to know about me. He knew of how I spent my wealth and how I spent my time. I shared everything with him, although, it seems he didn't do the same to me. He was perhaps, a kinder husband than he was a friend or ally."

"And you're sure of that?" Reginald persists.

"Why?" I feel my forehead furrow in thought.

"I'm just asking. Everyone else here, apart from Rebecca, has been forced to admit to some action they'd sooner keep quiet. It stands to reason that you must have had your own secrets as well."

"If I did, I'm unaware of them. But, perhaps if we find the stash of documents Bertie held on everyone, then we can prove the truth of that."

"Then you don't know where they are?"

"How can I? I know nothing about this. I think you forget that I was locked-up when Bertie's will was read, and his possessions distributed. I am, once more, the last to know of these things."

I feel eyes on me, none of them kind. But, I don't owe them an apology. It was Bertie who did all these things.

"Anyway, we're discussing who everyone believes killed Bertie. So tell me Edmund, who do you think fired the pistol?"

"I suspected it was Hector," Edmund admits, holding the shocked eyes of Hector as he makes his assertion. "Of us all, I believe he had the most to lose, as it would have been his career that I suspect was threatened. And, well, I knew he had his pistol on him that night."

Once more, all eyes swing to Hector.

"How did you know that?" he asks Edmund.

"I saw it, inside your suit jacket. And I had no idea why you'd need a pistol at a dinner party."

"It was not for the dinner party," Hector's quick to reply. "In fact, Bertie gave it to me. He was uneasy. He thought something might be afoot, and he asked me to take hold of the pistol so that no one could kill him with it."

I gasp at the words. I'd known Bertie was distracted, but surely not because he feared someone would harm him.

"And yet, we have only your words that this is what happened?" Edmund persists.

"If you wish, you can see it that way. But, I see it that of everyone there that evening, Bertie trusted me above all others. He wanted me to stay close to him."

The words sting, I can't deny it. But then, I'd arrived back from collecting my new motorcar so late, perhaps Bertie hadn't had the time to speak with me about it.

"So, how did he end up in his study, all alone?"

Hector looks stricken at the question.

"He told me to listen at the window, from outside at a certain time. He said that I was to listen to what was said, and bear witness to it. But when I went outside, I couldn't hear the conversation. It was muffled by the thick curtains and the even thicker glass. He told me he'd leave one of the bay windows open, but he must have forgotten. I was torn, unsure what to do. I left my post, and made my way back inside the house. But by the time I was outside the study once more, there was no noise coming from inside. The door was open, but there was no sign of Bertie in there. I went looking for him, but I never found him alive."

"And did you see who he'd been talking to?" Reginald queries.

"No, but it was a woman. I saw the swirl of a skirt disappearing behind a door in the darkness, but I can tell you nothing about its design, fabric or colour. There were no lamps in that corner of the hall. I made attempts to check what everyone was wearing, but it was impossible to say, one way or another."

"And of course, it might not have been a skirt, but a cloak, or some such," Olive offers. "It could have been a man in disguise," she explains more slowly when Hector looks at her with narrowed eyes.

"Yes, it could have been anyone of the guests, or even the servants. When the cry was given, I was devastated to have failed him."

"But, you just said that this secret conversation didn't result in Bertie's death?"

"Not at that time, no. I don't know if the murderer went back to kill him, or if it was someone entirely different."

"So, we're still no closer to solving any of the cases," Amelia casts her hands up in frustration. I feel as confused as she does.

Lady Carver, Reginald, Edmund, Hugh, Lilian, all of them seem to have a motive for killing Bertie. But had any of them had the opportunity? I'm beginning to fear I might never know the answer to that.

# Chapter 15

When Aldcroft returns sometime later, an uneasy calm has fallen between us all. We're too exhausted to talk anymore, and what, after all, is there to say? The fire has been continually restocked by the housemaids. Yet I feel cold. Aldcroft looks grey, exhaustion weighing him down, and yet his voice is firm.

"Lady Merryweather, will you accompany me." I stand, bemoaning my aching muscles and follow him once more to the study. I'm unsurprised to find Lilian there, scowling furiously, the constable keeping a firm eye on her.

She eyes me with loathing.

"What's she doing here?"

"Lady Merryweather has been assisting me on this investigation, as you well know."

"Well, I'm not speaking while she listens." Aldcroft nods, as though expecting the answer, and sits down all the same. I'm unsure what I'm supposed to do.

"Lady Merryweather, do take a seat," he instructs me. I slide onto the one remaining chair. With the four of us in the room, it feels quite tight. I also have no idea what Aldcroft is hoping to accomplish by keeping me here when Lilian has already said that she'll say nothing while I'm in the room.

"As you know," Aldcroft directs this at me. "I've been interviewing Mr Hugh Bradbury with regard to the murder of Lady Margot Bradbury. And in doing so, I've discovered some information that I wish to share with you." His eyes are bland, hands steady where they rest on the desk before him. He doesn't even consult his notebook. I nod. Whatever's happening here, I'm happy to go along with it, for now.

"Mr Hugh Bradbury informs me that Miss Lilian Braithwaite was well known to him before she sought employment at Cragside with Lord Bradbury." Aldcroft doesn't take his eyes from mine, but both of us are aware that Lilian startles. My mind is busy, once more assembling the pieces of this puzzle. Lilian, it appears, has been angling to become Lady Bradbury for much longer than any of us could have foreseen.

"She and Mr Hugh Bradbury were in a relationship for about twelve months when they were younger. It was Miss Lilian Braithwaite who broke off that relationship. The next time Mr Hugh Bradbury laid eyes on her, she was here, working for his uncle, or rather pretending to work for his uncle while trying to win his regard."

"Mr Bradbury spoke to his uncle about her, while being slightly sparing with the details, but he was not to be moved on the subject. Mr Bradbury was unwilling to admit to another improper union, following the problems of his annulment to Lady Carver. Not, I hasten to add, that he and Miss Lilian Braithwaite were married, as he had been to Lady Carver."

I risk a sideways glance towards Lilian. Her slim hands are fists in her lap, her shoulders held so rigidly I think she'll have back pain come the morning. Hugh's conversation with Aldcroft hasn't gone quite as she'd expected. What then does Lilian know about Hugh?

"Mr Bradbury then informed me that he'd been forced to endure her presence here ever since because she's been blackmailing him, as well. It seems that Mr Bradbury, as well as indulging in indiscreet love affairs, also had another reason for failing in his career as a solicitor, and Miss Lilian Braithwaite knows what that is. Mr Bradbury never completed his degree."

"Now, Miss Braithwaite," and Aldcroft finally looks at the younger woman. "I would welcome your comments on what Mr Bradbury has said." Slowly, my mind's beginning to decipher the intent behind Aldcroft words. Surely, if Lilian pedals in secrets, as Bertie had done, then they might well have clashed. Yet, I can't move away from the knowledge that the police surgeon has refuted claims that Lady Carver has been murdered, and not just him, but two other experts as well.

"I will say nothing," she announces firmly. "I'll have a solicitor present, as no doubt Mr Bradbury and Lady Sunderland have had, and I'll take their advice."

"So, you don't wish to refute anything that Mr Bradbury has said?"

"I do not, no." Her chin is high, filled with defiance.

"Then I'll continue."

I hadn't expected there to be more.

"It seems that Lady Bradbury had her suspicions about Miss Braithwaite as well, and she was not as inhibited as her nephew in sharing them. In fact, Mr Bradbury suspects that Lady Bradbury had uncovered much of your life story. In turn, she was using it against you, so that she could be assured you wouldn't marry her husband, after her unfortunate death. Mr Bradbury informs me that he saw you, with Lady Bradbury, in the stables this morning."

No denial issues from Lilian's mouth. I find this more interesting than if she'd simply accused him of being a liar.

"He also apprises me that you have a key for Lord Bradbury's desk, and that Lord Bradbury has forgotten about this."

The words fill the room, but still Lilian doesn't speak.

"Mr Bradbury also asserts that you're a regular on the shooting trips, and that on more than one occasion, there have been bullets missing when the gamekeeper ran his inventory afterwards."

Still there's silence.

"Mr Hugh Bradbury, in short, believes you killed Lady Bradbury to keep her silent because you were experiencing a little of the same that you'd applied to him. He also advises me that Lady Carver had been trying to assist him; that you and she had arranged a meeting, to take place at the basin tank on Friday afternoon."

Somehow, I manage not to gasp at this list of denouncements which seems to entirely incriminate Miss Lilian Braithwaite.

Her knuckles are white with the pressure of her clenched hands.

"Well, we all know that Mr Hugh Bradbury is a liar and a fraud," Lilian finally states. "And I confirm that I'll say nothing else without a solicitor present."

Aldcroft nods, as though expecting the answer.

"Constable McStewart, will you take Miss Lilian Braithwaite to the police car please. I'll be along in a few moments. We'll take her to Rothbury police station."

"Very good, sir," he rumbles, a slight Scottish burr to the words, to be expected so close to the Scottish border.

I stand, to allow easier access to the door, and watch Lilian escorted from the room, her hands in cuffs before her, her back rigid, her eyes on where she's going. I can just make out one of the housemaids goggling at the sight as she dusts the wooden rail that runs along the wall.

Aldcroft moves to my side. "I've kept Mr Bradbury in custody. Not all of his story can be correct. I've rung through to the university for confirmation of Hugh's status as a graduate, or not, and now I have three people in my custody. I'm still not convinced that any of them are truly guilty."

"And yet you said all those things to Lilian?"

"I did, yes. I'm curious to see if she'll buckle with the knowledge that she's lost control of another of her underlings she held in her thrall by knowing things about them they didn't want widely broadcast."

"Are you disregarding the police surgeon's suggestion that Lady Carver died in an accident?"

"I am yes, it doesn't fit, and equally, it would be far too convenient to a number of individuals if that's what happened. Tell me, what are the remaining guests saying? Do you suspect them of being involved?"

"At the moment, I feel as though I suspect everyone here,

perhaps even myself." I laugh a little at that admission.

"It's too easy to second-guess ones actions after the fact," Aldcroft concurs as though he finds the statement plausible.

"I'll be back shortly. I've had word that Detective Inspector Davidson hasn't yet returned to London. That makes me suspicious, so I've had a quick word with your man, and would ask you to be alert for anything strange. Despite this whole can of worms we've uncovered here, Davidson is still convinced of your guilt."

The news unnerves me. "My thanks," I offer. By now, we're in the hallway once more, and I can see, through the open door, and thanks to the house lights, where Lilian is being helped into the police car. I'm unsurprised to catch sight of Williams through the doorway. I can only imagine the expression on his face. The cold of the winter's night seems to bellow in through the door, and I shiver, wrapping my arms around my waist.

I move forwards, eager to talk to Williams, and at the same time, I see Mrs Underhill. She emerges from her kitchen, no doubt to see what's happening. I offer her half a smile. She arches an eyebrow at me, and quickly makes her way back into the kitchen. Outside, the rumble of a motorcar engine fills the night time air. I listen to the wheels scrunch over the gravel drive.

Only then do I move on.

"Williams," I call to him, and he looks up, already making his way towards me.

"My Lady," he tips his cap.

"What are you doing out there?" I ask.

"I've been checking on a few things, speaking to people and also looking at the places where the victims have been found. And, I have information to share with you. But not tonight. It's late already, and it's too dark to see beyond the tip of my nose."

"Then I'll meet you here, first thing in the morning."

Williams nods, and quirks an eyebrow at me.

"Sleep well, My Lady. You should, now that so many potential murderers have been hauled away to Rothbury police station."

"Perhaps," I offer, before turning aside. It's too cold outside.

The promise of a frost, or perhaps even some ice, to come in the morning. I'll be making sure I dress warmly.

# Chapter 16

"**G**ood morning," I greet Williams. I'm huddled inside all of my warmest clothes. The windows are etched with thin tendrils of ice and I can't see that it's going to warm up anytime soon. Not with the cloudless sky, and distant sun.

Another day spent here, at Cragside, with suspicions all around me, but I feel freer once I've skipped through the doors.

"Did Aldcroft speak to you about Davidson?"

"He did, yes. Has there been any sign of him?"

"No, not at the moment, but the estate is huge, and I can't be everywhere at once," Williams cautions.

"I appreciate that. Now, what do you want to tell me?"

"I've been speaking to the staff down at the stables, and at the big house. One of the stable hands tells me that they did see a horse drawn cart being led up to the house. It was filled with supplies. There's nothing unusual about that, other than they believed the supplies were brought to the house on Friday and so there'd be no need to bring more until next Friday. And, they said hello to the cloaked figure directing the horses but received no response. He thought it was a bit strange at the time, but put it down to the fact that old Bellows who normally performs the task is hard of hearing."

"And what did Bellows say?"

"Bellows knows nothing of it," Williams confirms.

"So, we know how Lady Bradbury's body was returned to the house?"

"We suspect half of it," Williams qualifies. "How that body would have been dragged to the elevator with no one knowing is beyond me. They'd have had to get the body past the kitchen, and if not the kitchen, then past the study along the inner hall. It would have been a terrible risk."

"Do you suspect whoever it was had an accomplice?"

"I think they must have done. And they would have needed to be strong as well. It's no mean feat to carry a dead body."

"I've learned that Bertie hoarded people's secrets, although I suspect you know that, and that Lilian was little better. She used what she knew to blackmail people into doing what she wanted them to do. Hugh was one of her victims, if his words are to be believed. And, he had a relationship with her not long after he'd married Lady Carver. It seems that Lady Carver was assisting Hugh in trying to bring an end to her demands on him. Lady Carver and Lilian had arranged a meeting at the basin tank."

"Is this what Hugh has been telling the Detective Inspector?"

"Yes, it is. I accept it might well be an attempt to muddy the waters."

"Potentially, but it still strikes me that Lilian isn't quite the sweet young woman she portrays herself to be in front of Lord Bradbury."

"No, well, he's seen the light as well. He says he has no intention of marrying her now that Margot's dead."

I haven't been looking where we're going, but now I look at Williams quizzically, as we're about to once more take the steep incline behind the house.

"I think we should have a look at the basin tank."

"To see if Lady Carver was murdered or died by misadventure?"

"Exactly," Williams confirms.

Once more, I feel the steep climb in the back of my legs and consider just how fit someone would have to be to run up this hill. Not, I realise, that it's the only means of reaching the basin tank.

The estate is criss-crossed with pathways. The unwary can

become very lost amongst them, but the individual who knows their way around, there's no end of surprises and stunning views to happen upon. My favourite view is close to the quarry, looking down on the valley that runs southwards. A farm at the tip of the estate there has sheep and cows grazing in the fields, and it's always struck me as idyllic. While I appreciate the sweeping views of the many lakes, and the vista of the heath, it's that small area that calls to me.

Williams continues to speak as we climbed higher.

"But, it's possible that, once more, the consensus of the group is leading us to look at Lilian as the culprit."

"Yes, I realise that," I huff. I don't want to come to a stop, but it's hard going trying to walk, breathe, talk and think all at the same time.

"If Lady Carver wasn't murdered, then really, no matter what Hector says, Lilian simply can't be our murderer."

"No, she can't, but I'd be curious to know what she was up to during that time."

"Indeed." By now, we've reached the top of the slope once more. Only yesterday we'd followed the trail along to Cragend quarry, although I realise now, we'd not actually made it all the way there. Today we turn left and head into the heart of the estate from a different view point. I pause, looking down on the roof of the fine house, lit up with the electric lights that Cragside estate is so famous for because it's still early in the day.

"I'm impressed Lady Carver could walk here," I admit, feeling the burn of the cold day and the exertion in the back of my throat.

"Yes. I'd have expected her to keep to the lower paths, and out towards Tumbleton Lake. If she'd wanted to come this way, I'd have thought a horse or even asking one of the chauffeurs to drive her."

This is something I've not truly considered. I know the walkways are rugged, the going difficult in places. More than once, in earlier days, I've returned to the main house with walking boots clogged in the thick, black mud of the estate,

177

and with feet so wet, they were blue when I removed my boots and stockings. Cragside is a beautiful, but wild and unforgiving place.

We walk on in silence. I don't have the breath to speak and Williams is busy looking all around him. And what a feast it is for the eyes. Wide white mushrooms lurk in the dampest sections of the walkway, which never seem to drain, and in the slighter drier areas, bright red mushrooms broadcast their deadliness. Creatures rustle through the undergrowth, pheasants making their strange, half-strangled cries just out of sight, the tree tops filled with birds busy about their tasks. I pause, looking upright as cones tumble to the floor. My eyes alight on brightly coloured birds harvesting the goodness from the cones before discarding them.

Williams grins at the sight. It's a feast for the soul, and then we emerge next to the basin tank, and I shiver, despite myself. What a cold and lonely place it is to have died. Despite the cold, but bright sky overhead, the water of the basin tank reflects nothing but blackness. I move as close as I dare, wary of slipping on the undergrowth that creeps close to the stone-lined side of the built pool. I don't want to end my days the same way Lady Carver did.

"She was found, face down, floating in the middle of the basin tank." Williams recounts, before I can ask. "The police had a good look round the sides but could find no signs of any disturbance. They couldn't even see where anyone had walked close enough to get a good look. But, if you turn, you'll see our footsteps have made no impression either.

I glance behind me and quickly confirm for myself what Williams has noticed.

"So, anyone could have been here, and they'd have left no mark?"

"It seems that way, yes." I walk away from the basin tank, to the edge of the plateau on which the basin tank nests and peer down. There are twisting paths lower down, coming up from all directions close to the house, and some which even allow access from the west of the estate. And there are ferns and pine everywhere as well. Some of them mask the view, others don't. At a certain angle, you might suspect that no one will see what you do in this secluded location.

"I did notice something, though." I haven't realised what Williams is doing. Now I rush to his side, ready to grab hold of him if I need to, from where he stands, perilously close to the side of the basin tank.

"If I can just reach it," his words are muffled, his neck close to his chest as he reaches down the side of black pool. I'm there, ready to haul him if I need to, but I wish he'd warned me what he was doing, or even brought a rope so that I could keep a firmer hold on him.

"Be careful." The words leave my mouth unbidden. I know they're a foolish thing to say. They'll hardly make him behave any more carefully. Williams is a good man, but he does have a high belief in his abilities to do anything he sets his mind to. The fact he's not yet cleared my name fully with regard to Bertie's death is a failure that bedevils him, although it's not his role to clear my name.

"Ah ha," and he rears backwards, clutching something that drips black water into the basin tank.

"What is it?" I ask him.

"I don't know, but I caught sight of it earlier when I was up here with the police. I didn't want to draw attention to it."

"So, you thought to keep information from the police." I'm reminded of Aldcroft's directive that Williams isn't above the law.

"Not at all, My Lady," his formal words remind me that sometimes I speak too freely to him. "But I did want to see it before they got their hands on it."

"Well, come on then," I urge him. He's fumbling with the rope tied around what can only be called a sack, perhaps used for garden refuge. Water streams from the hessian material and I consider that if someone wanted to keep something hidden, they really should have wrapped it in treated canvas, or something like that. I don't doubt that the contents will be ruined.

"Here," and the sack finally springs open and we both peer inside it.

"What on earth?" I breathe. Williams sighs in disbelief.

Inside the sack is a pile of soggy but easily identifiable bank notes, huge ones of denominations that few people will see in their lifetime, and besides them all is a pistol.

"Well, who left that here?" I'm astounded by the vast sum of money. All of the notes seem to be for one hundred pounds, although, until they're dried out, it isn't possible to say for sure without risk of ripping them.

"I've no idea. It isn't what I was expecting to find, that's for sure."

"What did you think it would be?"

"I thought it would be Lady Carver's bag, or something like that, in which incriminating evidence was stored, something that Lilian wanted destroyed. This looks like someone's life savings, as though they were meaning to make a huge purchase, or escape to somewhere else and start a new life."

"Yes, but not even Bertie would have been able to gather so much cash together, and he was wealthier than every other person here."

"Apart from Lord Sunderland," Williams interrupts.

"Yes, apart from Lord Sunderland, perhaps, and maybe Lady Carver. This could have been her money. This could account for why she was here?"

"But why would she place her money in the basin tank? She only arrived the day before you. Are you saying that she came here on Thursday and sunk her money into a watery hole?"

"I don't know, and also no. That bag won't have lasted for long. The bank notes would have begun to come apart."

"Yes, they would have done. They're not far from doing so now."

"Do you think someone else found the money and put it in a different bag? Or perhaps, it was never meant to fall in the basin tank? Maybe she came here to meet someone and buy their silence?"

"If that's the case, that only makes it more likely, not less likely, that Lilian was the person she was meeting."

"Perhaps, or Lord Bradbury?"

"Really, it could have been anyone."

"Or, maybe she was leaving the money here, and someone else was going to retrieve it later on. That could be why she slipped into the basin tank, if her death was, indeed, by misadventure."

"So why the gun? Did she mean to protect herself with it? And if she did, why is it in the basin tank, and why is the money still here?" Williams shakes his head as he attempts to dry his cold hands on his overcoat.

"We need to hand this over to Aldcroft."

"Yes, we do," Williams agrees, but he looks unhappy about it.

"This isn't what I came here to find. I was sure that there'd be something that finally made it clear who the murderer was."

"If there was a murderer," I feel I have to clarify.

"Yes, if there was. No matter what that police surgeon says, unless Lady Carver was doing what I just did, then I can see no reason why she'd have fallen into the basin tank, unless by a great misfortune. I still believe she was murdered, and perhaps for a great deal of money."

I purse my lips, eyes flicking from the sack of nearly ruined bank notes to the darkness of the basin tank. I shiver once more, just thinking of touching the inkiness of its depths, and take a few careful steps backwards. Williams is right, I believe, to dismiss the police surgeon's summary of what's happened here. And yet, there's very little to show anyone has ever been here. And I will be adding my words to the gamekeepers call for the tank to be fenced off. It's a deadly location in what's already a challenging landscape.

Not here the perfectly kept lawns and flower beds of my London home. Admittedly, the formal gardens on the other side of the valley offer those charms, but Cragside is all about its wildness, its vastness and a desire to tame the untameable.

I admire the ambitions of Lord Bradbury's ancestor who purchased this land and made it what it is. It had required the ability to see far into the future, to what the estate could become, as opposed to what it was right then, more than seventy years after the first stone had been laid to build the hunting lodge.

"There just seem to be more questions, not less," Williams bemoans.

"I quite agree," I confirm, pleased to be away from the basin tank and once more on the footpath. Williams carries the sodden bag in his hand, and it continues to stream water from its sides. By the time we make it back to the house, I foresee the money being scrunched tightly. And what it certainly doesn't do is prove that Lilian murdered Lady Carver.

"Ah ha." We're almost within sight of the house once more when the bushes in front of us come alive. I'm almost unsurprised to find Detective Inspector Davidson standing in front of me, his eyes gleaming as he takes in the sack in Williams hand. He's dishevelled, and hasn't shaved since I last saw him.

"So, you thought you'd return to the scene of the crime, did you? Reclaim what you left behind."

Williams growls low in his throat, but before I can stay his actions, he's dropped the sack and is rushing at Davidson. I shake my head and tut, dismayed by the scene unfolding before me.

"Williams. No. Don't give him the bloody satisfaction," I shout, raising my voice to a level I've only used when racing my motorcars. Immediately, Williams stills, no more than three steps in front of Davidson, who doesn't even seem to notice he's about to be attacked, his jubilant eyes focused only on me.

"Lady Merryweather. Not content with the murder of your poor husband, you continue to murder people who might think themselves your friends."

"I've murdered no one," I offer quickly, my voice restored to its normal level. "Tell me, Detective Inspector Davidson, have you been hiding out on the estate, watching everyone come and go."

"I have, yes." He sounds proud of his achievement.

"And tell me, when did you arrive on the estate?"

"Saturday morning," he confirms. He seems almost too eager to answer my questions.

"So, did you see who murdered Norman and Margot?"

"I did yes, and it was you."

"Was it?" I ask, my voice dangerously low. If he's noticed, he makes no show of it.

"Yes, it couldn't have been anyone else. I saw you, on the patio just before Norman was killed." I can feel Williams eyes on me at that. It's impossible, and yet, it's brought about an intriguing possibility.

"How did you know it was me? And where were you hiding?"

"I knew it was you because I recognised your hat and your coat and that particular way of walking you have – the confidence in every step, the complete assurance in your right to be in places you shouldn't be."

"And what? You witnessed me with a knife?"

"I did yes. I was too far away to do more than shout an alarm, but no one heard it, and then you were gone, just like that."

"And you reported the crime?" I ask.

"No, not at all. I waited. I know how you murdered your husband, and I knew you'd come back, check that he was completely dead."

Again, I'm aware of Williams watching me. I hope he's beginning to understand what I am.

"And Lady Bradbury?"

Now Davidson smirks, his eyes wild. What's happened to the poor man, I don't know, but the leaves on his coat and his dirty boots speak to me of a man who's been sleeping rough in the estate, and what a terribly cold night it was last night. I was grateful to return to my bedchamber and find a fire had been laid for me. Is he truly so determined to convict me that he's abandoned all reason? What has he done with the two police sergeants he brought with him from London? And the police car?

"I saw her walking to the stables. I heard the gun shot and I witnessed you two throwing her on the cart and carrying her back into the house. I'm here to arrest you," he continues. He's holding a pistol before us. I wouldn't worry, but his grip is poor and I'm not at all convinced he'll manage to shoot anyone, not the way he's swaying from side to side.

"Again, how do you know it was Williams and I? Were you close enough to hear us speaking? To catch a glimpse of our faces?"

"No, nothing like that. Again, you wore that coat of yours, and your hat, while Williams had his black chauffeur's hat and smart coat on. I'd recognise the pair of you anywhere. Anywhere." He shouts. Spittle flying from his mouth, and for a moment, I realise he's more than half-crazed. I feel sorrow for him. His career is entirely ruined, but more than that, I worry for his health, for that of his family, for his future. I can't see that the police can possibly continue to employ him in any capacity.

"Then, come with us. You must inform Detective Inspector Aldcroft of what you've discovered. He's desperate to find some evidence to convict us."

A slow smile spreads across Davidson's face.

"I will, yes I will. The fool is determined you can't be responsible. He even set someone to watch over me, to make sure I went back to London, but I over-powered them easily enough. And now I have my proof. I'll see you hang, you bitch." The word rings so sharply through the trees, that a handful of sparrows flutter into the air in surprise, terrified by the unusual sound.

"Yes, of course," I confirm, catching Williams eye to warn him not to punch Davidson, just yet. I need to get him back to Aldcroft, and more, I need to share what Davidson has seen, and also what he might not have realised he's witnessed, with Aldcroft. I have a witness to the murders of Norman and Margot, and despite what Davidson thinks, he's not watched me do those terrible deeds, but rather someone pretending to be me, and that makes the list of suspects, even smaller than ever before.

# Chapter 17

Detective Inspector Davidson escorts me to the main house with surprising ease. While Williams glowers behind him, no more than five steps away, I make it appear as though I'm coming willingly, and have, indeed, carried out the terrible deeds Davidson has accused me of doing.

At the front door, Underhill opens the door to my bell ring, shock on his face.

"Aldcroft?" I ask.

"In the study, My Lady," he quickly informs me, and without discarding my boots or coat, I stride down the short hallway. With Aldcroft here, this should go far more easily than if Davidson were alone.

Underhill follows Williams, adding his reassuring heft to the small procession. When I knock and gain entry, both eyebrows are arched on my forehead, as Aldcroft looks on at first with pleased surprise and then in consternation.

I wait for everyone to enter the small room, which smells of damp and cold on the winter's day.

"Detective Inspector, Williams and I have made a discovery at the basin tank, and then Davidson appears from beneath the hedges and apprehended me. He's witnessed me murdering Mr Harrington-Featherington and Lady Margot Bradbury, while camping out on the estate." I hear Underhill exclaim with outrage at my statement.

"Has he now?" Aldcroft replies slowly, quick to understand what's happening here. I do think that the dishevelled state of

Williams makes it more easier to gain the trust of both Aldcroft and Underhill in disbelieving Davidson's assertion. Not for the first time, I'm relieved that I'd been apprehended for the murder of Lady Carver on Friday night and into Saturday. And that Norman had been killed in my absence. If I hadn't been away from the house, I might well have had to put up with Davidson's half-cracked ideas with no recourse to the truth.

"Sit, Davidson, sit," Aldcroft instructs the other man firmly. Davidson sinks into a chair, the smell of him is most obnoxious. I imagine he's inadvertently rolled in fox excrement, or something as equally unpleasant. He's no better than Lord Bradbury's dogs in that regard.

Davidson leans forward, dropping his gun onto the desk. Aldcroft immediately grips it and places it in his own overcoat pocket. I breathe a sigh of relief then. I haven't felt truly in peril, and yet it's good that the gun is no longer an option for Davidson. I do notice that Williams has taken up station behind Davidson, with Underhill close to hand as well. Aldcroft makes no comment as to whether he approves or not of the arrangement, but he does notice it.

"As I was telling Lady Merryweather, I saw her, out on the rockery, with her knife, wearing her very distinctive blue coat and hat. I was too far away to help the poor man, but I saw the blood well enough. It flew through the air." Davidson shudders at the memory. "I've never seen such blood before," he continues.

"Mr Harrington-Featherington hit the stones with a thud I heard even from where I was hiding down the lower road, that runs opposite the river. I watched her peer all around, and then dash away, not inside the house, but rather, back along the top road. I could hear her breathing heavily, and her boots thudding with the noise. I tried to follow her, to grab hold of the knife, but she disappeared along the paths that criss-cross through the estate."

"And did you see her face?" Aldcroft presses him, to all intents and purposes, receptive to the words Davidson is sharing with him, his notebook on the desk before him.

"I saw her mop of blonde hair, yes. And she has a particular way of moving, that I recognised, and of course, she was killing someone, so it had to be Lady Merryweather." He speaks with triumph. Why, I think he's not admitted to this sooner, I'm unsure?

"But you didn't see her face?"

"No, I told you I didn't, but I didn't need to." There's an edge of suppressed anger to his words, as though he doesn't like being doubted.

"Tell me," Aldcroft leans forwards, his elbows resting on the desk. "Why were you in that location?"

"Because that's where I was told to be, of course."

Now Aldcroft's voice dips lower. I don't think one of us dares breathe. We're so close to finally solving this. I'm aghast that the murderer has managed to subvert Detective Inspector Davidson to their cause. As much as I dislike him, perhaps he's been as much a victim of this as I have been.

"Here, look," and from the depths of his overcoat, admitting a foul stench of unwashed body, Davidson moves to grip something. From his jacket pocket, he pulls forth a much tattered postcard. I lean over to see what's written on it, but Aldcroft has his hand on it first.

His lips move as he reads the message to himself, and then he fixes me with a firm look.

"To witness Lady Merryweather killing again, you must be within sight of the rockery, close to the main door, Cragside, Northumberland at 3pm on Saturday afternoon." Aldcroft pauses, I think a little dramatically and then continues, turning it from one side to another as he does so. "It was sent to you at Scotland Yard and has a postage stamp on it that reads last Wednesday."

"Wednesday?" I gasp at the date, and the implication. This had all been set up long before I'd even been invited to attend the party. Who then could have known of it?

"And that's not the only one. This one as well."

"You must also bear witness to more of Lady Merryweather's

murdering instinct on Sunday at 12noon, by the stables, Cragside, Northumberland." Davidson reads this one before handing it to Aldcroft. "I've fulfilled my task as a detective inspector. I've witnessed these crimes, and now Lady Merryweather must pay with her life for taking the lives of others, and with such planning as well."

"Tell me," Aldcroft asks into the tense atmosphere. "Who do you think sent these to you? Lady Merryweather?"

"Of course not, it must have been someone else," Davidson dismisses contemptuously.

"But who? And how would they know Lady Merryweather's intentions?"

"What?" Davidson's forehead creases in thought. It's as though he's not even considered the problem before. "Someone who wanted to see justice done, ensure there was a witness this time to Lady Merryweather's crimes, and one who could never be dismissed by a court of law. A police officer, no less." Davidson speaks as though Aldcroft's a child.

"Yes, but who?" Aldcroft persists.

Again, Davidson's forehead furrowed.

"It doesn't matter, man, it doesn't matter. All that matters is that Lady Merryweather has killed, three times in as many days. She must have a real thirst for it."

Davidson's fumbling once more in his pocket. I'm unsurprised when he pulls forth a set of handcuffs.

"Let me have the honour of arresting her," he crows at Aldcroft.

"Not just yet," Aldcroft words are as steel, as he meets my eyes. "Tell me, did you also receive a postcard informing you of events on Friday afternoon, at the basin tank, with Lady Carver?"

"No, just these two. I wasn't in Northumberland on Friday," he confirms.

Only then does Aldcroft raise his eyeline from examining Davidson, no doubt communicating with Underhill and Williams what's to happen next.

Slowly, I lift myself from the chair, moving aside, inching

towards the door. I don't want to be caught in the affray when the handcuffs are slipped over Davidson's hands and not mine.

As I expect, Davidson goes wild when Aldcroft moves to detain him. I can't detect the words Aldcroft uses in slipping the cuffs over Davidson, but I hear the chair he's been sitting on crash to the floor, my back to the commotion, a wet sound and 'huff' of pain, speak of someone being punched.

Then, the door opens and Davidson's escorted from the room. I really don't think the local police station can have enough room to keep everyone locked up. Once the men have left the room, I pick up the discarded postcards from the desk.

They're plain white things, well, more cream really. I run my fingers over the cardboard, noting the thickness of the paper. Then I move to the window to examine the writing and the postage mark. The stamp shows the king but it's the postmark I'm most curious to see. Has our murderer truly been foolish enough to post the cards from somewhere that'll help us determine who they were? But no, the postage mark's impossible to decipher, smeared from where it's been stamped onto the paper, obscuring the one penny stamp. But the handwriting is interesting.

It's a squat flat form of writing, capitals letters used throughout the message which has been written in black ink. I want to recognise the writing, but I don't. Not, I realise that I'm an expert on such things. How often do I receive letters, handwritten ones, and take the time to consider the words painstakingly written down? Not that often. I'm not a good communicator, unless it's to do with a fine motorcar or a thoroughbred horse. And then, I prefer to communicate via the telephone or in person.

Aldcroft walks back through the door first, shaking his head. Williams follows quickly behind, although not Underhill.

"Well I never," Aldcroft sinks onto the chair I've been sitting on, leaving me on the far side of the desk. Williams lifts a hand to tentatively touch his cheek, and I realise he's the one who's been punched.

"I got him back," Williams glowers furiously. "He's not hinged," Williams continues.

"No, it seems he's not. But, someone has toyed with him. I imagine when we investigate further we'll discover these aren't the first such postcards he's received. Or perhaps he's been sent other information. Someone out there really doesn't like you, Lady Merryweather, and they're determined to see you hang."

"But who?" I ask.

Aldcroft runs his hand over his eyes, his lips in a tight line of unease.

"It seems to me that it could have been anyone, but that person must be organised, methodical, able to plan in excruciating detail." I think Aldcroft will continue then, but he pauses.

"What's that terrible smell?" He looks around him, and then I remember. In all the excitement of Davidson's reappearance, I've forgotten about the sack of money.

"Look what Williams found in the basin tank."

Williams pushes the sodden sack towards Aldcroft with his boot.

"It's stuffed with money, and it has a gun in there as well."

"Where was it?' Aldcroft looks from Williams to me.

"It was hanging on the side of the basin tank. I don't know who chose such a poor hemp sack for the task. The water's ruined all of the notes. They'll need to be dried out."

"Yes, they will, won't they?" Aldcroft grimaces and reaches into the sack.

"Here's the gun," and I place it on the desk. But it's the money that fascinates Aldcroft for now.

"Why so much money? And why the basin tank? Do you think that might be what Lady Carver was doing up there? Had she been enticed to collect a huge sum of money and fell in the process? She was murdered, no matter what the police surgeon says."

I'm inclined to agree, and not just because Lilian is the prime suspect, and her alibi has proven to be utter rubbish.

"Or maybe this is what Lilian was looking for, and she encountered Lady Carver, or Lady Carver found it first, or even, the money was never supposed to end up in the basin tank."

Aldcroft looks up from the pile of sodden bank notes and frowns again. "I'm not going to pull any of these out. They'll only tear. Now, what does the gun show us?"

He handles it carefully, checking first to ensure there are no bullets in it. I realise I should have done that straight away.

"It's a pistol, very similar to the one that Lord Bradbury kept in his desk."

"It is yes," Aldcroft agrees. "Could it be the same pistol used to shoot Lady Bradbury?"

"If it is, then it seems the pistol can't have been put in the sack until after her death."

"A good point," I concur. "And therefore the money might not have been there either."

No one talks as we muse the possibilities.

"I think we should focus on the postcards, for now. Who could have sent them?"

"They have a London postage stamp on them. That doesn't narrow it down," I mutter with frustration. "And it's hardly news that Davidson was investigating my husband's murder. His name has been listed in all the newspapers, and one need only telephone Scotland Yard to find out who it is."

"Maybe we should turn our attention to who could have been pretending to be Lady Merryweather. Someone must have snuck into her room to retrieve her blue hat and coat."

"And then returned them as well," I interject. I'll not be wearing that particular hat and coat combination again.

"And who would have been able to wear the hat and coat?"

"Lilian," I exclaim. "As well as Amelia and Rebecca. Not Gwendoline as she's too tall and broad, and not Margot Bradbury who would have been too wide." I sum up the physical description of the women so as to prevent the men having to do so. It would only embarrass them.

"Lilian has already been detained," Aldcroft muses. He's not yet told me what she's said to him while in the police station. It makes me think that she's refusing to say anything at all.

"Or it could have been someone else entirely? Perhaps one of the maids." I dismiss Williams suggestion with a shake of my head.

"The staff here are so loyal to Lord and Lady Bradbury, I just can't see them wanting to bring any scandal to the estate. I can't imagine them wanting to dirty their hands with something like this, not even for all the money in the world. Hard enough to murder someone you know, but even harder to murder someone you don't, surely?."

Aldcroft fixes me with a pensive look. "I don't know about that," he argues. "I just believe it's hard to kill any living creature, whether I know them or not."

"Amelia and Rebecca are staying in bedrooms close to mine, in the Red bedroom and the Morning room," I change the topic slightly. "They'd have been able to sneak into my room if they'd wanted to, and especially as I was not here at the time."

Aldcroft growls with frustration.

"What we need is some sort of proof, and that's impossible to come by, at the moment."

"As you already hold Lilian, it might be a good idea to start with her. Interrogate her to see what she says."

"She's refused to say anything. I won't waste my time with her. I will," and he bounds to his feet. "Get this money stored securely, and then I'm going to invite Amelia and then Rebecca to speak with me. I'll tell you everything after I've spoken with them."

I nod. This seems as good an idea as any other.

"I'll also have the pistol examined. I just hope no crimes are being committed elsewhere throughout Northumberland, because I must have all the police officers of the Northumberland County Constabulary working for me at the moment." His words are filled with outrage, and I agree with him. What's supposed to be a peaceful weekend in the countryside has turned out to be anything but that. And the answers feel no closer, even with Lilian, Hugh and Gwendoline in custody.

I follow Williams into the hallway as Aldcroft disappears with the sodden parcel of money. I wince to see the foul water spilling over the wooden floor and expensive rugs, but I can hardly call him to task for that.

"Come with me," I say to Williams. I walk to the library. The huge expanse of the room is a shock after the close confines of the study. In here, I feel I can breathe deeply, and don't give two hoots what people think of me inviting Williams to join me. At least I can trust Williams. He hasn't done anything other than try to assist me in finding the real murderer.

"What now?" I say, standing beside the window and peering towards Tumbleton Lake.

"I'd try and stay alive, if I were you," Williams words are doleful.

"I think out of everyone here, I'm the one person who should worry about that the least. All this seems to have been concocted to remove me from whatever it is I have that this person wants."

It's taken me a long time to determine that this is what's happening.

"And what is it that you have?" Williams asks.

I shrug a shoulder. "It's impossible to know. Do they want money? Do they want my property? Do they want my motorcars, my horses, my influence?"

"I think you must know something that they don't want you to know," Williams adds thoughtfully.

I scrunch my face in thought. "And just what might that be?"

"They must suspect you know something that your husband knew about them. I can think of no other reason."

"It must be pretty terrible, and I'm sure I'd know what that was if it was something quite so scandalous."

"I don't know," Williams comments, settling before the fire, and holding his hands out towards it. "Maybe you know only part of it, but if you share that with anyone, they'd then connect the two dots and reveal all."

"Do you think it must be something stored in Bertie's safe-deposit box?"

"If it is, I'd expect them to have done all this in London, where they could at least take you to the bank and remove whatever this piece of information is."

I sigh. My head hurts, and I just can't think what I know.

"It's perhaps better if you don't try and work out what you know," Williams suggests. "As long as you don't know it, then you can't be in any more danger than you already are."

I shake my head furiously. In the hallway, I can hear the murmur of voices and believe Aldcroft must be interviewing either Rebecca or Amelia.

"But, I didn't even know my husband had all these secrets stored away. If I didn't know he had them, then how can I know anything about them?"

"You did talk, you know. Maybe he let something slip or perhaps this person only suspects you know. Tell me, if you die, who inherits the estate? Who would have access to your papers and those of your husband's?" The question is a prickly one, and I don't really want to answer it, but know I must all the same.

"I have an older sister, living in New York. We were separated as children, and most people have forgotten that she even exists. In the event of anything happening to the other, we inherit each other's estates, and hers, I have to say, is larger than mine." Williams opens his mouth to ask something, and then shuts it once more. He earns my regard in that moment. I don't like to speak of what had happened between my sister and I, or rather, our family, that brought about our separation. Sometimes, even I forgot I have a sister.

"So that gives us no answer then. No one here can know of your secret sister."

"No," I concur. They can't. We hardly communicate with one another, and if we do, we make no mention of our relationship, making out we're friends, nothing else.

"Unless, someone suspects they'll inherit?"

"No, I've given no indication. While the newspapers might

speculate on who the estate will go to, there's no truth to any of the rumours."

"So, do you have any enemies?" Williams asks. I purse my lips.

"I think you know as well as I do that I have many enemies, but in the sphere of automobile collection and thoroughbreds. Certainly, other than the two jealous women who wanted my husband for themselves, no one else. Lord Bradbury and I were friends since childhood. Hugh, I tolerate as his heir, Amelia and Rebecca because of Hugh. Lilian, again, because of Edmund. Indeed, many of the people here are related to Edmund, and not me at all."

"Apart from Hector, Lord and Lady Sunderland and Olive," Williams interjects, ticking them off on his fingers.

"Apart from them. But none of those four could have pretended to be me, even from a distance."

"No, they couldn't."

"What if it's two people working together, just as we thought?"

"You mean Lilian and Hector?"

"I do, yes. Hector has seemingly implicated Lilian with his outburst, but it doesn't mask what we know. They returned to the house together on Friday, and they were both wet, for some reason."

"But why Hector? Why Lilian?"

"They both have their secrets. Perhaps they expect me to know more about them."

From the hallway, I again hear the murmur of conversation, and realise Aldcroft is changing his interviewees. I consider that he might discover nothing from them.

"I'm going to speak to Hector again." I announce, already walking towards the door.

"Is that wise, My Lady?" Williams hastens to divert me.

"I'll find out the truth," I round on Williams. "If Lilian won't talk, then it's Hector who must. And," I pause now. "I'll also telephone my solicitor. Perhaps he might know what my husband has locked in his safe deposit box, because I certainly don't. I'll ask Underhill if I might borrow his telephone."

"And I'll escort you." Williams seems much happier knowing he isn't about to let me out of his sight. I'm grateful for his support, even if I find it a little overpowering on occasion. I'm an independent woman. My husband let me do as I wanted. I'm not used to someone thinking they know better than I do.

To reach Underhill's room, I need to either walk down the hallway towards the front door or, and this is the route I chose to take, walk through the dining room, and through the outer hallway that takes me close to the kitchen.

Inside the dining room, I note that the table's set ready for a lunch. The large, polished wooden table dominates the room, apart from the huge fireplace, which beckons to me with its enticing warmth, and carved words which announce, 'East or West hames best.' But I skirt it, sniffing appreciatively of whatever's being prepared in the kitchen by Mrs Underhill as I walk along the outer hall. I missed my breakfast. I'm looking forward to my luncheon.

"Mr Underhill," he looks up from where he's sorting through a pile of paperwork, and looks at me with faint surprise on finding me in the butler's pantry.

"Lady Merryweather," he inclines his head. He's older than I am, and yet he has the vigour of a man half his age. Living and working at Cragside has ensured he spends a lifetime breathing the clean, fresh air of northern Northumberland.

"I don't wish to inconvenience you, but might I have use of your telephone to make a private telephone call."

"Of course, My Lady. I need to consult with Mrs Underhill anyway regarding the dinner this evening."

I smile at him. I know he doesn't need to, but he's eager to help me, and I appreciate that.

"I'll find you when I'm done," I assure him.

"No, need My Lady. I'll be gone for fifteen minutes." His eyes sweep to the large clock on the wall, and I smile once more. My own butler could do with some lessons from Underhill. He's a rock, and a stalwart, having begun life as little more than a page boy, and having seen Cragside transformed into the wonder it is now. On a good day, and with a glass of sherry to hand, it's possible to have him recite the tale of the first time the hydroelectric lamps were turned on inside Cragside, and his own part in the monumental moment.

I pick up the receiver, and wait for the operator to answer.

"Whitehall, 2167 please." Quickly, I feel the line being connected, and then a bright, young voice answers the telephone in faraway London.

"It's Lady Merryweather. Is it possible to speak to Mr Rogerson, please?"

"I'll see if he's available." I wait. Williams stands as a guard at the door that opens into the hallway close to the front door. He has his back to me, perhaps pretending he can't hear my conversation.

"Lady Merryweather?" The voice is filled with surprise and concern. "I've been hearing about all these deaths in Cragside. They even detained you at one time." Rogerson is breathless with shock.

"Yes, yes, the local police up here, but it was quickly resolved. But these other deaths, I can't help believing they're connected to Bertie's death."

"Really?" I detect the iron in Rogerson's voice as he considers my words. He's my solicitor, not Bertie's, and yet, he knows a great deal about the estate, as I've had him take control of all legal matters after Bertie's death.

"Yes, I understand my husband liked to collect and store secrets. Tell me, do you know what he kept in his safe deposit box? I can't help thinking that the answer must lie there."

There's a heavy silence from the end of the telephone, Rogerson's laboured breathing coming to me, and then I hear him cover the mouthpiece.

"I've had Miss Angel leave the office. What I must share with you isn't to be heard by anyone else. Are you entirely alone?"

"Williams is protecting me," I confirm. My heart fluttering. Will this finally be the end of all these deaths, all this confusion, all this not knowing?

"Well, that's good, but be careful how you reply to what I say, for fear you may be overheard and the other person will know what we're talking about."

I nod, and then speak, as he can't see me from London.

"I'll do what I can."

"Very well, My Lady. You may not know, but Lord Merryweather, Bertie, had a number of safe deposit boxes throughout London. You gave me permission, and informed the banks, that I was to be allowed to access all of them as we were seeking out deeds for the properties he holds."

"He held safety deposit boxes with five banks in all. Most of these merely contained legal documents pertaining to the houses, in London and in the Midlands, to his investments, share certificates, financial documents, that sort of thing. But in the fifth box I visited, I did find some altogether different items. Not one of them was in his name."

"Whose name was on the documents?"

"An assortment of names. I didn't note them all down. I confess, they unnerved me, and I meant to discuss them with you, but we've not met in person for some time."

"I quite understand," I demur.

"There was a mortgage for Cragside, in the name of Lord Bradbury, showing that he'd borrowed heavily against the estate, if not the house itself. It seems he doesn't have the head for figures that I would expect from him. There were also other legal documents in his name, one of which was him transferring ownership of a smaller property in Jesmond Dene to a Miss Lilian Braithwaite."

"There were also documents pertaining to Mr Hector Alwinton, and he too had transferred ownership of property to Miss Lilian Braithwaite as well. This time, it was a larger property, on the Kent coast. And there, the documents became more worrying."

"There was a birth certificate in the name of Rebecca Barlow, listing her mother as a Miss Esme Rainbow, but not her father.

I don't remember the date of birth, but it was at the end of the previous century. Not as scandalous as such a thing might once have been, but why it was there, I don't know. There's a mortgage agreement in the name of Norman Harrington-Featherington for a flat in London, in Kensington, and Lady Millie Carver was a co-signature on the deed. Equally, there was also an agreement between Lady Sunderland and Lady Bradbury regarding some fine paintings which were to be transferred from Lady Bradbury to Lady Sunderland on Lady Bradbury's death. There was a marriage certificate, but I didn't recognise either of the two names, a Maisie Dairy and a Robert Howard. This marriage took place in 1902."

"It was, I confess, a most irregular collection of documents, and there was also some sealed correspondence, which I didn't open. The letters, I noted, had been posted in various places around the United Kingdom. They all had typed addresses on them."

"So somewhere amongst all of those legal documents, is something that led to these events."

"I wouldn't know that, My Lady. But, as I said, it was a strange collection of items. I did some small research afterwards. I can confirm that the transfers of property are legitimate. Equally, I found mention of a Miss Esme Rainbow, quite by chance, in an obituary that I recently saw in The Times of London."

"And where did she die?"

"In France, I don't remember the name of the place."

"Hum," I muse. There's a great deal to try and unpick with this.

"I'd also say that I confess, my curiosity did get the better of me, and I attempted to determine what became of the child born to Esme Rainbow. It seems that the child lived only for six months, and no more."

"Also, Esme Rainbow was married when she died, to a Mr Harrison Alwinton. I only caught sight of her maiden name quite by chance." Mr Rogerson offers, laughing with embarrassment because he's actually done quite a large amount of work to try and make sense of this fifth safe deposit box.

"And anything else?" I think to ask. Perhaps there's more to these connections

"Yes, one final point to note. Miss Lilian Braithwaite had insisted on another name being added to the transfers of her properties. I discovered this when confirming ownership of the properties with the Land Registry people. I have a contact there, you know, so I was able to ask them to confirm the details for me quite quickly."

"And who else was named on the deed?"

"A Mr Davidson. Your Detective Inspector Davidson, as far as I've been able to ascertain."

"So she knows him?" I don't mention his name, for fear it might conjure him before me, even though he's been taken away on the orders of Aldcroft.

"Either that or she's decided to share her properties with a complete stranger."

"None of this makes sense to me."

"No, it doesn't to me either. I feel sure that there would be a connection, and when it failed to materialise, I didn't pursue the matter with you, as I perhaps should have done."

"But there are worrying connections between many of the people here, financial links, and I'm curious about the birth certificate you found as well. There's a guest here who shares that name."

"And how old is this woman?" my solicitor queries.

"Perhaps the correct age, certainly no older."

"Then, she's not who she appears to be."

"No, no she's not, but equally, many of the other guests are hiding matters as well."

"Would you like me to revisit the safety deposit book and search the documents once more. I didn't make a full accounting. As I said, I meant to discuss it with you when next we spoke."

"I don't know. It might be relevant, or it might not."

"Then, with your permission, I'll nip over again. I still have your signed letter of authority."

"Thank you," I confirm, pleased he's made the decision for me. "Telephone me back if you have any further information to share with me, but please don't leave any sort of message other than asking for me to telephone you back. Not that I think I'll be away from the house."

"Very well. I'll get back to you within the hour," and the telephone line goes dead.

I stand, checking the clock, aware that Underhill will be back shortly, and keen to be gone before he's discomfited once more.

"Anything?" Williams asks, turning to face me now I've disconnected the telephone.

"Many things, none of them particularly easy to disentangle, but I need to speak to Aldcroft about what one of our guests said to him."

I retrace my steps through the dining room. I once more take notice of the inscription above the fireplace. It brings a smile to my face. Edmund's relative, who built Cragside, had truly seen something magnificent in the stark location. I know from drawings I've seen, that not too long ago, the hillside was as barren as the heaths which surround it. Well, not barren, but filled with grasses, moss and heather. Not at all what the estate is like now. Such transformation requires someone with forethought. I've never thought myself capable of that. But, perhaps there's someone here who is imbibed with such far-sightedness.

I tap on the study door and Aldcroft voice rises to beckon me inside.

"I have some new information," I offer, sitting, while Williams hovers behind me. It's as though he's decided not to let me out of his sight.

"I do as well. You go first."

"Rebecca isn't who she says she is." I can see the surprise on Aldcroft's face at my revelation.

"How do you know that?"

"I telephoned my solicitor and asked him about my husband's

bank security boxes. He advised me, amongst other things, that there was a birth certificate in there, showing the mother of Rebecca Barlow, but that the child died soon after birth. The birth certificate was from the end of the last century. My man is going to check the exact date."

"Well, the date fits, doesn't it? I think Rebecca, or whatever her name is, is about that age."

"Yes, I agree it does. But that's not it. The woman who gave birth to the Rebecca who died, only recently died herself. Quite by chance Rogerson saw the obituary in The Times. She was married to a Mr Alwinton. I don't recall the name of Hector's father, but I'd be unsurprised to discover it was the same person."

"So, what, Hector's father was married to the mother of this Rebecca who died shortly after birth?"

"Yes. And there's no father listed on the birth certificate either?"

Aldcroft sits back in his chair, and then runs his hand over his face, pausing on his clean-shaven chin, his eyes narrowing as he thinks.

"I certainly had no idea that she wasn't who she said she was. Rebecca made no mention of her parents, but I didn't ask those sorts of questions either. Her acquaintance with Miss Amelia Clarke began about five years ago. They met while attending the theatre, a favourite past-time of both of them, and it quickly developed into a friendship."

"I didn't press her on the details. I was more interested in checking her whereabouts when Mr Norman Harrington-Featherington was murdered, and whether or not she might have been the one wearing your coat."

"And what did you decide?"

"Her alibi isn't firm enough for me to rule her out."

"And Amelia?"

"The same with her. And that means that it could have been any of the women; Amelia, Rebecca or Lilian."

I growl softly. We still don't seem to be getting anywhere

with this. "I've discovered that Lilian and Detective Inspector Davidson have a connection. He's a co-signatory on one of the property titles she extorted from Lord Bradbury."

If I thought Aldcroft looked concerned before, now he looks horrified.

"So one of the witnesses who decries you in the murder of your husband, is financially connected with the Detective Inspector assigned the case?"

"Or is now," I amend.

Aldcroft shakes his head. I can sense Williams has startled at the news. I turn to face him, a wary expression on my face.

"It's perhaps best that Lilian isn't here at this time."

"Yes, yes, it is," Aldcroft confirms but for quite a different reason to me.

I note that Williams has his fist clenched tightly. I well know what he's capable of if he feels I'm under attack.

"So, at the moment, we believe that Rebecca is a fraud, and that Hector knows this."

"Yes."

"We also know that Lilian has been given property by Lord Bradbury which is co-owned with Detective Inspector Davidson?"

"Yes, and she also has a deed transferred to her by Hector Alwinton. And that's not it. Lady Bradbury and Lady Sunderland have reached an agreement whereby some of the finer paintings will become Lady Sunderland's on the death of Lady Bradbury. There's a mortgage agreement for Norman Harrington-Featherington on a London flat that has Lady Carver as a co-signature, and there's also a marriage certificate but neither of the names are recognisable to Rogerson or myself. A Maisie Dairy and a Robert Howard."

Aldcroft's quickly writing the details down as I speak.

"Anything else?"

"I think that's more than enough, but as I said, Rogerson will telephone again once he's been through to the bank to check everything."

"How would your husband know all this?" Aldcroft asks. I shrug a shoulder.

"I only wish I knew. Apparently, I paid my husband too little attention and he filled it by discovering everybody's dirty secrets."

"It just seems to me," Williams interjects. "That there's no one here who wouldn't be keen to have hold of the contents of that safety deposit box. I don't like it, Lady Merryweather. I believe you should leave here." But I'm quick to dismiss his suggestion. I do appreciate his care for me.

"If we do that, then this'll merely drag on for even longer than it already has. No, I believe we must do something altogether more worrying than just staying here. I believe I should make myself a target for whoever this person is. We can ask questions until we're blue in the face, but it's getting us nowhere close. We have the bloody knife, but we don't know who wielded it, and while we have the money, we don't know who placed it there."

"No."

"No."

Both men are staunch in their denial.

"Then what shall we do? Wait until they try to kill someone else? I believe I'm the main target or suspect, but I have no idea who else of the guests has begun to realise this. Perhaps, now that so many have died or been apprehended, everyone is second guessing one another."

I allow that to percolate into their thoughts, and all three of us jump when there's a polite knock on the door.

"Lady Merryweather, a telephone call for you."

"That was quick," I mumble, following Underhill back through the drawing room with Williams at my back.

I can't think it's good news if Rogerson is telephoning me back so very quickly. He must have run to and from the bank, and a gentleman such as Mr Rogerson, should really not do that.

# Chapter 18

Overnight, snow has fallen. Not in a wild flurry or even with any great force, but instead I wake to find a gentle blanket of white coating the land. I turn to meet the bleary gaze of Williams. He's insisted in guarding my doorway during the night. I can't see that he's slept well, but I have, knowing he was there.

"I'm not happy about this," he hisses at me, and I grunt as I rise from the large bed.

"What makes you think I am, but I'll have answers, once and for all."

I dress quickly, behind the wooden screen, choosing my skirt of brown corduroy and thick woollen jumper for warmth, not fashion. I wear stockings, and over them, a pair of Williams socks. Then I make my way to the dining room. Williams keeps pace with me. I don't know when he's had time for his ablutions, but his aftershave is fresh. Perhaps one of the constables has relieved him briefly before I woke.

"Good morning," Edmund looks up from behind his copy of The Times newspaper to flash a dour smile in my direction. He's still a broken man following the murder of his wife. He drinks only coffee. His plate is bare of food despite the feast laid out before us.

We are, for now, entirely alone in the dining room.

"Well, you may as well eat as well," he directs Williams. Williams pauses and then hurriedly helps himself to a generous portion of scrambled eggs, bacon and sausages. He eats immaculately, and quickly at my side, his gaze flashing between the door that allows entrance from the kitchen, via the butler's room, and the short hallway down which other guests will need to come.

"Lord Sunderland is eating in his room," Edmund offers by way of an explanation. Only when Williams has finished eating, and is standing once more behind my chair, do the other guests arrive. The three women appear together, but only Rebecca and Amelia are engaged in conversation. Olive is huddled inside three cardigans and I wouldn't be surprised to discover she has her blanket in the bag she carries as well.

Not that it's cold in the dining room. Far from it. The fire has been built up high and crackles merrily in the background, the stained glass windows to either side, bright with reflection from the snow.

None of the women comment on seeing Williams as my guard dog. Edmund has his two hounds to guard him. A gentle buzz of conversation swells, all of us exchanging pleasantries on the snow and bright morning, perhaps, like me, they're just relieved to count the same number of guests this morning as had departed for bed last night.

But, when Hector appears, his heavy tread on the wooden floor alerting us all to his arrival, does the conversation drain away. He's ensconced in classic country-gentleman's attire, even down to the black boots he wears laced around his ankles.

"Good morning," he speaks to the room at large, and then sits beside Olive, and beginning to help himself to the warm food. We all watch, and I do with disbelief, as he spoons a mountainous amount of porridge into his bowl and then adds three spoonful's of honey to the mixture. He's entirely oblivious to us all watching on.

"And where is Lord Sunderland this morning?" Olive questions.

"Eating in his room. He's feeling quite out of sorts this morning. I've spoken to him this morning," Edmund confirms. His words are mournful. Both men have been badly treated by this weekend retreat.

"And where's the Detective Inspector?" Hector asks around a mouthful of his porridge.

"He's been forced to return to the police station to ask some further questions of his suspects." Edmund provides. I'm grateful not to be the one speaking.

"But the constables have remained?"

"Yes, there are six of them, some in the house, one with the kitchen staff and others in the grounds. We're quite free to walk out, if we desire," Edmund adds, as though conferring a great book. "Detective Inspector Aldcroft assures me he'll return at 3pm this afternoon, and then hopefully, we'll have our answers, and can dissolve the party."

His words are greeted with some pleasure by Amelia and Rebecca, although Olive shudders as though a blast of cold wind has blown through the room. It's clear she doesn't wish to leave the comfort of Cragside now the weather has turned even more wintry.

"I'll be going for a walk," I announce. "I haven't yet been to the lower part of the estate. I think it'll be easier underfoot than trying to follow the carriage drive."

As I suspect, no one offers to come with me on such an endeavour.

"I hope to finish my knitting," Olive holds her bag high as though to assure us of what it contains.

"Rebecca and I have decided to listen to the radio this morning. It'll be good to hear some music," Amelia offers, her gaze taking in Edmund as though he might object.

"If I can," and Hector directs this to Edmund. "I'd like to make use of the telephone. I was meant to be at a business meeting today, but alas, I've been unable to leave the property."

"Of course. I'll make it available to you," Edmund replies. That leaves only Lord Sunderland to decide what he'll be spending the day doing, and as he's absent, I'll have to hope that word of my plans reaches him by other channels.

I pause, to look back at the house. It sparkles beneath the brilliant, if cold sunlight. It's going to be a beautiful day. Behind me, my footsteps have carved shapes in the snow, leading anyone, if they didn't already know, straight to me.

I shiver inside my big, blue coat, the one that has been used against me so many times this weekend, and resume my stroll. I swore I'd never wear it again, but to bring about a resolution to these tragic events, I've decided it's best to do so. After that. Well, after that, I'll be gifting to someone I don't like.

My breath plumes before me, my heart thudding loudly in my chest. While I know I should feel safe, I don't. I feel as exposed as when I was placed in the women's jail, with all those cold, hard faces of the other women who looked at me and laughed at me for thinking my station in life would protect me from justice. They didn't consider I was innocent. None of them were, so why should I be?

Around me, the estate is alive, despite the snow that's fallen overnight. A robin hops to and fro, as though thinking to approach me and then deciding not to. A pheasant makes it's strange half-strangled cry, somewhere off in the distance, and small indentations in the snow assure me I'm not the first to venture to this place.

And down the slope I go, towards the Debdon entrance to the estate, as opposed to the one close to Tumbleton Lake. In the far distance, I might normally expect to hear the engines of motor vehicles, but there's nothing today. The whole world sleeps, apart from me.

I think back to Mr Rogerson's telephone call yesterday afternoon. He'd been all a flutter, and I'd not been surprised when he'd shared with me what he'd learned from a more careful examination of the documents my husband had gathered. With the information before us, so much of what's happened now makes perfect sense.

If only we'd known before. But of course, I'd been carted away by Detective Inspector Davidson before my husband's personal collection of items was known. It seems now, that had been intentional. I was only lucky that despite it all, the law of inheritance meant that my husband's possessions couldn't just fall to anyone, not until I'd been convicted, and that, thankfully, had never happened.

Now I wait. I know someone will come for me. I just don't yet know who that someone will be.

Despite the fallen snow, and the realisation that there'll be prints left in it, I know it won't be a deterrent.

Overhead, the trees grow ever thicker, the path I'm taking becoming more and more treacherous. I consider how far I'll go to bring this to an end, but I have to carry on. This has taken over enough of my life.

And then there's a sound I don't expect to hear over the rumble of the burn on its way to the power house at the bottom of Cragside estate. I turn, fearing to see who follows me and who claps quite so loudly that overhead, snow slithers from branches to pool on the ground, leaving little white mountains on the crisp snow.

"Lady Merryweather," I observe the woman before me, eyes wild, no attempt made to disguise herself. Not this time.

"Rebecca," I incline my head in greeting, pleased she's stopped clapping, the loud sound making me cringe. She reaches for something in her pocket, which I know will be a pistol. The one used to shoot Lady Bradbury in the stables. It wasn't Edmund's pistol, or the one we found in the basin tank.

"You thought you were so clever in putting the pieces of the puzzle together, didn't you?" It isn't a question. I make no response to her triumphant gloating.

Her breath rasps, whitely in the cold air. It almost masks her, a cloud of her own devising. But, all the same, I know who she is, and why she's done what she's done.

At least, I think I do.

"Why?" I ask her, just to be sure, pleased my voice sounds smooth.

"It doesn't matter now, does it? With your death, no one will know the truth."

I hesitate. "That's not quite right."

"What do you mean?" She comes closer now. I look down and see she wears men's boots. Rebecca thinks of everything. She's also been walking in my tracks and still does, coming closer, gun in her hand, pointed at me, even while she watches where she steps. I make no attempt to move. If I do die here, then no one will be able to determine how many people have passed this way.

"My solicitor has opened the files, and informed Scotland Yard of their contents. Even now, Detective Inspector Aldcroft is on his way to arrest you. Didn't you hear the telephone ring this morning? That was him informing me of what was happening."

"No," the cry is half-strangled, and for a second, the gun drops low in her hand, her grip lessening as she sees the outcome of all her schemes coming to nothing. I could have made an attempt to evade her, but there's still more I need to hear.

"No," she says again, voice desolate. I think she'll drop to her knees, but instead she straightens, raising the gun and looking directly at me.

"It doesn't matter. Scotland Yard will do nothing about it. I have that on high authority. Your Detective Inspector Aldcroft will be as ridiculed as Davidson has been until now. He'll lose his position for drawing such far-fetched conclusions."

"I don't believe that Detective Inspector Davidson is a police officer anymore. My understanding is that he's been removed from duty. Permanently." Once more, the gun wavers, and I can tell, just from watching her, how she's trying to contend with this piece of information. She's weighing it up, deciding if it's true or not. What could happen if it is true. What would happen if she ignores the knowledge and shoots me any way, which I believe she intends to do, regardless.

"You lie," she hisses, her mind made up. "You've done none of those things, and with your death, the matter will come to an end."

"If you like," I mollify. "But first, tell me all about it."

She shakes her head, her curls turned white by the snow as

she wears no hat. Perhaps she hasn't thought of everything after all.

"No, I'll not play your games," and she lifts her pistol. I brace for the impact as the sudden sound of a shot being fired echoes through the still valley, sending the birds fluttering from the tree branches, more snow cascading from the heavy boughs. I feel as though the sound could be heard as far south as Newcastle. But I don't fall.

I expect another shot to fire. When it doesn't come, I open first one eye and then another. I can make no sense of what I see, for Rebecca is lying, bleeding on the ground, her hand clenched to her belly, and over her is another figure I don't recognise, swaddled in a huge coat.

"You bitch," Hector screams the words, as he turns to face me. I flinch because the words wound more than the gunshot. He's dressed for the weather as well, but his chest heaves with the effort of his words, although not as much as it might have done. He's cast off his extra layers of clothes and now he stands before me, half the man I'm used to seeing. This confuses me, but shouldn't.

"Why can't you just forget about it. Wasn't it enough that they freed you?"

He glances down at Rebecca, and she whimpers beneath his scrutiny. I want to go to her, help her as the snow around her turns ever redder, but the answers aren't complete. Not yet.

"I didn't start killing people," I retort. How any of this can be my fault is beyond me.

"Perhaps," Hector agrees. The sunlight flashes from his pistol. Is everyone here carrying a firearm other than me?

"Why did you shoot her?" I ask.

"If she shoots you and you die, then all this is over."

"What?" I'm incredulous. "You believe you still have some control over me to hand over the documents you require."

I don't enjoy the smirk on his face.

"I do yes, and you know what that control is, don't you?" I don't but I'm happy to be educated. There are still parts of the puzzle that Aldcroft, Williams and I have failed to put together even with Mr Rogerson's help.

We know that Rebecca and Hector clearly know one another, and that Rebecca isn't his long-lost step-sister. Who she actually is hasn't yet been ascertained, but I feel we'll know soon?

"Your husband wasn't the only person capable of collecting people's secrets," Hector continued. "When I realised how valuable they could be, I began to seek out my own. It's surprising what you can infer from half an overheard conversation."

But, I still have no idea what he speaks about.

"So what did you discover?" I prompt him. I'm getting cold, and the clouds overhead are turning greyer, promising more snow, sooner rather than later. Rebecca continues to whimper, but the sound is becoming more and more faint. I fear for her. Surely, enough people have died? Whatever she's done, it doesn't need to end like this for her, dying, in the snow.

"Hah, how you play these games. You're not such an innocent as you make out, are you?"

Still, I don't know what he speaks about. I'm even more confused when Reginald emerges from the side of the road, to stand beside Hector, a smirk on his familiar face. He too is bundled inside a thick winter coat, a fur hat covering his head.

"I'm sorry, dear. I had no choice but to share what I knew about you."

Now my eyes narrow. I've not led a blameless life, but I know I've done nothing to deserve these three individuals murdering my husband. Or thinking to force me into giving away information I don't even know I have control over.

"You had no choice," I say, playing for time, and for them to tell me more.

"There are few people who know of your first marriage, of the child born from that union."

My heart stills at this pronouncement. I think back to the marriage certificate with the two names I don't recognise. "And of course, Lilian is the child of that union." I laugh then, the sound burbling from my mouth, hectic and musical in equal measure.

"Who told you this?" I demand to know. I'm finally getting to grips with what's happening here, and they're so wrong, so very, very wrong, and my husband has died for this. I can't comprehend it.

"Lilian, of course," Reginald comments as though this makes perfect sense. "She confided in me some years ago."

"And what proof did she have for her statement?"

"A birth certificate showing her father was a Robert Howard and her mother was Maisie Dairy. Not very ingenious names, but I know your middle name is Maisie. I can only assume you chose the dairy to make it appear as though you were from a lower class."

"And then who was Robert Howard?"

I ask him, but I fear I know the answer.

"I was my dear, you know that. My middle name is Robert." I recoil at the thought of Reginald's hand over my skin, of what had almost happened between us all those years ago, when we were young, and I was foolish. But good sense saved me from the precipice I would never have stepped back from. It seems that Reginald has been convinced into thinking something happened between us which hadn't.

"Then Lilian is your child?"

"And Rebecca is her sister, in real life. She's not Rebecca but Mary, twins raised in poverty because you cast them aside."

"I can assure you, if I'd managed to birth one child, let alone two, I'd remember that fact."

"What?" confusion sweeps over the faces of both men. I hear Rebecca start to laugh around her pain.

"You fools," she gasps. "You truly believed the lies you were told by that whore, Lilian."

Hector looks from Rebecca to Reginald, confusion on his pinched face.

"You aren't Lady Merryweather's daughter?"

"Of course I'm not," and she continues to laugh, the sound

becoming a low moan of pain as it goes on.

"But Lilian?"

"Lilian told you what you wanted to hear to gain your trust, your greed. She promised you a slice of the estate didn't she? She promised you that you'd profit from assisting her in her grand plan. See how well it's done her now?"

And I duck low, another sharp report echoing through the still day. Rebecca's silenced, this time, a small hole through her forehead adds more blood to that which she's already shed. She won't live to recover from such a wound. Already, her eyes stare forever upwards. At least, I think, her last sight was of something beautiful, the snowy sky and the decorated fire trees.

Aldcroft has been as good as his word. He'd released Lilian the night before, saying there was no evidence to continue to hold her. Now she glares at me from just in front, triumphant, blond hair wild, face blue with cold. I harbour the suspicion she might have spent the night on the estate, just waiting for her chance to kill again. Where she's gotten the gun from, I'm unsure, although I harbour my suspicions.

Hector watches her, Reginald as well. They both wear expressions of confusion, but no remorse. Neither of them even looks at Rebecca, or Mary, as I'd just been told she was called. It's clear to see who's been Reginald's favoured 'child.'

"Don't listen to what Mary said," Lilian crows, gun trained on me, and also on Hector and Reginald. Reginald staggers backwards, tripping over the prone body of Mary, and losing his balance to land with a crack of bone on the driveway. A shriek bursts from his mouth, and then he whines. He tries to stand, but his one leg is useless to him. His hat has come askew and his trousers are drenched, his coat bunched beneath his bottom. He looks pitiful.

"But she said," Hector states, refusing to believe Lilian's words.

"Every word that burst from her lips was a lie. Always," Lilian spits, fury turning her face rosy despite the chill that hangs around her.

"And you didn't?" I feel the need to defend the woman

although she was nothing to me.

"I told what lies needed to be heard to get me what I wanted."

"Then tell me, who is Detective Inspector Davidson to you." But I know. How I've not seen it before, I can't say. It's evident in the sneer that plays around her lips. I've seen it before. Many times.

"He's my father," she gloats, delighted to have played such a deceit on us all.

"What?" Reginald moans. I shake my head. Gwendoline might have thought she loved my husband, but Reginald has managed to conjure up not one, but two children, from one inappropriate kiss over thirty years before. He's more deluded than his wife.

"My father is Detective Inspector Davidson, my mother was Mrs Annie Davidson. My sister was Mary Davidson, and I am Lilian Davidson."

Hector's face bunches with fury.

"But Rebecca's my step-sister."

"No, no she isn't. Your step-sister died as a baby. Rebecca was just pretending to be her."

"How did you know all this?" I think to interject. Records of births, deaths and marriages are hardly secret and yet they're not easy to come by either.

"I worked for the registrar," Lilian gloats. "I took great pleasure in looking through the old entries, in making connections where others hadn't made them."

"But how did you know about Reginald and I?"

"I had no idea, but old men are particularly susceptible. Younger men as well." The look she casts over Reginald and Hector fills me with loathing towards her. My friends might have conspired to murder my husband, but it would never have happened without someone to pull their strings.

"So tell me, who killed who?" I try to make it sound conversational. Hector's eyes open wide at the words, while Reginald continues to moan in pain.

"It doesn't matter, not when you're dead and I have what I want."

"Didn't you hear me inform Rebecca, sorry Mary, that the documents have been handed over to the police."

"Didn't you hear me inform you that my father would ensure they're dismissed as evidence." Her eyes gleam with triumph, the brightest thing on the estate, even with the snow lying on the ground, and the sun glinting coldly on it.

"Detective Inspector Davidson, your father, has been arrested. Or rather, he's been apprehended. They say he may be held under the criminally insane act."

"No." Lilian bellows, stamping towards me, the gun in her hand aimed directly at my heart.

"You made a mistake when you involved him in detaining me. Despite it all, he's a good man. He knows what you're doing is wrong. It's driven him insane." I relish the words, despite the gun aimed at my chest.

So many emotions flutter over Lilian's face that it appears as though she finds it impossible to determine how she feels.

"It doesn't matter. He was always a weak link." With that, she moves her finger on the trigger of the pistol. I consider falling to the ground, or running away.

"How did you do it?" I ask instead, voice quiet.

"What?"

"Kill my husband?"

"It was easy. I shot him. Hector and Reginald gave me an alibi. I hid the gun. We all blamed you. It was even easier because I didn't realise how much Reginald's wife despised you. And when she was happy to blame you, Lady Bradbury joined in as well. You really have very few friends," Lilian spits at me.

"But why?"

"Because of what he knew, of course. I couldn't have him making all the connections and putting an end to my union with Edmund."

"Why Edmund?"

"Why Edmund? Look at all this?" and she lifts her left hand to indicate the estate at Cragside. "And he has Bamburgh Castle as well. And in time, all this will be mine."

"And now?"

"What do you mean, and now?"

"He won't marry you. Don't you know that?"

"Of course he'll marry me. I killed his wife for him, and now he'll be mine."

"But Lady Bradbury was dying anyway."

"She suspected things, I couldn't have her getting in the way."

I shake my head. Lilian still believes Edmund will marry her. She's even more deluded than her father.

"And Lady Carver?"

Now Lilian smirked.

"Tried to bribe me, silly woman. She wanted money for her silence. She saw me, on the night of your husband's murder, in her bedroom, looking through her documents. Hector said it was him, but it wasn't. She told Norman. They both had to die."

"So, you did push her into the basin tank?"

"Yes, with the aid of Hector. He kept her talking while I crept up behind her. She died pitifully, gasping for air, drowned by the weight of that damn fur coat she insisted on wearing everywhere."

"But you were seen?"

"No, not at all but Lady Carver had told her old lover of what she was about. Norman approached me, said he would inform Aldcroft of what was happening. He had to die."

"So, you did kill everyone here then?"

"I killed most of them, yes. I'll kill you as well. But Reginald and Hector assisted me when they could. Reginald helped me return Margot's body to the elevator, positioned it as though she'd been shot in the house."

"Why did she need to die in the house?"

"Because you'd not been seen at the stables."

"But I hadn't even arrived when you murdered Lady Carver?"

"Yes, a slight miscalculation, but easily remedied by having my father arrive and raise a fuss when they released you from the police station."

"So, what? If they hadn't released me then the others would

still be alive."

"They wouldn't have needed to die quite so quickly, no," Lilian confirms. It's as though she speaks about dead-heading flowers for her collection and not of killing people. Her callousness astounds me. I gain an even greater insight into why Detective Inspector Davidson is in the state he is. Bad enough to spend all day hunting down criminals, but to know he's fathered one must be traumatic.

"And now, you mean to kill me, Hector and Reginald as well? How else will you keep your secret?"

"I'll do what must be done to ensure Edmund marries me and I have all the wealth denied me for all of my life."

"I say," Hector complains. I risk looking at him.

"Why have you been pretending to be so much fatter than you are?" I ask him, my curiosity allowing me to ignore the gun aimed at me.

"The perfect means of hiding in plain sight," Hector retorts. "It was Rebecca's idea."

"I just bet it was." I shake my head at the folly of men I've known nearly all my life.

"And now, it's time for you to die," Lilian crows, her pistol trained on me.

For the briefest of moments, all I can focus on are the trees above my head, the pristine white of the snow, and the thought that if I do die, here and now, then at least I'll see my husband again. I miss him. Every day is an agony without him, and it doesn't matter how many motorcars or horses I purchase to fill the void.

"Lilian, there really is no need." It's Hector who thinks to plead for me, and I'm astounded.

"What?" she hisses, looking over her shoulder at him, while the gun remains trained on me.

"This is over. We'll all go to prison and no doubt, to the hangman's noose as well for our part in this scheme. It's all fallen apart. You must allow Lady Merryweather her life."

"No," and I wince at the rupture of her voice in the echoing silence.

"She'll die and I'll regain control over those documents."

"How?" this confuses me.

"I have a contact in your solicitor's office. Until now it's been impossible to reclaim the documents, but now that your foolish solicitor has actually withdrawn them from the safety deposit box, they'll come into my hands."

I smile then, relief making me giddy.

"Oh Lilian. They haven't been returned to my solicitors. They're still in the bank. He's taken the police to them, and not vice versa. It's safer for them to stay where they are than withdraw them."

Lilian's triumphant smirk falters at the news.

"Then I'll have to continue with my quest then, won't I? What are a few more deaths to ensure I get what I deserve."

And now she doesn't pause, but moves her finger on the trigger. I drop to the ground, springing sideways as I do so.

I hear Hector cry out, Reginald as well, but the sound I'm relieved to hear is that of Williams, colliding with Lilian, sending the gun askew with a metallic clatter even in the soft snow, so that they land in a tangle of arms and legs, Aldcroft assisting him and Lilian shrieks, her hands and legs pounding on the floor. But it's no good. She's captured, and then more police constables flood from their hiding places and take control of Hector and Reginald as well.

Edmund rushes to me, from where he's been waiting in his Rolls Royce Phantom 2. The heat of him assuring me that the car will be warm when I'm allowed inside it, as I stand, with his aid, and dust down the hem of my detested blue coat. I shiver.

Edmund meets my eyes, unimaginable sorrow in them. I'm unsurprised when he strides to Lilian, standing between Williams and Aldcroft. I watch him, while his body shakes, considering what he might do to her, and then he turns aside.

"You're not worth it," he mutters beneath his breath, threading his arm through mine, and leading me away.

It's over.

At last.

Thank you for reading Cragside,
A 1930s murder mystery.


Please do consider leaving a review if
you've enjoyed the book. Reviews help
keep me writing. Thank you in advance.

# Historical Notes

Cragside is a nineteenth century country house in North Northumberland. It's renowned as the first home to be powered by hydroelectricity, and its owner, Lord Armstrong has an equal reputation. Cragside is now in the care of the National Trust. Today, the descendants of the Armstrong family continue to own that even more famous landmark, Bamburgh Castle. For fans of the Last Kingdom series, this is Bebbanburg.

I've chosen to inhabit Cragside with a fictious cast, although I've 'borrowed' the attributes of some of the people who lived and worked at Cragside. For me, the purpose of this story was to write about Cragside estate, a place I was lucky enough to wander through at least once a week during the Lockdown of 2020. It's hardly my fault if, as I went, I began to see places where a body could be easily concealed. I did not wish to tell the story of the Armstrong family, and I certainly didn't want anyone to think that the estate and family had harboured a murderer at any point in their story. But, the estate is as I know it, and the interior of the house, is as I've seen it.

I've made use of the Cragside Guide Book for details of the interior written by Henrietta Heald. It's proven to be an invaluable guide, and where I've mentioned furniture, the details have come from the guide book. I am really not interested in the history of furniture or decorations.

For details on policing in Northumberland in the 1930s I was lucky enough to discover 'Constable – A History of Northumbria

Police' by Frederick C Moffat in my local second hand book shop. It's not a modern book (published in 1983, and very clearly typewritten), but rather written by someone who was in the police force from 1946 onwards. It's filled with wonderful detail that only an eye witness would have access to. I particularly appreciated the comment that police officers were required by law to wear their overcoats from November to April in the Northumberland County Constabulary. I'm not surprised.

This book informs me that there was no 'proper Crime Department' until 1937 and that the five detectives appointed in the 1930s had received no training. A fingerprint and photography department was included in this department but I've chosen to set this novel in the early 1930s, so we have the detective but no department to support him. Police officers were supposed to live in the town they served, and could often be asked to move with very little notice. The Chief Constable from 1900 to 1935 was Captain Fullarton James who lived in Morpeth and who had the new recruits mow his lawn as part of their fatigue duties. The first motorised police vehicles in Northumberland arrived in 1923 because of a royal visit to Alnwick, but a car was only added in 1927, alongside 4 motorcycles. Most police walked or had a bicycle. There was a horse and cart for the 'super' at each of the six divisions within Northumberland at this time. For those who are interested, Berwick upon Tweed was only amalgamated with Northumbria in 1920.

My decision to include many tedious legal documents resulted from seeing a large number of deeds and conveyances from the 18th to early 20th century, and they are things of beauty, affixed with seals and stamps and written on vellum and paper. The Land Registry in England and Wales has taken over a century to accomplish its intention of being a registry for all lands and properties within England and Wales. Public searches are quite a recent invention from 1990, which is why my solicitor needs a contact in the Land Registry office. And having worked on Census 2021 in England, I am also more than aware of the historical documents available from the period.

I've been visiting Cragside for at least twenty years, but it's only since Lockdown that I feel I've come to know at least some of its secrets and beauty, and there's still much more for me to discover. Those who only visit Cragside for the house are missing an absolute treat, so bring your walking shoes, and get a map (you'll need it) and take to the carriage drive or the many, many interconnecting paths and absorb the beauty of a place like nowhere else on earth.

I chose to include mention of the prominently displayed statue of an enslaved woman in this story because on a trip to Cragside, with my then, very young, daughter, she was horrified by the statue. I remember her asking me about the chains on the lady. She probably doesn't remember, but her question has stayed with me ever since. For more information, I can inform that Lord Armstrong himself purchased the statue in 1870 and placed it in a custom made niche, where it remains today. It's entitled Daughter of Eve, by John Bell.

As a final note, I wrote this novel during November 2021. Devastatingly, as I was drawing to a conclusion with my final draft, Cragside was struck by Storm Arwen and many, many of the trees damaged. My last walk around Cragside as it 'was' took place on that very day, Friday November 26th 2021, with gusting snow and a biting wind. I wouldn't have wanted it any other way, although I do wish the winds had become less fierce as the night had carried on and that a place which gave me so much comfort during Lockdown hadn't been so catastrophically damaged, that even now, the estate grounds are still not open to the public and may not be for a very long time. It's strange to think I might have been the last person to see many of those trees still standing proud.

# Cast of Characters

Lady Ella Merryweather

Lord Bertie Merryweather, Lady Ella's husband, now deceased

Reginald, Lord Sunderland, friend of Ella Merryweather

Gwendoline, Lady Sunderland, friend of Ella Merryweather

Lord Edmund Bradbury, owner of Cragside Estate

Lady Margot Bradbury, Lord Bradbury's wife

Lady Beatrice Carver, friend of Ella Merryweather, now deceased

Hugh Bradbury, nephew of Edmund Bradbury

Amelia Clarke, engaged to Hugh Bradbury

Rebecca Barlow, friend of Miss Amelia Clarke

Hector Alwinton, friend of Bertie Merryweather

Lilian Braithwaite, secretary to Edmund Bradbury

Olive Mabel, friend of Lady Bradbury

Norman Harrington-Featherington, friend of Edmund Bradbury, now deceased

Detective Inspector Aldcroft from Northumberland County Constabulary

Constable McStewart from Northumberland County Constabulary

Detective Inspector Davidson from Scotland Yard

Williams, Lady Ella Merryweather's chauffeur

Mr Rogerson, Lady Ella's solicitor in London

Miss Angel, Mr Rogerson's receptionist

Mrs Underhill, the cook at Cragside

Mr Underhill, the butler at Cragside

Patrick Cooper, the gamekeeper at Cragside

Alice, housemaid at Cragside

<u>Millicent</u>, housemaid at Cragside
<u>Ada Mitchell</u>, Lady Bradbury's lady's maid
<u>Bellows</u>, the carter at Cragside

# Acknowledgements

I am once more grateful to my beta readers for their support even when I write something completely different to my usual stuff. ST, CS, AM and EP, you both rock and are very supportive and never fail to keep me right. I would also like to thank my StreetTeam for their advanced reads:)

I must also thank my cover designer, Shaun at Flintlock Covers. I think this was a hard task but the finished result is fabulous.

Huge thanks, and massive respect to all the staff at Cragside House and Estate, including the staff who front the property (Alan, you know I mean you). You kept it open all the way through Lockdown and you do such fabulous work. Thank you, thank you, thank you.

# Meet the author

I'm an author of historical fiction (Early English, Vikings and the British Isles as a whole before the Norman Conquest, as well as three 20th century mysteries) and fantasy (viking age/dragon themed), born in the old Mercian kingdom at some point since AD1066. I like to write. You've been warned!

Find me at mjporterauthor.com and @coloursofunison on twitter. I have a newsletter, which can be joined via my website.

Books by M J Porter (in chronological order, not publishing order)

## Early English Historical Fiction

Gods and Kings Series (seventh century Britain)
Pagan Warrior
Pagan King
Warrior King

The Eagle of Mercia Chronicles (with Boldwood Books)
Son of Mercia
Wolf of Mercia

The Ninth Century
The Last King (audio book now available)
The Last Warrior (audio book coming soon)
The Last Horse
The Last Enemy
The Last Sword

The Last Shield
The Last Seven (coming soon)

The Tenth Century
The Lady of Mercia's Daughter
A Conspiracy of Kings (the sequel to The Lady of Mercia's Daughter)
Kingmaker
The King's Daughter

Chronicles of the English (tenth century Britain)
Brunanburh
Of Kings and Half-Kings
The Second English King

The Mercian Brexit (can be read as a prequel to The First Queen of England)

The First Queen of England (The story of Lady Elfrida) (tenth century England)
The First Queen of England Part 2
The First Queen of England Part 3

The King's Mother (The continuing story of Lady Elfrida)
The Queen Dowager
Once A Queen

The Earls of Mercia
The Earl of Mercia's Father
The Danish King's Enemy
Swein: The Danish King (side story)
Northman Part 1
Northman Part 2
Cnut: The Conqueror (full length side story)
Wulfstan: An Anglo-Saxon Thegn (side story)
The King's Earl
The Earl of Mercia
The English Earl

The Earl's King
Viking King
The English King

Lady Estrid (a novel of eleventh century Denmark)

**Fantasy**

<u>The Dragon of Unison</u>
Hidden Dragon
Dragon Gone
Dragon Alone
Dragon Ally
Dragon Lost
Dragon Bond

<u>As JE Porter</u>
The Innkeeper

**20<sup>th</sup> Century Mysteries**

The Custard Corpses – a delicious 1940s mystery (audiobook now available)

The Automobile Assassinations (sequel to The Custard Corpses) (audiobook now available)

Cragside – a 1930s murder mystery (audio now available)

Printed in Great Britain
by Amazon

12516070R00139